BETWEEN THE RED & RIO GRANDE:
ROUSING EXPERIENCES ON THE TEXAS FRONTIER
1836-1875

BY WILLIAM R. WHITTEN

Author's Note

Thanks very much to Jeremy Pessoa, a graduate student in English at Texas Christian University, for his very capable editing help; and to Mindy Reed, The Authors' Assistant, in Austin, Texas who provided the final editing and publishing assistance when Jeremy moved to California. I also want to thank my daughters for their encouragement and the encouragement of others during the writing process.

I want to express my gratitude to the members of the Fort Worth Freelance Writers' Network who provided a lot of constructive criticism. I am also grateful to the libraries and librarians at Texas Christian University and The University of Texas for providing verification of historical facts.

This is a novel, but I have tried to be both historically and geographically accurate. I did use some literary license in the location of Cuthand Creek.

The first eighteen years of my life was spent in Northeast Texas between the Sulphur and Red Rivers. (Sulphur, as in Sulphur River is spelled correctly). My friend, John Howison, of Bogata and Paris, Texas showed me where Jonesboro was located before the Red River changed course and took the town away.

This is a work of fiction and the main characters are products of my imagination. This is not a biographical representation of persons living or dead.

This book is dedicated to my two daughters:
Peggy W. Watson PhD, and Rebecca W. Provenza

CHAPTER 1

Tom Williams
1828-1835

Waiting was the hardest part.

Tom Williams fixed his eyes on the valley below; the campfire was glowing so brightly he could just make out the shadowy outline of the three Comanche Indians crouched around the flames. He wanted to move and anxiously waited for the small dark cloud to his right to drift over a bit more and cover the face of the moon. Tom rubbed a calming hand over his horse's muzzle, as it looked around nervously. Even with night vision far superior to his, his horse needed time to adjust to the different levels of darkness.

As much as he tried, Tom couldn't get the nightmare of earlier that morning out of his mind; rising pillars of black smoke, the charred ruins of the Vanegas ranch house and the mutilated bodies left strewn by the Indians in the dry, red dirt.

The carnage had been so recent that their bodies were still bleeding when Tom found them and the horse tracks fresh.

He had set off immediately, following the murderers at a safe distance all day as they brazenly drove the stolen herd of twenty horses. They led him here to a valley carved centuries earlier by the Medina River just northwest of San Antonio. There behind a thicket of huisache bushes, Tom waited patiently until night fell.

Now it was time.

With his knife in one hand and a hatchet in the other, Tom drew a deep breath and clapped his spurs sharply into the animal's sides as he charged forward, the hoof beats partially muffled by the tall prairie grass.

As he approached the campfire, the Indians jumped to their feet, startled. Tom leaned forward in his saddle, sliding his hand roughly on the horse's right side, and yanked on the right rein. The animal turned sharply and in one swift and fluid movement Tom sprang from the horse, slitting the throat of one Indian and splitting open the head of another with his hatchet. After a few minutes grappling on the ground, he gripped his knife, making short work of the third.

Rage spent, Tom walked past the stolen horses to the river, which gleamed silver-black in the light reflecting from the moon, now shining brightly and freed of cloud cover. He wiped his brow, red glistening off his fingertips as he held his hand up to the moonlight. Tom was covered in splattered blood, too much to be just his own. He bent down over the river, wincing as the water washed over the tomahawk slash on his arm. Ripping off part of his sleeve, Tom wound the strips of cloth around his arm, bandaging the wound.

Tom, cradling his arm, walked over to turn the stolen horses and turned them loose. Then he mounted his own horse for the long ride back to San Antonio. *I'll take it slow*, he told himself. There was no longer a need to push himself or his horse. There was no one to return to, no one waiting for him.

❧❧

A summons came from the Alcalde's office the next morning. As promised, Tom received a land grant from the Mexican government for past service. Partial payment for two years spent fighting the marauding Comanche's around San Antonio. Tom knew that after days committing murder, rape and theft, the Indians were sure to retreat west, away from retribution. He also knew better than to report the previous day's exploits because he shouldn't have followed the Indians alone, foolishly risking his life by attacking the three young Indians without help.

All the killings over the last two years had taken their toll on him. His dreams were haunted by countless bloody murders. Death and murder had become commonplace and he knew he needed to make a change. Now, with the land grant in his hand, he dared to hope for a better life. Tom would have a ranch of his own.

As he loaded his pack mule at the livery barn, he overheard the boisterous voice of a stranger telling the blacksmith about his home in Tennessee. Tom approached the men to get a better listen.

"White's Creek, did you say?"

The man turned to face him. "That's right. You know those parts?"

Tom grinned. "Tennessean born and bred. The name's Williams. Tom Williams."

The stranger's warm smile vanished quickly. "Not Clovis William's boy?"

"You know my pa?" asked Tom.

The man released his words with such hesitation that Tom was sure something bad had happened. "Lord, I hate for you to hear it from a stranger, son, but your father's dead."

Without delay, Tom made preparations to go to Galveston where he could catch a boat sailing for New Orleans and from there a riverboat up the Mississippi River. It would be the fastest way to reach Natchez Trace and his home in Tennessee. So he sold his livestock and boarded the first available boat bound for New Orleans. It wasn't the future Tom Williams had planned for himself, but he figured it was his responsibility to care for his mother, now widowed.

CHAPTER 2

Effie, Tom, and Jake
1836

Effie Thompson felt herself blush when her father first brought Tom Williams to their home. *Well now* she thought, *what a man. Mature, handsome, tall, nearly six foot with reddish-blond hair and an even redder beard;* this kind of rugged masculinity appealed to her. His bright blue eyes, which twinkled with a hint of mischievousness, only added to his appeal.

Effie's blush didn't escape Tom's notice. He felt a tinge of embarrassment at what raced through his mind. Just looking at her tall shapely frame, her thick blond hair modestly pinned up at the nape of her neck as befitted a proper young lady, made his heart beat faster. Many years earlier, Tom had made a vow to stay single until he could be sure he found the right woman. Tonight, he might have just finally found her.

Jake Thompson, a prosperous horse trader in Nacogdoches, had met Tom Williams when he came to see him the first week in

February. Tom had traded him three good horses in exchange for four strong young mules. When Jake asked Tom where he came from and where his family was, he was impressed with Tom's mannerism and thoughtful reply.

"Well, let's see, I left home in Tennessee in 1823 when I was twenty-two years old, came to Texas down the Mississippi to New Orleans, then traveled by ship to Indianola. I spent some time at Austin's colony and then in San Antonio, until a man brought news from home that my father had died. I went back to Tennessee to take care of my mother, but she passed away last fall. I sold the Tennessee property, came south down Natchez Trace and returned to Texas." Tom's lips formed a grin, which they didn't do often, and added, "It's a detailed answer to your question, Mr. Thompson. I apologize for being so long-winded."

"Not at all, Mr. Williams, call me Jake."

"Fine. And it's Tom."

They were an easy fit; there was an instant kinship between these two men from hardscrabble backgrounds. Tom had no way of knowing it, but within two minutes of meeting Tom, Jake Thompson thought of his daughter, Effie, and what a good husband he might be for her. Quality men with character weren't easy to come by in the Texas frontier. And only the best would be good enough for his daughter.

"May I offer you a cup of coffee, Mr. Williams? It's freshly made."

Though the question was simple enough, Tom had barely processed her words. He had been mesmerized by the gentle lulling, the rich, low sound of her voice. It was lower in tone than that of most women, but was easy on the ears, almost soothing.

"Mr. Williams?"

"Oh yes, Miss Thompson. Thank you kindly."

Effie blushed again and then smiled. He knew he was smitten.

"Take a load off, Tom," Jake said, with a chuckle. He had not failed to notice the momentary spark as it passed between his Effie and Tom Williams.

Jake adored his sixteen-year-old daughter, who cared for him after her mother's death from stomach fever back some years before. Several people in the community died of the infection that year, including Effie's two younger brothers and a baby sister. Although Effie devoted time and energy caring for her hard-working father, she often thought of someday having a husband and a home of her own.

On Sunday afternoon, two weeks later, standing at Jake's front door with his hat in his hand, Tom asked Jake if he could court his daughter.

Jake played it straight, hiding his enthusiasm. He nodded slowly and said, "All I want to know is what took you so long, Tom?"

Tom looked startled. "What's that, Jake?"

"I've been watching you through the window, pacing up and down the street, not only today but yesterday and Friday, too. I wondered when you'd work up the nerve."

"Well, I just—"

Jake roared with laughter. "Tom! There's no man I'd trust more than you. I'd be proud to have you courtin' my daughter. Don't look embarrassed; she's out back, tending the garden. Come on in, have a seat, and I'll let her know you're here."

Thereafter, Tom took every opportunity to pay a visit to the Thompson house until he was finally able to work up the nerve to ask Effie to marry him.

Jake even put off going on a trading trip and stayed close to watch the courtship. Not because he didn't trust Tom; it was just the way things were done. You didn't leave your young child alone without someone to mind him, and you didn't leave your grown daughter alone with a man, no matter how decent you knew him to be. Effie and Tom were alone only twice, when they went horseback riding.

"You like him, don't you?" Jake asked his daughter one

evening.

She was surprised by the question. "Why, I love him, Papa," she said simply.

Although Jake already knew this, he needed to hear it from her lips. He kissed her gently on her forehead and bid her good-night. Adjusting to the idea of Effie marrying Tom and having a family took time. As the courtship progressed, the two young people developed the easy, comfortable manner he remembered from his courtship with Effie's mother. Tom obviously was a good match, but Jake felt somewhat reluctant to lose his daughter.

Effie and Tom were different from one another. She liked to talk and often found Tom's quietness a little disconcerting. Effie loved everything else about him and thought that perhaps his quiet manner was the product of spending so much of his life alone. Finally, she asked him plainly, "Is there some reason why you are so quiet?"

He replied, "I don't know, Miss Effie. I guess I don't have much to say."

Meantime, something else had been on Jake's mind, too. One night, while they were playing cards and discussing the current problems with Mexico, Jake asked, "What are you doing for the war effort, Tom?"

"What exactly do you mean, Jake?"

"Not a hard question," Jake said with a shrug. "For instance, I made a gift of two hundred fifty dollars to help the war effort, not to brag or anything. And last summer I served on the Committee of Vigilance and Safety. We housed volunteer companies passing through here and helped provision them."

"Sounds like good work."

"The first of this month we selected four delegates to the provisional government convention scheduled at Washington-on-the-Brazos next month. If you ask me, I think they'll declare independence."

"You think so?"

"Yes, I do, and I hope they put Sam Houston in charge of the Texas army. Rumor has it, Santa Anna's marching up from the South with a huge army. If you don't mind my saying, Tom, I'm a little surprised a single man like yourself isn't planning to go help."

Tom frowned. "Here's how it stands, Jake. I'm not young anymore, and I want to get married and settle down. And as far as fighting goes, let's just say I've already had too much killing. I spent two full years, killing Indians around San Antonio."

Jake nodded. It wasn't easy getting Tom to talk at such length about himself, so he listened.

"You see, back in '29, the Mexican government gave me a land grant because of my Indian fighting west of San Antonio. But now, I don't want to kill any more than I want to get killed."

"So what do you aim to do now?" asked Jake.

"If Effie will marry me, I'll take her and go look for land between the Sulphur and the Red Rivers, north of here. A man in Natchez said he'd hunted and trapped there and liked the area. If Effie and I like it, we'll build our home and raise our family there. I'm thirty-five years old and it's time I got a place for myself. Also, it's a long way from where the fighting against Mexico is probably going to be, and hopefully, I can avoid getting very much involved."

Tom stayed in Nacogdoches and continued to court Effie patiently until she finally agreed to marry him. They had gone for a late afternoon ride, dismounting to watch the sunset fill the valley skies with every hue of orange imaginable. He decided it was time to ask her to marry him. Her soft cheek blushed with becoming modesty; she whispered an answer of "yes." The adoring look in her serious grey eyes confirmed to him that she truly loved him. As he gazed back into them, Tom couldn't imagine being happier.

Two weeks later, they were married. The wedding took place in the morning, and Effie had insisted that Tom have the mules packed and the horses saddled, so they could leave immediately after the ceremony and spend their wedding night away from her father's home—just the two of them.

Effie had always dreamed of being married by a minister, but since none was available, Tom persuaded her to let Judge Sterne marry them.

"He's as fine a man as I've ever met," Tom told her.

"Then that's good enough for me, Tom," Effie replied.

She now called him Tom. It gave him a little thrill hearing his Christian name from her lips. During their courtship, she only allowed herself to call him Mr. Williams.

A light south breeze and bright, spring sunshine yielded a beautiful wedding morning. Jake Thompson and a few neighbors attended the small, yet wonderful ceremony.

All were blissfully unaware that later the same day, March 6, 1836, the Alamo would fall in San Antonio and the war for Texas independence would become a central theme, changing their lives forever.

CHAPTER 3

Tom and Effie
1836

Tom and Effie left soon after the wedding, taking the trail north out of Nacogdoches. They had discussed the route with Effie's father and he had referred to it as "Trammel's Trace." Jake had often used it to bring stock purchased in Missouri back to Nacogdoches. "Follow the trail until you cross the Sulphur River. As you bear west, you will eventually come to a vast territory of unsettled land." Jake had also suggested that they take a look at the area along the Red River near the Trace. "A few people have built themselves homes there. It's a nice enough spot."

Jake added that some years back, the trace, originally an Indian trail, had been made wide enough for a wagon to travel. "It goes all the way to Red River to an old buffalo crossing at a place called Pecan Point. It's easy to follow. A branch of the trail goes on northwest to Jonesboro. You'll have yourself quite a pick up there."

"Thanks for the help, Jake," said Tom, as he folded up the

well-worn map.

Tom and his new bride rode a pair of bay mares and led four heavily loaded mules packed with their possessions. Jake and Tom had made sure that the couple would be well equipped with weapons for protection along the open trail. Both Tom and Effie carried long Kentucky rifles, shot pouch, and powder horn. Tom also carried a hatchet and a butcher knife with a ten-inch, razor-sharp blade. Effie rode on the new soft leather sidesaddle her father had given her as a wedding present, smiling at Tom beside her.

Their slow-paced travel gave them an opportunity to talk. It was only the third time they had been alone and Tom wanted Effie to be comfortable. He still had some difficulty with most conversations, but found Effie easier to talk to than anyone else.

"Tom, what kind of place are we looking for?"

"Good farm land, near timber, water, and plenty of game. We're going to have to live off the land. Is there something you'd particularly like for us to look for?"

She thought a long time before answering. "Well, the rivers seem muddy. I hope we can find a place with clear water, trees, and wild flowers; a good, pretty place. Look at the redbud tree up ahead. See how the purple-pink flowers give life and color to the darker trees?"

Tom smiled; he hadn't thought about flowers, but then that's what made Effie a woman. And he sure liked her femininity. "Effie, I promise you we won't settle anywhere you don't like."

On the trail outside of Nacogdoches, a dog suddenly appeared from out of nowhere and began following them as if he was a part of their caravan. He was big with brindle coloring, at least thirty inches tall, and likely weighed over a hundred and fifty pounds. The dog didn't get very close, but he sure wagged his tail when they spoke to him. Effie eventually christened him Bull. "His head looks like a bulldog," she said, and laughed quietly. "The scars prove he's a fighter." When they stopped to have some lunch along the roadside, they offered Bull some of their beef sandwiches. He finally lost his timidity and lay right at their feet savoring their offering.

Tom said, "Well, you know Effie, a good dog is handy to have around. I like dogs and if you like him too, I hope he stays with us." The dog seemed to sense their decision and wagged his tail in delight. He had found himself a home.

The air turned hot and humid as they continued their journey. The dust from the trail clung to their skin, their clothes, and virtually everything else. Tom soon realized he had underestimated Effie's hardiness and maturity. All of the horse trading trips she had made growing up with her father had taught her how to handle livestock and make camp.

Tom broke what had been a temporary silence between them. "I hope I packed everything we'll need."

"If there's something we don't have, we'll have to get along without it," she responded. "Papa never packed enough salt and I bet you didn't either."

Tom gave her a piqued look, which made her laugh in a high-spirited way that he had never heard from her before. It seemed that their setting out on their new life, or maybe just traveling the trail, had awakened a thirst for adventure he never knew she had. It was exciting to realize she was his wife now. He would have the rest of their lives to get to know her better and he knew he treasured her more than he had when they first exchanged their vows. However, he still wondered if it was possible to have a greater love for her than he did at this very moment.

About ten miles out of Nacogdoches, they left the trail and followed a little creek for a half-mile upstream. Hardwood trees and pines grew up alongside the banks of the creek. Tom looked past the branches and saw the water was clear, despite the red soil, it was running through. And soon, they found a natural clearing near the water.

"I'd say this is a fine place to setup camp," Effie declared.

Tom unsaddled the horses, unpacked the mules, and hobbled them so they could graze. While he located the supplies they would need for the night, Effie gathered wood and prepared to build a fire. She carried with her the same flint and steel she had used so many times when making trips with her father.

The wide-spreading limbs of the few hardwood trees and the tall pines around the campsite cast long shadows across the whole clearing. White buttercups covered the ground and the branches of a large dogwood tree blew in the gentle breeze from the west, its white blossoms quivering.

Effie smiled at Tom. "This sure is a pretty place to spend our wedding night. Wish I could fix a special supper for us, but we don't have any fresh meat."

Tom grinned and picked up his rifle. "Let's see what I can do about that. " Effie smiled back and returned to building the campfire.

The way Bull moved close to Tom as they set off, you'd think the two of them had been hunting together many times before; and quietly, they disappeared into the woods. Effie didn't hear anything else until fifteen minutes later, when a rifle shot rang out, echoing across the clearing. Tom returned a few minutes later with the hindquarter and loins of a young deer.

She raised her eyebrows at the sight of the meat. "Nice job," she said, impressed.

Tom talked to Effie about the possible Indian problems they could face along the trail. Since he had already fired his gun in the area, he figured it would be a good time for her to get some practice. Shooting his rifle would probably be more dangerous later on when they were further away from a settlement. In the quiet wilderness, a rifle shot could be heard for miles around.

Although he knew Jake Thompson had taught Effie to shoot, Tom wanted her to be able to fire the long Kentucky rifle. He was well pleased when she hit a spot the size of a hand from fifty paces.

"Don't look so surprised," she said as she reloaded. She was an amazing woman. Tom wondered how he could have been so lucky to have her.

The red glow of the fire made the shadows bounce on the trees. Tom and Effie wrapped a blanket around their backs as they sat by the fire. They had kissed before, but not like tonight.

Effie's eagerness made it difficult for Tom to be slow and gentle. Though neither of them really knew what they were doing, their passion made up for their inexperience. Effie's legs went limp at Tom's touch and he trembled.

After the fire began to die, they moved to their bedroll and buried themselves within the blankets; and once they were spent, they slept soundly in each other's arms.

At sunrise, they were back on the trail. They wanted to make good progress today. The first big stream they crossed was the Sabine River. Since it wasn't flooded, as was often the case during this season, fording the river didn't present a problem.

Bull had been trailing behind them, but was now leading them from about a quarter of a mile ahead. Around noon on the seventh day, Bull stopped suddenly and the hair on his back nearly stood straight up. When they got closer to him, they heard a deep guttural growl.

"What is it Bull?" asked Effie.

"Shh," Tom said.

After checking their rifles, they moved forward with caution. Jake had warned them it wasn't unusual to encounter Caddo Indians near the Cypress Bayou. As they approached the bayou, two braves suddenly came into view standing at the edge of the tree line, about fifty yards away. "Effie, don't look at them; just ignore them. They can see we're armed. These are Caddo Indians; I talked to your father about them. He didn't think they'd attack us."

Bull stayed within ten or fifteen feet of the horses, between them and the Indians, marching stiff-legged, hair still standing on end.

As they rode forward, the Indians froze until Tom and Effie

were out of sight, and they both breathed a sigh of relief when no other Indians were seen that day.

Jake had told them the Indians around the Cypress Bayou would steal anything available. Being more concerned with their supplies and livestock than about their personal safety, they traveled as long and as far as they could. Distance was desirable and when they finally set up camp for the night, they didn't make a fire. They kept their packs close and all their stock nearby.

Red soil and slim pines gradually changed to gray soil and hardwood trees. Some days later, they reached the edge of the Sulphur River bottom. Tom and Effie chose the spot to stop for the night, not wanting to try to cross the river in the darkness.

Sulphur River's heavily timbered bottom, or flood area, extended for almost two miles on each side of the river. Since it had overflowed recently, deep and thick black mud made for slow and difficult traveling. It stuck to the hoofs of the animals, slowing their progress. Whenever higher ground was available, they rested the stock. The thick tree cover kept out the sun and the whole dark area smelled wet and rotten. It was nearly nightfall by the time they got out of the mud and over to the other side.

About a mile away from the river bottom, they camped beside a stream and set to cleaning the mud off the horses, mules, and themselves. Bull's eyes were the only spot on his body not caked with mud. He generally didn't like to be touched, but he somehow managed to stand still while Effie washed off the grime. His big brown eyes looked up into hers and he licked her hands in appreciation.

Their camp was in a small clearing in the woods with good grass. Deer and turkey were plentiful and Tom shot deer for fresh meat, promising Effie that once they built their new home, he would construct a smoke house so she could cure the meat he would obtain with his hunting.

"This branch of the trail goes more to the west. Your father suggested we go this way. I'd like to go to the Red River and look over the land there. Jake said he thought two or three families had settled northeast of here, near the river. I think we'll be west of them, but we can take a little detour to go by and meet them and see how they're doing if we want to."

"I'm willing, Tom. I would like to see a real river. Sulphur River is shallow and muddy. The rotten egg odor drifting through the air is so bothersome."

Tom laughed. "The rotten egg smell is the smell of sulfur. That's where it got its name." Tom tugged on a stray curl that had fallen on her forehead.

"All right, I promise we'll not settle where a river can flood nor near one that smells like sulfur. No mud, no stink." Effie stood on her toes and kissed his cheek.

They headed northwest for two more days. Late the next afternoon, they were surprised to come upon a settlement near a spring. A tall tan man emerged from a farmhouse and welcomed them, introducing himself as James Clark. After talking for a while, he invited them to consider settling nearby.

Tom thanked Mr. Clark and explained their plan. "We'll want to see the area toward Red River before coming to a decision."

"Fair enough," Mr. Clark replied. "You are welcome to stay with us while you study the area. Why don't you leave some or all of your mules here and ride to the river? We'll be happy to care for them. The closest route to the river is northeast. It'll take two days to go to the river and back. Come back here and spend the night. When you return, we can talk and perhaps I can convince you to build your home in the area. We need more fine people like you to settle here. I know you're anxious to explore the land, but maybe when you return for your animals, we can have a good meal and a long visit. We'd love to hear the latest news from where you come from."

Tom replied, "We'll be glad to come back and visit. I'll take you up on leaving the mules. We are much obliged."

Effie and Tom reached the Red River late in the afternoon.

Once they saw it, they understood its name. The surging river, almost tumbling out of its banks, looked to be a half-mile or more wide and the water itself was red and muddy. Because they saw no sign of settlers, they decided they must be west of the folks Jake had mentioned. Effie and Tom spent the night on the banks of the Red River and then returned to the Clark settlement.

"Effie," Tom said as they neared the house. "Mr. Clark says he wants us to settle here. We'll listen, but let's not make a decision until we go a little west of here. I'd like to find even richer land."

They camped near the little settlement that the settlers called Clarksville. The Clark family invited Tom and Effie to super and as expected, tried to convince them to settle nearby.

"We're much obliged for your hospitality. It'd be good to have close neighbors and we may be back. But for now, I think we'll be heading west in the morning to see some more country."

Tom paused for a moment and then changed the subject. "You know, we haven't seen any Indians since the Cypress Bayou. Have you had any Indian problems?"

Clark shrugged. "There are some semi-civilized tribes in this section of the country. Kickapoo, Shawnee, and Delaware migrate seasonally into the area at one time or another. So far, they haven't hurt anyone. But mind you, they are all thieves, so watch your livestock and other property."

"Thanks for the warning."

"Well, if you find a place to settle, don't forget where we live. Come back to see us. And Tom, you have some good-looking livestock. Be sure to make a trip to see me when you decide to trade off a pair of those mules."

Clark leaned back in his chair and scratched his chin. "Now, if you go southwest, you'll cross a creek with some timber. That creek runs south into Sulphur River. It's called Cuthand Creek after a Dakota Indian who had all his fingers on one hand cut off. And that prairie you crossed going to Red River—we call it Blossom Prairie. It curves around and goes west and southwest of here. The land southwest of us is woody, sandy loam for the first fifteen to sixteen miles, and then you'll reach Blossom Prairie again."

Tom nodded his head and Clark carried on. "So tell us what you heard in Nacogdoches about fighting Mexicans. You're the first folks to come through here in some time, so we haven't heard anything recently."

Tom and Effie told them what they heard—about the huge Mexican army rumored to be marching in from the south.

The next day, Tom and Effie left Clarksville and moved southwest through low, rolling hills and scattered areas of hardwood trees. The blooming Indian paintbrushes, bluebonnets, and buttercups highlighted the bright green grass and the hardwood trees either had buds or tender young leaves. Spring was a beautiful sight in these parts.

By late afternoon, they came to a small clear stream with thick trees stretching a mile or more on each side. They set up camp on a hillside that sloped gradually into a natural clearing by a big spring. Along the stream and around the spring, maple trees stood among other hardwoods. The water from the spring, clear and cold, appeared to be the main water source feeding the little stream. On the north side of the clearing, a mockingbird sang and a blue jay fussed from the south side. Behind the campsite, bluebonnets bathed the hillside in a swath of blue. Spreading maple, oak, gum, hickory, and other hardwood trees covered the rise across the spring from their camp. Light, orchid-pink redbud and white blooming crabapple dotted the ground around the hardwoods.

Old ashes from a half dozen campfires lay cold. "Tom, look at the campfire ashes; it looks like it's been a while since anyone passed through here. This is by far the prettiest place we've found. I know that everything is young, fresh, and prettier in the spring, but I'll bet this place looks good anytime—even in the dead of winter."

"Effie, this also looks like a favorite camping spot for Indians. The placement of the different fires looks like an Indian tribe has camped here. We haven't seen any white men since we started out early this morning."

Effie shrugged and said, "Should we call this Campfire Spring, Indian Springs, Ash Springs, or Maple Springs? I think I like Indian Springs best."

"I think Indian Springs would be most appropriate."

Before sunup the next morning, they were packed and on the trail again, as they soon left behind the woods for flat prairie land. As the sun rose, they stopped and took in the view before them.

The prairie stretched for miles around them, and nothing but grass grew for as far as they could see. The young, fresh green grass gave way to occasional patches of wildflowers that dotted the landscape. A herd of ten or fifteen deer grazed off in the distance.

"I don't like the prairie. It's too open, too exposed, and not as inviting. Could we go back to Indian Springs? It's such a pretty place."

"I think you might be right. The soil was very rich there and I don't think that stream would ever flood. The spring is a good source of water and there's plenty of wood for fuel and building."

"I'd say it has everything we could ever want or need." She tried not to be overly enthusiastic in case Tom wanted to continue exploring, but Tom saw the light in her eyes when she spoke of their "Indian Springs."

"Yeah, I'll bet the spring where we camped never stops flowing. Game is plentiful, too. I don't think I've ever seen more quail anywhere; not to mention the turkey roost we passed before we left the trees." He only had to mull it over a few seconds. "You're right, Effie. Let's go back."

CHAPTER 4

Tom and Effie
1836-1837

Once they got back to the spring, Tom unpacked the mules, took the animals to the prairie, and hobbled all except his riding horse, leaving the animal to graze nearby.

After hobbling the stock, Tom immediately began work on an open-fronted shelter, which he would make out of saplings. Trimming the limbs from two small trees about ten feet apart, he tied a three-inch pole between the two trees as high up as his arms would allow and leaned small saplings against the crosspiece to close the back and ends.

They moved their belongings under the shelter and made it relatively waterproof with a wagon sheet cover. Tom then placed another wagon sheet across the open side, creating a makeshift door.

Heavy, dark grey clouds had been collecting in the western sky all day and were now blowing closer still. Effie and Tom worked quickly to move all their belongings under the shelter and that night, as the cold rain fell, they snuggled close under their hand-made quilts, grateful that they and their belongings were warm and dry in the shelter Tom had labored tirelessly to build. It had been a labor of love, and Effie knew she had been right to accept Tom's proposal for marriage.

Over the next few days, Tom built a corral near to their shelter. During the day he hobbled a mare and released the mules, which stayed near the mare as they grazed on the fresh green grass. At night, however, Tom corralled all the animals.

Bull had no trouble staking his claim to their new home, scouting the entire area about a mile around. His days were full of adventure, like the time when a mocking bird dived at him. Bull snapped at the bird, but it kept on harassing him, swooping down to peck at his back. Bull usually slept near the corral; but when it rained, he would retreat into the shelter, spraying Tom and Effie as he shook the water off. In spite of these instances, they were quite happy to have him around and hoped he would warn them if a threat ever came near the shelter.

At night, owls hooted, cicadas sang and wolves howled. These wilderness sounds often gave Effie an excuse to snuggle close to Tom, wrapping her arms around him. Her love for Tom had grown as the days passed and she was thrilled at being held close by him. She had now become accustomed to his quietness, and felt less self-conscious about his long silences. She loved him and just enjoyed being with him, even though at times he was a man of few words.

On days when it rained a lot, Tom knew to put the stock out to graze in the sandy areas. This was because the wet black soil on the prairie became very gummy when it rained, and balled up on the hoofs of the animals. By the last of April, the rain had slowed enough for Tom to begin cutting trees for their house. He planned to build a one-room cabin, fourteen by fourteen feet. After he cut down the trees and trimmed off the branches, Effie would tie a rope around the end and use one of the mules to drag them to the building site. Tom squared the logs and dovetailed the joints at the corners. By the end of June, their cabin was nearly finished. Shingles made up of thinly split longs covered the roof, which Tom had to strain to reach when he lifted his arms.

Sometime during the building of their home, Tom and Effie found clay from a mile or so downstream. After Tom had dragged the clay to their home site on a sled, Effie mixed it with water and small twigs to serve as building materials for their fireplace. They also mixed the sticky clay with grass, using it to fill the cracks between the logs.

As they labored together day after day, building their home, the two of them found it easier to share their ideas and dreams. They often stopped to rest, talk and have a drink of water by the spring. "I wish I could find some rocks around here. A rock fireplace would be safer than what we're building.

Effie smiled back shyly. "Well, I'm just glad we're this far along with the house. I'd like to be able to do some sewing. I don't have a thing for the baby to wear."

Tom's eyes widened, "A baby! Why didn't you tell me?"

"I'm telling you now. I might be in the family way, and I hope we have our baby by Christmas. And by the way, I'm hoping for a girl."

"It's going to be a boy," he corrected her. "I'll name him Clovis after my father." He thought a minute longer. "You've got no business working on the chimney and doing all the other things you've been doing. Effie, you have to take care of yourself and the baby!"

"Phish-posh," she said with a wave of her hand, "The work's good for me. Besides, I want to help you finish this house and get settled in before winter. We'll want to keep our baby warm."

Tom had made it a daily habit to stop working on the building long enough to plow and weed their garden and the corn patch. Once finished with the plowing and weeding, he brought in the stock from the prairie where they had grazed all day. Effie moved the things they brought with them from their makeshift camp to the cabin and built a fire outside to cook supper. "Say, Tom, if I had a prairie chicken I'd cook it for supper. Have you checked your traps lately?"

"No. I'll go check now."

Tom set traps a mile or so west of the cabin. Prairie chickens and quail abounded in this area. Bull followed Tom to the prairie. Coming back, about a quarter mile from the cabin, Bull growled and ran homeward as fast as he could go.

"Tom!" Effie screamed.

He jammed spurs to his horse and as he came out of the trees, saw two Indians, one pinning Effie's arms behind her and the other heading for the corral. Bull attacked Effie's captor, as Tom swiftly brought his horse to a halt, jumped off and shot the one opening the corral gate. By the time Tom reached them, Bull and the first Indian were rolling on the ground. Tom swiftly buried his hatched blade deep in the attacker's head.

"Effie! Are you all right?" asked Tom as he took Effie into his arms, cradling her as she trembled.

"I don't think I'm hurt. Thank goodness for Bull. I didn't see or hear a thing 'till that savage grabbed me."

"I think maybe you should lie down for spell. I need to check the Indian at the corral and patch up Bull. He's bleeding from where the bastard cut him."

"I'm all right. You go see about the Indian, I'll check Bull."

But Tom's immediate concern for Bull urged him to leave the two Indians on the ground where they lay dead, and gently put the wounded dog on a blanket by the fire. Effie quickly set to sewing up the gash on the side of poor Bull's head and another on his rib cage. Bull stayed still most of the time and seemed to understand that he was being helped. Tom wrapped him in the blanket and placed him on the floor by their bed, his rifle, hatchet and knife close at hand.

Effie looked at Tom, "Do you know what kind of Indians those were? They don't look like the Caddo Indians we saw."

"Tom's eyes narrowed. "They're Comanche. Mr. Clark said some semi-civilized Indians were in this area. I'm not sure what semi-civilized means, but I do know these two won't bother us again. I just hope—"

"What, Tom?"

"Well, I just hope they're alone and we don't have any more trouble tonight." Tom paused for a moment and lowered his voice. "They look like the Comanche I fought in South Texas."

Because it was almost dark, Tom dragged the two dead savages to the edge of the woods south of the house. He didn't think it would be wise to bury them in the dark. Tom sat up awake until the early morning hours watching the entrance of the cabin, alert and listening for any sign of movement.

The next morning, the bodies of the attackers were gone. Neither he nor Bull had heard any noise that night; the Comanche, if that is what they were, must have come very quietly to go undetected.

As soon as Bull had healed enough to travel, they saddled their horses, led all four mules, and set off to see James Clark. They needed coffee, a mulch cow, chickens, and hogs. Mr. Clark had liked their mules and they hoped to trade a pair of them for the things they needed.

Clark and his neighbors were surprised to hear about the Indians.

"We recently traded some blankets, worn-out knives and old pots to some Shawnee Indians for corn. From your description of the attackers they may have been renegade Shawnee, but I'll wager they were Comanche."

Clarksville had grown with two or three new families and they gathered together for supper and fellowship. Tom and Effie enjoyed the social interchange. The dominating topics of conversation were those about the war, the battle of San Jacinto, and Sam

Houston.

Before moving south and starting a settlement of their own, the Clarks had lived on the Red River in Jonesville. James recalled the story of how Sam Houston rode through Jonesville, on his way into South Texas, staying with them as houseguests.

"They were all gentlemen," Mrs. Clark remembered with a smile. "Folks say Houston is a rounder and drinks heavily, but when he stayed with us, we found him to be a gentleman in every way."

"If a boat could come up the river and bring Sam Houston, why don't they still come up the river?" asked Effie.

Clark shook his head, "As I recall, the Sam Houston party came by horseback and then crossed the river by ferry. You see, logs, trees and other debris often block the river, and boats can't always get upstream. A man told me the raft was very large, and had been there long enough for trees to grow on it. Boats do get up the river, when the water is high enough. But then you have to get around the raft."

"I know Texas is an independent country now, but I think I would feel better if we were part of the United States. I'm hoping that they honor my Mexican land grant, " Tom said.

"I'll bet your grant'll be honored. I've heard we may have trouble with Mexico again. And if we're a state, we'll have the U. S. Army defending us."

After a two-day visit, they drove home in a borrowed wagon home with several chickens, three pregnant sows, a mulch cow with a calf, and a young black boar-hog with a white left ear. New supplies filled the wagon: garden seed, a better plow for the garden, two barrels for water, wooden buckets, coffee, corn, and salt. The Clarks had been generous in their trade for Tom's pair of mules.

On the way home, Effie seemed wrapped in thought. "Tom, did you see the box the Clarks had by the side of their house, the one with the barrel hanging over it?"

"Yeah, it's a box for ashes. What about it?"

"They use it to make soap."

"Do they?"

"Yes. I asked Isabella Clark and she told me. They fill the box with fresh ashes from oak wood. The barrel above it drips water into the ashes and when the ashes become saturated, the water drips out the bottom as lye—"

"That's right, only we called it potash."

"Oh, you know about this?" asked Effie as she raised an eyebrow.

"No, Effie, I would like to hear you tell it."

"Alright then" she responded with a smile. "They catch the lye, and then they mix it with hog fat to make soap. Isabella told me how to do it. Can you make me a box like the one she has? I'll have to have soap for the baby-and us. People stay healthier if they keep clean and wear clean clothes."

"My mother had one like it," Tom said. "It looked like an upside down pyramid. I can use small tree branches to make it."

"Oh, can you?"

"Sure, that's easy. You know, Effie, one of the sows is going to have pigs any day now. So on a cold day this winter, we'll kill the pigs, cure the meat, and you can use the pork fat to make soap. I'll turn the hogs loose in the woods and they'll get plenty fat on acorns. We might be able to use bear fat, too. If I can kill a bear before winter, we'll try it."

About two weeks later while Tom was working on some deer hides, Bull began to bristle and growl. Tom quickly slipped his knife into its sheath on his belt, and picked up his rifle. A man on horseback rode into sight from the west. While the man was still fifty or sixty paces out he held his hands out away from his body to show they were empty, and yelled, "Hello, the house! Can I come in?"

Bull growled and crept a few steps forward, but Tom silenced him with a harsh whisper.

He motioned the man over and met him across the spring, away from their cabin. He was a tall, thin man about forty-five years of age. He had ridden in on an old jug-headed roan horse. He was dressed like a farmer, like Tom, with buckskin pants, homespun shirt, and a floppy black hat.

"I'm Luke Gault. We're looking for a place with water to stop for the night. My family will be coming up right behind me. We've been traveling across the prairie, looking for a place to settle."

Luke got off his horse, and Tom introduced himself and Effie when she joined them. Within minutes, a covered wagon pulled by six oxen came into view through the trees. A big white female dog that had been trotting beside the wagon took one look at Bull and jumped up into the back of the wagon. She was almost as big as Bull.

"You're the first people we've seen in weeks. Looks like you have a good setup here," said Luke.

Luke then went down the line, introducing his family. "This is my wife Sophie, and our four children-Matthew, Mark, John, and Mary."

The oldest boy, Matthew, drove the wagon and Mark rode an old gray mare driving two cows and a calf. The youngest children were John, who was a year and a half old, and Mary, a new baby less than three months old.

Bull, not liking so many strange people at once, bristled, growled, and stood close to Tom. Finally Tom became exasperated with the dog and said, "Bull, shut up! Lie down, now!"

Effie's bright smile betrayed how glad she was to have company. Sophie Gault, a wide, tall woman—at least twice the size of her husband—beamed with friendliness. She looked at Effie and asked, "Is there some place close where we can camp?"

"Well now, you'd be welcome to camp right here. Tom killed a deer yesterday so we have plenty of fresh meat. Just come on over when you finish. You must be tired traveling with two little babies."

Sitting by the campfire after a supper of venison stew and biscuits, Effie shared her thoughts with the Gaults.

"It's awful lonesome here and we need good neighbors. This is a very good place to settle because there's plenty of game, and trees for building. Tom and I call this place Indian Springs. There is another area, south of here on the spring branch. We'd be pleased to have you as neighbors," she said.

So the Gaults agreed to settle nearby.

Within days they began building their cabin down the spring branch where Effie had suggested. Luke, like Tom, worked hard and they helped each other. Sophie and her little ones spent most of their time with Effie while the men worked on the house. Although Effie and Sophie became fast friends, Sophie still felt uncertain about Effie's husband. "Tom isn't friendly like you. Doesn't he like us?" she asked.

Effie smiled back indulgently. "Oh, yes. He's just quiet and doesn't say much. Don't pay him any mind. After spending so much time alone before we were married, Tom finds it difficult to talk with others."

Effie's pregnancy had been bothering her for some time, but she kept her concern from Tom. Having heard women talk about the agonies of childbirth in Nacogdoches she decided to discuss her concerns with Sophie. "Is having a baby really so difficult? "I've looked forward to having a healthy child, but I've been getting a little scared lately."

Sophie was direct. "I won't lie to you, Effie. There is nothing easy about child bearing. Sure it hurts real badly at the time, but after it's over we forget. You'll see; the joy of your new little one makes up for it. Remember, I'll be here to help; and besides, you look healthy as can be."

With Sophie Gault's assistance, Effie Williams gave birth to a son at noon on January 1, 1837. She and Tom named him Clovis. They couldn't have received a better New Year's present. Effie loved Tom dearly, but she thought her heart would burst at times when she looked into the little eyes of their sweet son. Parenthood suited them both very well.

CHAPTER 5

Tom and Effie
1837-1841

By mid-February, the weather had grown cold. Tom and Effie's breath came out in white puffs as they sat by the fire; Effie wrapped Clovis in extra blankets as he squirmed tiredly in her lap. Startled by a knock at the door, the baby began crying despite his mother's efforts to quiet him. Effie watched over her shoulder as Tom answered the door to reveal a haggard and scrawny-looking man astride a black gelding. Beside the stranger stood a mule heavily loaded with hides and supplies.

"My name is Fred Prewitt, I ain't had no coffee nor salt for months, and I'm sho' tired of my own cookin'," said the man.

Tom offered to put the man's stock in the corral and Effie fed the grizzly visitor, whom they soon learned was a trapper-hunter, a meal of fresh venison, cornbread sweetened with molasses, and wild onions that she had kept in the underground storeroom Tom had dug for her out by the side of the house. As Prewitt set to drinking nearly a pot of coffee and finishing the last of the cornbread, he talked incessantly-as if he hadn't seen people in a long time. "I heard tell you wus here. The Indians call you 'Red Beard with Big Dog.' You got big medicine when the four of them Comanche come smelling around and you killed two of 'em. You didn't see the other two of 'em you didn't kill, 'cause they went down the creek seein' if they could steal somethin' there. When you shot, they come back here to see what happened. The Shawnees were followin' them and told me about it."

"Have you had a lot to do with the Indians?" asked Tom.

"Some. I run into them now an agin and git along with the Shawnee most times. Two year ago, around here, I hunted with a Shawnee and hid a bunch of hides about fifteen miles or so southeast of here near Trammel's Trace. I meant to pick 'em up, but I ain't got no way to take 'em to Nacogdoches. My packin' mule is totin' about all he kin handle. Two years is a long time to be gone from white folks."

Later, while the trapper snored in front of the fire, sprawled in Effie's rocking chair, Tom and Effie talked softly, their whispers low and hurried, as she nursed their son in a distant corner of the room. "We could loan him two of our mules on the condition that he take our hides to sell in Nacogdoches," Tom said. "And if he goes to Nacogdoches, your father, Jake, is sure to recognize our mules. Do you think we can trust Prewitt with our hides and the loan of two mules?"

"Well, let's try it. It could be a good opportunity to get those hides to market, and I'd love to get a letter to my father."

They nodded in agreement, and then Tom cleared his throat loudly in an effort to get Fred Prewitt's attention. "Well, Mr. Prewitt, if you'll take our hides along with you, I'll let you take the two mules I have. Effie's father, Jake Thompson, lives in Nacogdoches. He will act as our agent if you will take our letter with you."

Fred Prewitt was surprised, but didn't take a second more to think about the offer. "I'd sho' be happy to take your hides for trade and be much obliged for the loan of the mules. I could prob'lay have them back here after the spring thaw." He then proceeded to ask a lot of questions, most of them concerning the war. Although it had been a while since Tom and Effie had news, they told him everything they had heard from their last trip to Clarksville.

When Prewitt left the next day, he took the two mules, Tom's hides, and the letter. Effie also gave him enough fresh baked cornbread and coffee to last until he got to Nacogdoches.

"Fred said he hadn't seen white people in two years," Effie commented after their visitor left. "I don't think he's taken a bath since then either. There is no excuse for anyone to go around smelling as bad as he does. He could wash in the creeks, even if it is cold. His beard looked like a rat's nest."

Tom chuckled and gave Effie a little kiss on the cheek.

Tom reviewed their supply situation and discovered that it was dire. They were running out of the essentials. Marriage and a child had created new needs, and Tom scrambled to meet them. He needed a forge, iron, seeds, nails, salt, rope and a bigger plow. Effie needed calico, and a better steel grinder for coffee and corn.

The letter Tom and Effie had entrusted to Prewitt announced the arrival of Jake's new grandson, Clovis, and listed the supplies they needed. It requested that Jake send them back with Prewitt on his return trip. Before he left for Texas, Tom had sold the Williams property in Tennessee for good U.S. dollars and had left some of the money with Jake. Tom was hoping that their trust had been well invested in their new friend. Effie was a pretty good judge of character, so Tom determined to hope for the best. They needed the supplies, but Tom couldn't justify leaving Effie and little Clovis alone.

Being that game was plentiful, Tom had the good fortune of killing a bear in the woods and a buffalo out on the prairie. They had managed to smoke most of the meat. The fall season provided black walnuts, pecans, hickory nuts, persimmons, and wild grapes; the early summer months brought wild plums, Indian peaches, dewberries, blackberries, and other things as they ripened. Tom even robbed a bee tree and plenty of honey provided them with a sugar substitute. Even still, there were some things nature didn't provide.

In June, Jake Thompson and Fred Prewitt arrived at the Williams' cabin with a wagonload of supplies. Fred drove the loaded wagon, pulled by six young oxen. Jake rode a stallion and led Fred's black gelding and the mules.

Effie cried with joy as she fell in her father's arms and Jake cried as he held his new grandson for the first time.

"Effie, I would have come sooner if the weather had permitted, but we had to wait for the rivers to be fordable. Hopefully everything you need is on the wagon."

"Oh Papa, you brought more than enough," she said, wiping away a tear.

"I've given it a lot of thought, and I really don't like being so far away from you and Clovis. I plan to stay for a month or so, if that's okay. And when I return to Nacogdoches I'll sell my property, come back and settle nearby unless you and Tom object."

"It would be wonderful to have you here! Being so far from you is hard and I would like for you to be around as Clovis grows up. You and Tom could help one another out, go hunting together and plant crops together, and—" Effie didn't need to say anything more to convince Jake; she could sense the excitement in his eyes. The sooner, the better; he didn't want to miss any more of his grandson's growing up years.

Fred Prewitt didn't look like the same man. He was now clean; his hair was cut and his beard shaved. A new hat and new buckskin clothes completed his new look. Prewitt left the following day, announcing "I'm going to try heading northwest, away from people, but iffin' I don't find good furs, I'll be back.

Jake left and returned once again in November, and this time with a surprise for Tom and Effie: a new wife. She was a widow named Hannah; her husband, Joe Crawford, a friend of Jake's, had passed out plowing in the fields one morning and never woke up from it. She appeared to be a little younger than Jake and was a fine-looking lady. They brought with them two wagonloads of tools, equipment, supplies, and food. They even brought a few pieces of furniture. Clearly, they had come to stay. Hannah drove one wagon and Daisy her Negro slave drove the other. Nell, Daisy's fourteen-year-old daughter rode on the wagon with her. Jake rode a stallion and drove six bred mares, twenty bred cows and a bull.

Bull didn't like the pregnant yellow striped cat Hannah had brought with her, but the cat soon proved she wouldn't be intimidated, arching her back and hissing whenever he came near. However, it seemed she avoided Bull out of preference, not fear.

Tom and the Gault family helped Jake and Hannah build their cabin. Because Jake wanted to be close, they built his cabin about a quarter mile upstream from Tom and Effie. Jake's home in Nacogdoches had stone fireplaces, an elevated rock foundation and a fitted log floor. Since there were no rocks in the area, the houses had to be built on the ground without wooden floors. Dining table legs and the legs for everything else that held food now sat in saucers full of water to keep away ants and other insects. Milk and other perishables were kept in covered buckets and lowered into the cool spring water or in the water of the creek.

"You know, I'm tired of horse trading," said Jake. "The horses and cattle I brought will reproduce real well because they're from fine stock. So here's what I've been thinking. There's a good market in Nacogdoches for oxen. If Tom agrees, we might raise and break oxen and take them to Nacogdoches to market. And we don't have to worry about a market for horses because there's always a need for saddle stock."

Tom also built a cabin for Nell and Daisy. The Williams now had the two dwellings, a side room for cooking, an outhouse, a one-sided shelter for stock in the corral, a smokehouse, and a corncrib with room for harness and saddles.

Eventually, more families moved into the area and homes

were built and babies born. Everybody farmed, raising corn, wheat, oats, cotton, potatoes, beans, and other garden vegetables. Because corn didn't spoil and fed both humans and animals, it became the most important crop within the community.

Actual money was scarce so they took what they produced to Clarksville, and sometimes to Nacogdoches, to make trades. Instead, most commerce was conducted by barter. Tom had decided on raising hogs, a fairly simple job since all he had to do was turn them loose and watch them grow. Recently, he had made a trade for four more sows and in time, it paid off. The next fall, when he and Jake went to Nacogdoches, they took hides and thirty pigs to trade for some much needed supplies.

In 1837, Mark Epperson, a farmer along Trammel's Trace, established a ferry across Sulphur River on the Trace, reducing travel time to Nacogdoches. The legislature voted to pay Epperson a league of land to provide ferry service to deliver mail between Nacogdoches and Clarksville.

During their time in Nacogdoches, Tom and Jake saw the arrival of heavily loaded freight wagons, pulled by six to twenty oxen, or six to eighteen mules, hauling freight to and from Galveston and Indianola.

All of the family livestock had done well and reproduced, and now they were reaping the benefits. Tom and Jake eventually built a bigger and stronger corral at Jake's house for breaking young horses and oxen. The stock ran loose and rarely strayed far because the area provided everything the animals needed.

In the spring of 1838, Sophie, Tom and Effie's first daughter was born. Twins, Maude and Claude, were born two years later in October. All of the children became sick with the flu before Christmas that year, and they lost little Maude. Effie was crushed, but thankful that Sophie Gault came to provide her with comfort and assist her when she felt too grief-stricken to get out of bed.

Tom and Jake made a small coffin and little Maude was placed in the big room of their cabin to be viewed. Effie was loved by everyone in their community, and all of the neighbors came to tell her how sorry they were. Nell was as crushed as Effie and her tears continued to fall as she tried to take care of the other children; Jake and Hannah stayed with Effie every minute they could. Jake was almost as tearful as Effie, but tried to remain strong for his only daughter.

Tom didn't say anything but held Effie close when he could, and she slept in his arms that night.

The next morning, Tom went out and set aside land for a cemetery. Effie picked the spot for Maude's grave under the wide branches of an oak tree, less than half a mile from their cabin. Being that there was no minister in the community, Luke Gault offered to conduct a prayer service by the grave.

Effie realized that life had to go on and she had other children who needed her. Tom quietly asked Effie if there was anything she needed him to do. She smiled wanly and shook her head, and so he went back to work. Whether he liked it or not, he still had the responsibility of supporting his family.

In December, when little Maude died, the oak was bare of leaves and the cemetery seemed cold and lonely. But in the spring, when the leaves came out and the bluebonnets bloomed, the cemetery became a beautiful, quiet, and peaceful place. In addition to the bluish hue of the bluebonnets and pale buttercups, bright orange Indian paintbrushes spotted the area. Effie visited the site often, letting her tears fall on the little girl's grave before she had to get up and tend to the other children and the list of household chores that seemed to grow longer by the minute.

In the fall, the family was once again short of necessities and so Jake went to Clarksville for coffee, salt, and flour. He also took with him a big sack of corn to the gristmill to be ground into meal. He returned with startling news. "The capital of Texas has been moved."

"What?" Effie said, as she cleaned baby Claude, pinning a new bib into place. "What are you talking about; it 'moved'?"

"President Lamar moved the government from Houston to a location near a little settlement called Waterloo, on the Colorado River. The new capital is named Austin after Stephen F. Austin. The talk in Clarksville is about President Lamar irritating Mexico and there seems to be concern he'll get us into war. I'll tell you one thing though: I'll be glad when his term is up and we can elect Sam Houston again."

Effie sighed, as she was not very interested in politics. "Did you happen to talk to Isabella Clark? She was so nice to us when we first came here and I haven't seen her since I heard her husband died."

"Yes, I did. She asked about you and asked me to tell you she married Dr. George Gordon. She would like for you to come see her when you can."

Tom continued to pay little attention to his children, totally ignoring the boys. Effie knew that Tom loved them, but he seemed to think the children were the women's responsibility; he had plenty of other responsibilities himself. His duty was to provide and protect. And he had been a good provider. Effie had no complaints along that line. After Maude's death, he had held Sophie tightly, but soon was back to his old habits. Grandpa Jake paid much more attention to the children than Tom did, and Hannah often took one or two of the children home with her for a day or so.

Because of their work, Tom and Jake spent a considerable amount of time together. One day, Jake finally raised the question that had been nagging at him. "Tom, is there some particular reason why you don't seem to like your children?"

The question seemed to irritate Tom but he replied, "Jake, I just don't know what to do around children. I think it's best if Effie handles them and I just focus on making a living." Jake was not satisfied with Tom's answer, but decided not to make further issue of the matter. He didn't want to have problems in relation to Tom. It would be best for everyone if they could get along amicably.

All of Tom's livestock did well and continued to increase in number. The hogs reproduced until there were so many near the house that they became troublesome. Tom eventually had to drive half the hogs to Cuthand Creek bottom and turned them loose there. They became fat and matured rapidly from eating the abundant acorns along the creeks. That December, Tom and Jake spent a week killing their hogs, curing the meat with salt, honey, and smoke. Some of the neighbors came to pitch in and filled their smokehouses with ham, bacon, and sausage, and the women made lard and soap from the fat. There would be plenty for all to have a share, and maybe even for Tom to sell at market.

With time, Tom grew even quieter than the early days and was often gruff and abrupt. Little Clovis liked to follow Jake around, but kept a distance from his father, as did all of his other siblings. Tom would move heaven and earth for Effie, but she doubted he would do the same for the children; he seemed to avoid even their touch. Now and again Jake would try to talk to Tom about his attitude, but Tom would just clam up and walk away. No one knew of the demons that haunted him-not even Effie, although she had her own suspicions.

What kind of man, she often wondered, *doesn't like his own babies?* She imagined it must have been something terrible that happened to him long ago, maybe when he was a child himself. And yet, in that cold stare she sometimes thought she detected a flash of dread—or fear, maybe that kept the natural love of a father locked as tight as a steel drum. She began to feel something for Tom she had never felt before—pity. It didn't make her love him any less, but it made her love her children even more.

CHAPTER 6

Tom, Effie, and, Family
1842-1849

Effie, as always, enjoyed life. She loved Tom and her children, and couldn't have been more pleased when their daughter Helen was born a few years later in 1842. The newborn baby girl was sickly, however, and only lived a month. So Tom and Jake built another coffin and now Effie had two reasons to go to the cemetery. It was another two years before a second daughter was born and Effie was grateful she was a healthy baby. She and Tom named the child Elizabeth.

Over time, six more families built homes in their area near the biggest spring and before long, everyone began calling the little community "Indian Springs." Although the new families didn't know what to think of Tom, Effie's friendly disposition made her especially popular and well liked. Also, it turned out Effie had become the obliging doctor of the area. Out of necessity, she had adopted and further refined a number of things she had learned from an old Indian woman in Nacogdoches.

She used willow bark and quinine for fever, crushed mistletoe and prickly pear on wounds and rashes, sassafras tea for female disorders, whiskey and honey for coughs, tincture of opium for severe pain and calomel for everything else. Whenever Tom went to Nacogdoches, she had him buy quinine, calomel and tincture of opium—items she needed for her remedies.

Effie was a strong believer in keeping things clean. She boiled the material she used for bandages and scrubbed everything, including wounds with lye soap. Through experience she had learned that if everything was clean, patients would do better.

A circuit-riding Methodist preacher began to visit the community every two months and conducted services in people's homes. Tom only went to services on occasion, and as a result of Effie's insistence, but stayed to himself and didn't talk unless someone approached him. On the Sundays when the preacher didn't come they usually had a prayer service, led by Luke Gault. Gault had become prominent because of his friendly manner and probably further due to being married to the unanimously loved Sophie.

Every fall, Tom and Jake took a wagon to Nacogdoches to restock their supplies. Steamboats had begun to come through Caddo Lake and dock at Jefferson. By 1846 they were able to get all of their supplies in Jefferson, reducing their travel distance from two hundred miles to only eighty miles.

The settlers began making the trip together every fall in several wagons pulled by mules or oxen. Most transactions were still by barter, so they brought what they had to trade. The Jefferson round-trip, with no improved roads and no bridges, could take up to three of four weeks. If it happened to rain a lot, or they had bad luck, it could take twice as long. Also, as Clarksville grew into a trading center, getting essential supplies became much easier.

Tom and Jake did well with their saddle stock and oxen, with the help of a good cash market in Jefferson for both. Jake knew his share of horse traders and some had become accustomed to trading with him and Tom.

Things were going well and Tom began hauling back lumber with every trip to Jefferson. Although rough lumber was available locally in Indian Springs, dry finished lumber wasn't. A newcomer named Richard Ashley started making bricks from the same clay deposit Tom and Effie had used to make their chimney in their original one room home. Tom traded him hogs for bricks and started stockpiling them to use when he might begin building a new home.

Claude was now six years old, and as sociable as could be, and visited every house in the settlement nearly every day making his rounds to the neighbors' homes to visit with them. He inherited Effie's happy disposition, which proved to be simply contagious.

Claude was also an attentive listener and remembered everything he heard, often sharing the local news and interests with the family. "Mama," he said one day, "Mr. Ashley doesn't make the bricks. Wash makes the bricks and delivers them. Also, Wash isn't a slave like Nell and Daisy. He's free and just works for Mr. Ashley. His whole name is Washington Hill."

Effie knew Washington as the Negro man who delivered Mr. Ashley's bricks, but that was the extent of it. He was always polite in her presence and seemed to be fond of Claude.

Clovis, now ten years old, weeded the fields, milked the cow, and did many other chores as directed by his father. Tom was in the habit of giving out orders to his sons, but never complimented them when they did a good job and rarely said anything pleasant or friendly.

Effie and the little girls did the cleaning, washing, spinning, and cooking. They also tended to the vegetables in the fields. Nell had become particularly good at making moccasins and she kept the whole family in footwear year round using hides prepared by Tom.

Effie loved Tom and found it difficult to disagree with him, but she also couldn't bear to see him lose contact with their children. One day, Clovis asked Jake if he could go with him and his father to Jefferson. When Jake made mention of it to Tom, his immediate and definite response was, "No."

"Tom, why do you always say no to Clovis and Claude? Don't you like your own sons, don't you want them around you?" asked Jake.

Tom didn't reply. In fact, he didn't say a word to anyone in the family for a week. And in the end, Clovis didn't go to Jefferson.

Effie had a habit of twisting her hair with her left hand when irritated. Lately, she had been twisting her hair a lot.

When he wasn't working, Clovis spent most of his time with Jake and Hannah. Jake taught him to hunt and fish, as well as other things boys needed to know. Although he was a few years younger, Claude was often included in their minor expeditions.

Hannah, being the most-educated member of the family, took over the education of the Williams children, as well as several of the other children in the settlement. Clovis and Sophie were quick to learn and could read and write well by the time they were eight years old. Numbers were easy for Clovis, and he could work most math problems in his head. Claude didn't have time to learn; exploring the woods and playing, left no time for boring and unnecessary school. However, even as an indifferent student, he did learn to read and write, although his skills were poorer than Clovis', and his handwriting was cramped and messy compared to his brother's immaculate cursive.

Little Sophie was loving and talkative, except when around her father. She seemed to be afraid of him and said absolutely nothing in his presence. Hannah enlisted Sophie to help teach the other children, which led her to begin dreaming of one day becoming a schoolteacher.

Bull had become stiff and arthritic and spent most of his old age sleeping in the breezeway. Effie loved the old dog, but told Nell, "He's getting old and cranky. His disposition reminds me of Tom."

The family now owned two other dogs. Bull sired both with

the big white dog belonging to the Gault family; one of the off-spring, a brindle dog, looked and acted like Bull and stayed close to Tom. The other, white like his mother, followed Effie when she left the house. Because Bull sired several litters of puppies, there was an abundance of big dogs in the settlement.

In 1847, another son named Jake Thompson Williams joined the family. Sophie Gault had become the area midwife. While everyone else cooed over the new infant, Tom appeared indifferent as usual. When told Effie and the baby were all right, he came in, touched Effie's hand, glanced at the new baby, and went back to work in the fields.

Nell and Effie worked side by side and became very close. When Nell said she wanted to marry Washington Hill, Effie encouraged her. Her second and most serious disagreement with Tom came when she told him the news. "Wash is free and we'll have problems over ownership of their children," he said.

Effie was shocked at his attitude. "I don't want to own Nell, or her children. I think of her as my best friend, not as a slave! She has helped me and has become an important part of my life and is very important to this family. The children look to her for help as much as they look to me."

"Effie, I'm telling you—"

"And what's more, Tom, you rarely carry on a conversation with me or the children, and I don't know what I would do without Nell's friendship and help. If she and Wash want to get married..."

"I am ordering you to leave the Negroes alone!" he loudly replied.

Effie ignored him. There was no time for arguments anyway, so she went about her work. As always, during the rare moments when her busy hands were free, her fingers would nervously twist her hair and it began to fall out into her hands in clumps.

Although Nell lived and worked with Tom and Effie, Jake had never executed a document transferring ownership of Nell to Effie. When Effie talked to him about it, he said, "If you want Nell to be free, I'll see to it."

That night Jake tried to discuss the subject with Tom. He said, "Actually, ownership of Nell hasn't been transferred, and I'm going to do what Effie wants me to. You shouldn't be upset about it. Nell and Daisy are going to be free. I hope they continue to work for us, but they'll be able to do as they please."

Tom said nothing. He stood up and stalked off into the night.

When he came back, the family was already in bed. He undressed and got in bed with Effie. Immediately she got up, made herself a pallet on the floor, and went back to sleep. The next morning Tom said, "Effie, if Jake frees Nell, I want her off my property before dark!"

Effie replied, "If Nell leaves, you will never sleep in my bed again. You have become cantankerous and unreasonable. I've told you what Nell means to me and don't see how this family can get along without her. Since the responsibility of rearing the children is mine, I plan to have Nell's help. When this conversation is finished, you won't hear another word from me until you get reasonable. You aren't the only person who can be silent. Nell and Wash are going to be married and live in Nell's house."

Effie talked to Nell and Wash, and they agreed Nell would continue working as usual, and they would live in her house. Wash said, "I would like to keep working for Mr. Ashley and try to save enough to eventually get some land."

After two weeks of isolation, and without apologizing, Tom gave in. "If it means so much to you, Nell and Wash can stay." Effie let him come back to her bed, relieved that the argument was over.

Between jobs for Mr. Ashley, Wash made bricks and built brick fireplaces at Tom and Effie's house, at Jake and Hannah's, and another at Nell's house. They quickly discovered Wash could do anything they needed done. Most people didn't know the extent of his abilities, but he was the best carpenter in the settlement.

Edna came in the fall of 1849. Tom knew the baby was due

but went to Jefferson as usual and when he returned, he didn't touch his new daughter at all. Effie was proud and happy of her pretty little baby girl. Nell wanted her named May, so Effie compromised and little Edna became Edna May.

Two months later, Nell's first son, Tommie Claude, was born. Claude was Nell's favorite of Effie's children and to keep names straight they decided to call him T.C. Sophie came and helped Nell just as she had Effie and all the other mothers in the area. And although there was some criticism in the community, Sophie and Nell did their best to ignore it.

When Nell was able to work again, they put Edna and T.C. on the same pallet on the floor and worked together as usual. If they had to work outside and Little Sophie was available, she watched them both, the babies cuddling together, as close as siblings.

CHAPTER 7

Williams Family
1849-1851

Luke and Sophie Gault had a son about the same age as Claude named Peter, and the two boys spent much of their time together, practically inseparable. They often fished in a hole in Indian Springs Branch that had been formed by the continual removal of clay for bricks. The twenty by thirty foot hole was about a half mile south of the Gault place and usually produced small perch that they caught using willow poles and worms for bait. Today, however, they hadn't caught a single fish.

"We need better bait," Claude said. "I heard baby wasps are good bait. I saw a big wasp nest on a limb of the willow tree about a hundred yards upstream. Why don't you run up there and get us some bait?"

Pete laughed. "Do you take me for a fool? That's not a wasp nest, it's a yellow jacket nest, and it's bigger than both my hands. Those things really sting. If you want baby yellow jackets for bait, you go get 'em."

"Scaredy-cat. Come on, let's go get some good bait," said Claude.

Pete refused to help; he didn't dare get close to the nest. Claude found a stick about four feet long and cautiously approached the yellow jacket's home. The hovering insects buzzed his head, but when he stopped and stood still, they didn't land on him. Emboldened, he threw the stick at the nest, knocking it off the tree limb. Instantly, the angry yellow jackets swarmed out of the nest straight at him. Claude turned tail, but stubbed his toe on a tree root. Once he fell, the yellow jackets were all over him. He jumped to his feet and ran toward Pete and the fishing hole. The yellow jackets kept apace, blinding his field of vision as he ran. He fell again. "Pete!" he screamed.

Pete had already spotted the swarm, now black as a wreath of smoke, and took off in the opposite direction as fast as he could go. By the time Claude made it to the fishing hole, the yellow jackets were stinging him all over his head and arms. He evaded them at last by diving into the water and swimming underwater to the other side of the creek. He came up, gasping for air, under a low-hanging willow. He lay still in the water for nearly thirty minutes as he watched the yellow jackets nearby. By the time Pete came back to help Claude out of the water, one eye was swelled shut and he could barely see out of the other. He screamed with pain as Pete helped him to his home not far off.

Sophie Gault sprang into action the moment she saw her son hobbling to the front door with Claude hanging onto his shoulder. "Pete, you go get this boy's mother. Run! Tell her he's stung all over!" Before Pete had disappeared from sight, Sophie began applying a stinky black ointment on Claude's wounds. Claude began to shriek with pain and Sophie ordered him to sit still; the sticky ointment she applied didn't seem to be helping a bit.

Both Effie and Nell arrived a short time later, frantic with worry. Effie took one quick look at Claude and told Nell, "Go to that sandy hill across the creek and bring back some prickly pear. Here, take this knife."

Not many prickly pear cacti grew in the area, but on occasion, Effie had relied on the plant to use in a poultice for puncture wounds, snakebites, and other remedies. When Nell returned, Effie peeled three pads of prickly pear, and pounded them into a pulp, making a poultice to cover Claude's swelling bite marks. She then covered him with a quilt, but Claude was in such pain that he quivered, shook, and cried. After a half-hour or so he began to feel some relief and in an hour after that he was able to fall asleep.

Effie got a lot of practice as the local doctor, thanks to Claude's reckless curiosity and tendency to be accident-prone. Not twelve months apart, he broke his collarbone after being thrown off a horse and his right arm after falling from a tree. Cuts, scratches, spider bites, stickers in his feet, burns, and an alleged water moccasin bite were among a number of minor inflictions that befell him. But no matter the damage, Effie could always find a way of fixing him up. Before long, Dr. Gordon in Clarksville began telling folks to go see Effie Thompson before making the long trip to see him.

Early in 1849, Sophie Gault's oldest son Matthew married Eula Fay Ashley, Richard Ashley's daughter. Shortly after the wedding, Mr. Ashley packed up his belongings and left for California to find gold and get rich. No one in the community heard from him again.

Mr. Ashley's leaving to California left Wash out of a good deal of work, and so he began working primarily for Tom, doing all of the fine carpentry for the Williams' new home. Theirs was the first frame house in Indian Springs, complete with glass windows, fitted doors, a brick foundation, a wood floor, a brick fireplace in every room, and some store-bought furniture. Wash got along alright with Tom because Wash never said anything and he quietly did as he was told. He and Nell had moved into the two rooms of the original Williams cabin, and Nell's old house was now used for storage.

Tom, being a good farmer, had cleared more land than any other settler. By 1850, he had Clovis working like a grown man, and Claude as well, when he could be found. Claude had gotten into a habit of disappearing whenever Tom needed him most, a pattern that irked his father to no end.

The prairie had always fascinated Tom. The rich black soil grew grass head high. When wet, the waxy soil shined and balled up on wagon wheels and feet. When dry, it became hard. Tom eventually decided to try planting corn on the prairie to see if it would grow. He sent Washington out to the prairie with a team of oxen and instructions to plow about five acres for a corn patch. But when one yoke of oxen couldn't pull the plow, Wash figured he should go and get a second team. With the second team, they broke the plow.

Washington explained the problem to Tom and said, "Mr. Williams, ifen you want me to take the time, I'll try to build you a plow strong enough break through the soil of that 'ole black prairie."

"Yeah? How's that?" Tom asked.

"The hardest wood around these here parts comes from them horse-apple trees. There's a big one growin' down by a gully at the edge of the prairie an' it has a crook in it. Ifen it's all right by you, I'll cut down the tree an' try an' make a plow frame an' cover it with some iron you have in the storeroom."

"Go ahead, cut it down and see what you can do," said Tom as he turned to walk away.

A portion of the horse-apple tree was shaped like a hook. It took Wash nearly a month, working in his spare time and on rainy days, to build the plow. The plow was heavy and hard to handle, but it worked. Wash hooked up six oxen and got Clovis to drive the oxen while he plowed the prairie.

By the time he made the plow and got the soil ready to plant, it was late in the season for corn, and yet the crop still did exceptionally well. But it hardly seemed worth all the trouble it had been.

It was Effie who came up with a better idea. "Well, why don't we try planting cotton?" she asked one day. "Just a row for now, to see how it does. I need the fibers." Tom put Effie's idea into action and before long the cotton plants grew to be four to five feet tall and were heavy with cotton bolls.

The next fall, Tom planted enough cotton on the prairie to fill the wagon that he hauled to Jefferson. He had now found a suitable use for the black prairie land from his original land grant and was looking to trade for some more. Tom realized if and when a reasonable method of separating the fiber, from the seed became available, he had the ideal place to grow cotton. He had already heard that a man was making a machine to gin the cotton and it was only a matter of time before someone in the area would get one. Then he could haul his cotton there and have bales made.

CHAPTER 8

Tom and the Boys
1851-1852

When Claude and Pete Gault could get out of doing farm work, they spent every spare minute together. Grandpa Jake had given Claude a little gray mare, and Pete could usually get the use of the horse his father kept at the house. One day they decided to explore all of Indian Springs Branch. They started early one morning and followed the little stream until it ran into Cuthand Creek. "Let's ride down the stream and see where it goes," said Claude.

But Pete hesitated. "My pa said it goes to Sulphur River. This whole creek bottom is dark and smells awful bad. The sun can't get through these thick trees, Claude; let's not go any farther."

"You're getting to be more of a scaredy-cat all the time. You want to stay home, work in the fields, and do chores for your ma?"

"Shut up, I'm no scaredy-cat!" Pete shot back.

"If you don't want to explore with me, I'll find someone else. Home it is. I'll race you!"

The next day, Pete relented. "Alright, Claude. If you want to explore the Cuthand area, I'll go with you."

"Good man, guess I don't need to find me no other partner," Claude said with a grin.

They left early the following morning and this time the boys headed southeast until they came to the stream bottom, where they turned to follow the water, traveling along the edge of it through the heavy timber. Every mile or two they would head back to the creek to make sure they weren't lost. They made several of these exploratory trips.

On one of these little excursions, the boys rode past a little rise in the creek bottom covered with bushes about six feet high. As they approached the brush, a big old boar-hog that might have weighed four or five hundred pounds came crashing out of the thicket. Claude's young mare wheeled suddenly, throwing him to the ground.

"Get up!" shouted Pete in horror.

Claude looked up just as the boar-hog began charging toward him and he gasped with fear, his mouth wide open. Unhurt by the fall, Claude climbed up the nearest sweet gum tree as fast as he could. His horse bolted toward home, Pete riding behind her as scared as Claude's mare. Claude's horse eventually slowed down because she kept stepping on the reins and Pete finally realized that he had to go back and see about Claude. He retrieved Claude's mare and went back to the spot where the old boar had bolted out of the thicket.

Claude clung to the tree while the boar rooted around the trunk. When Pete returned, the old hog slowly walked away and within minutes, it had disappeared back into the brush.

"You could have run him off if you hadn't got so scared," said Claude in disgust.

"Well, if you could ride a horse, you wouldn't have been dumped like that," Pete replied angrily. "I wasn't the only one scared; I saw you climbed up that tree in a hurry. Now let's get out of here."

Claude knew that cuts on ears identified ownership of hogs, and he recognized the markings as belonging to his father. He sighed. Claude knew he should tell his Pa about the hog but he didn't want to have to talk to him. It felt like Tom expected him to work all the time. His father simply didn't like it when he disappeared on one of his frequent outings. In addition to feeling uncomfortable around his father, Claude never seemed to be able to please him, so he sort of gave up trying.

After thinking it over for a while, Claude went to see his grandfather. "Pete Gault and I were down around Cuthand Creek yesterday and saw a big old boar-hog which may have weighed five hundred pounds. It looked real mean! But it had our markings on its ears; it was black with a white left ear."

Jake nodded slowly. "Yeah, sounds like it's a hog your papa's been looking for. Might be one of his original animals that he hasn't been able to find. Your Papa figured it'd probably died. So where exactly did you see it?"

"I can't tell you, but I can show you. It busted out of a thicket in the creek bottom about seven or eight miles from here."

"I'll tell your papa," Jake said. "He'll probably want to try and go get it."

Two or three days later Tom approached Claude. "What were you and Pete doing down on Cuthand Creek?"

"Nothing much. We just wanted to see what it was like. Did Grandpa tell you about the big black hog with the white ear?"

"Yeah. Go get Clovis and both of you saddle your horses. We're gonna go get that old boar-hog. He's been loose for too long."

Tom rode his big stallion, Clovis mounted his bay mare, and Claude straddled his little gray mare. As they neared the thicket, Claude told them it was about a quarter mile ahead. They stopped their horses, Tom loaded his long rifle and they continued with caution.

When they got to the brush, there was no hog to be seen. "I

can smell him. This right here is his bed and he probably isn't too far from it."

"So what's the plan?" asked Claude.

Tom cast his gaze around the brush. "Well, sometimes these old boars go the same way often enough to leave a trail. Let's move up and go around the brush. They often get mean, so hold on to your horses. We'll drive him home, if we can. But if he gets too dangerous, I'll have to shoot him."

Eventually, they found the vague formation of a trail going southeast, roughly following the course of the creek. So the three of them kept their horses at a walk, and spread out with Tom in the middle, Claude on the creek side and Clovis on the other side.

This area of the creek bottom was so heavily timbered that there was little underbrush, yet there were clumps of growth similar to the thicket the boar-hog had emerged from. They had just passed one of these clumps about four hundred yards down the creek when the animal came charging out once again, snarling and stamping its feet.

This time Claude was prepared and was really holding on tight to his reins. His gray mare was not a hog horse and with all of the commotion, she started to panic and tried to run. Realizing this, Claude held her head up, so she started spinning. The boar ran at him and his horse, but before it could reach him, Tom acted quickly, shooting him in the head.

The shot spooked Claude's horse even more. His mare spun about, crow-hopped, and tried to buck and run. Claude gripped a tight rein and held on with his other hand, as he wasn't about to fall off in front of his father. Once his mare calmed down Claude tried to ride her back to where the hog lay. She refused to get closer than fifty feet so Claude had to dismount and tie her to a tree. The boar was ugly, with four-inch tusks, its head and black hide mottled with scars.

"He sure looks old and mean," said Clovis.

Tom grunted. "It's probably better that I killed him; he

wasn't worth driving home. Old boar meat is tough and tastes strong. Effie could have gotten some soap from the fat, but that's about all."

He then turned to Claude and said, "Now if you think you can handle your little horse, we'll head for home."

CHAPTER 9

Tom and the Boys
1852-1853

Over time, Tom decided to make a trade for a bull, which he would only breed to cows that he intended for milking. The bull proved to be a wise investment and soon he built himself a reputation as the local breeder of mulch cows. And since raising cattle and horses had been profitable for him, Tom thought he might try his hand at improving the quality of his saddle horses.

On a trip to Jefferson in the fall of 1851, Jake Thompson introduced Tom to a friend of his named Carl Winters, who bought horses and mules in Kentucky and Tennessee and drove them down to Texas to sell. Tom told Winters that he wanted to raise better saddle stock and some good mules. "Jake and I come here every fall so if you'll watch for a big, exceptionally good stallion, maybe a Morgan, and a sizeable jackass, I'll be obliged and more than glad to pay a good price," said Tom.

"The stallion won't be a problem," Mr. Winters replied. "I

have a friend in Tennessee who has real good saddle stock. But right now, most good jacks come from Missouri. I don't plan on going to Missouri this year, but I'll be sure to keep an eye out for one. So I tell you what, as soon as I find a good one, I'll go ahead and get it for you."

When they went to Jefferson the next year, Mr. Winters had acquired a fine stallion and an exceptional yearling saddle mare. Tom bought both. He particularly liked the yearling mare and spent time petting and training her. Tom felt sure a colt from this mare and the new stallion would be an exceptional horse, but he wanted the mare to be more mature before he began breeding her.

When Tom came back from Jefferson the following year, in 1853, he brought with him a fine black jackass. The jackass had long ears, a white nose, and his black hide shined in the sun. One unexpected result from upgrading his stock was Tom found himself operating a stud service business. Settlers from ten to fifteen miles away, some even from the Clarksville area, brought their animals to be bred with his bull, stallion, and jackass. He eventually had to enlarge his corrals in order to keep these animals off the open range and to control their breeding.

Claude had always thought that Clovis seemed more like his father than he did. Clovis did what he was supposed to do and was silent about it. He talked to his mother and to his Grandpa Jake, but usually didn't say much to anyone else. He and Claude weren't particularly friendly because at that age, two years made a big difference. They didn't fight, but they also didn't have a lot to do with each other. Tom always kept Clovis working hard in the fields or elsewhere, but Clovis didn't like it; he dreamed of leaving Indian Springs and doing almost anything else.

Claude was almost fourteen years old. He and Pete Gault were into just about everything. They flirted with the neighborhood girls when they had the opportunity, went off hunting with their slingshots and explored the woods. Claude felt mature for his age and was pretty sure his parents didn't understand him. Some days he thought he was a full-grown man.

Claude's favorite in the family was Sophie and even though she was a few years older than him, they were very close. Sophie had plans to go to school in Clarksville in the fall and he knew he would miss her, but he never discussed her with Pete because he didn't think Pete would understand. He and Sophie had always been close and he didn't think it was any of Pete's business. When he and Pete did discuss girls, it never had anything to do with sisters.

The two boys had now reached the age where everything they discussed had at least a vague sexual implication. However, the implication was never vague with the big jackass. The boys thought that being a jackass was an ideal life. All he did was eat, loaf, and breed. "Our folks want us to work all the time but when we get away from work, like today, we have a lot more fun and life seems more worth living," Claude said to his pal, Pete.

The stock was kept separate in the corrals. The end corral housed the jack, and next to him was the stallion, while the young mare occupied the adjoining corral. The stallion was running up and down the fence opposite from the one the boys were leaning on; it was obviously excited and agitated.

"What's got into him?" asked Pete.

"You don't know? The mare's coming in season." Claude stared thoughtfully at the mare, then at the stallion, and then hopped off the fence. "Come on," he said to Pete.

The boys made their way over to the next corral and watched the stallion race back and forth. Pete said, "I wonder what would happen if we turned them together?"

"Actually," said Claude, "I was thinking about putting the mare in with the jack. I bet it'd be some sight to see. Come on, let's do it."

Pete laughed, until he realized that Claude was dead serious. "No sir! Your pa will kill us."

"You scaredy-cat," said Claude with a sly grin.

"If you're going to do it, Claude, I'm going home; I don't want to have any part of this. Your pa scares the living daylights out of me."

"Ah, nobody's gonna know. Just you watch, I'm going to do it."

Pete watched quietly as Claude went into the pen with the mare and put a halter on her. He carefully led the mare into the jack's corral, closed her in and then climbed up and sat on the top rail of the fence.

"Your pa's gonna kill you!" said Pete.

But he didn't leave either. Pete's curiosity had now gotten the better of his judgment so he stayed to look through the gaps in the fence while Claude sat on the top rail, clearly enjoying his joke.

The mare didn't seem like she was ready and tried to shy away from the jack. But the jack was as patient as he was determined and, after about thirty minutes, succeeded in his task. Just as the act was concluding, Tom Williams rode up behind the boys.

"What in the name of God Almighty have you done?" he bellowed.

Pete jumped up, fleeing the scene; he ran as fast as he could and didn't look back. But Claude had frozen on the spot. Tom rode up to where he sat perched on the top rail, grabbed him by the collar, and pulled him backwards off the fence.

"Damnation! Why, in all that's holy, do you think I've kept that mare penned up? Do you think I kept her in the pen to look at or to breed her to a jackass and get a mule? Now, you march yourself over to the corn crib and get what you have coming to you."

Claude couldn't remember ever being so scared. And while he had seen his father angry, he had never heard him talk like this before.

Tom yanked him along by the collar and led him to the corn crib where he bent Claude over a barrel. Without a word, he took a bridle rein from a peg, doubled it over and applied it generously to Claude's backside. Claude struggled briefly but Tom held him down by the back of his neck as he lashed him repeatedly with the rein.

After a while, Claude was in tears and his backside was bruised and bleeding. But Tom wasn't finished. He took Claude by the collar again and marched him out of the clearing and back into the woods. There he leaned Claude up against a tree.

This time Tom wasn't silent. He shook his finger under Claude's nose and said, "Boy, that licking was long past due. This is the first time I've ever laid a hand on one of my children, but I promise it will not be the last. You need to make some major changes in the way you behave around here. I demand you act like you're at least ten years old, and then we'll see if you're mature enough to stay out of the corn crib. Starting tomorrow, you come to me, daily to get your work assignment.

"Now, after you finish your chores tonight, get your Bible—which to my knowledge has never been opened—and bring it to me. You will start reading your Bible and I intend to question you to see that you understand what you've read. You're not to go see Peter Gault, and he is to stay away from here. If Pete shows up, it will indicate his pa can't find enough for him to do and I'll put him to work myself. Now, go see your ma and tell her you'll be doin' all the milking in the future. And, you will also feed the stock. Now get out of my sight."

Upon being released from his father's hold, Claude fled. When he managed to get himself under control, he went to see his mother as instructed. Effie listened and nodded her head, but made no comment at all.

The next morning after chores, Claude was sent straight to the corn patch. For a week, he hoed corn until just before dusk, and then it was home to do chores again. The only person he talked to was Wash, who would come to the cornfield to plow the row centers.

Wash listened, nodding thoughtfully. "We can't talk but a little bit. Ifen I was you, I wouldn't loaf. Two or three times a day yo' papa rides to where he can see you to be sure you ain't loafing. I bet he ain't going to forget what you done in a hurry."

When Claude finished hoeing the corn, Tom had him repair parts of the rail fences built around the fields, and after finishing that, Tom had him split rails. All gardens and fields were fenced to keep out free-ranging animals, so there never were enough fence rails. It was hard and hot labor, and Claude gradually became tan and strong. But as he labored in the heat of the sun, he longed for the days when he and Pete fished or sat in the shade. While Claude resented that his father never treated Clovis so harshly, he had to admit that his brother had worked this hard for years.

With this realization, Claude developed a new found respect for his brother, although it didn't make the work any easier. Clovis liked hard work; Claude didn't. Claude grew to hate reading the Bible, and not being able to understand it almost as much as he hated being mistreated by his father. Young as he was, Claude didn't really see himself a man of action. And the more he thought about it, the more he began to fear he might never get away from his father.

CHAPTER 10

Clovis and Claude
1853-1856

In 1855, Jake Thompson came down with the flu, and Tom needed to make a trip to Jefferson and so he took Clovis with him in Jake's stead. A strong young man of eighteen, Clovis had been doing the work of a grown man since he was thirteen years old. Although his father never paid him anything, his grandfather, Jake had helped Clovis startup in the stock business. Clovis now had a growing herd of horses, over a hundred head of cattle with his brand, and over a hundred head of hogs all with his own brand. The twenty head of young oxen he had raised and trained were big and strong.

Jefferson was a bustling town, and its streets were constantly crowded with freight wagons bringing merchandise from Indianola and Galveston. In addition to freight, boats and ferries arrived loaded with immigrants. Clovis had never before seen any place with this much activity. In fact, he had never been anywhere other than nearby Clarksville.

After they returned home from the trip, Clovis went to see Jake with the intent to borrow his largest wagon. "Well sure, you can have it if you want it. But what do you want with it, Clovis?"

"You wouldn't believe the amount of freight being hauled into and out of Jefferson. I'd like to take the oxen I've trained and try my hand in the freight business," replied Clovis.

Jake nodded slowly as he drew on his pipe. "I don't know much about the freight business, but I think it's high time you became independent. The wagon is yours. Good luck to you. I'll take care of your stock until I hear from you."

As soon as Clovis could round up a load of hogs he left for Jefferson, leading two saddle horses and all of the oxen that were not pulling the wagon. One of Bull's descendants, a dog they named Tip on account of him being all white with the exception of his brown-tipped tail, accompanied him. Clovis had trained him to be a good herd dog and he was fiercely loyal to him. When Clovis told his mother goodbye, she fretted over him, but said she understood and would pray for his success. He left without saying a word to his father.

"Where is Clovis? I need him to help me find some of our cattle today," boomed Tom as he burst through the door of their house. The room was quiet and so he turned to Effie. "Effie, have you seen him today?"

Effie didn't look up from her knitting. "He left, Tom. He's on his way to Jefferson. He took a load of his hogs with him. The way I understand it, said he was going to try the freight hauling business."

"He left, just like that? I'm his father; he should have said something to me. He's needed here and so there's no point in his traipsing off to Jefferson. Why, we just got back from there! Besides, I heard that a man set up a cotton gin in Halesboro and I plan on planting a whole lot of cotton next year."

"Well, why should he bother to say anything to you, Tom?

You never talk to him except when you order him to do something. Don't forget, he's already eighteen years old. And if you don't ease up on Claude, there'll come a morning when he won't be here either. And do you know why? You treat him worse than most people treat their slaves. And if you want to keep Wash around, you better start treating him with a little more consideration. You know he doesn't have to work for you. People can only take so much, Tom. You demand a lot from all of them but never have a kind word to say, and you never paid our sons a penny for their work. It's a miracle any of them have stuck by you this long. I won't say another word now about this, but please Tom, think about what I'm telling you."

Tom looked shocked; instead of responding to Effie he just turned on his heels and walked back out the door. Effie thought she noticed a new slouch to Tom's shoulders. She turned back to her knitting; her eyes were so full of tears she couldn't see, so she closed her eyes and said a prayer for her stubborn husband. He had a lot of flaws, but she still loved him.

Once in Jefferson, Clovis sold his hogs and was soon hired to work with his oxen, and wagon, for a freighter named James Doyle. Mr. Doyle, like most freighters in the area, had more business than he could handle on his own. Clovis' first freight job for Mr. Doyle was to transport a load of pine lumber to Indianola and bring back a load of barreled whiskey, all the while being led by an experienced teamster who had made the trip many times. From the first freight run, Clovis learned a valuable lesson: mules were significantly faster than oxen. So he sold all his oxen, his wagon, both saddle horses, and together with his earnings purchased a larger, newer freight wagon and teams of strong young mules.

Big young mules were expensive, even more so than oxen or horses, but he believed the investment would pay off. If he had learned something working all those years for his father, it was that courage and determination in a calculated venture often paid off. Tom had seen many successes when taking this same sort of risk.

Clovis would show his father that he could have his own successes. After all, he wasn't getting anywhere working for Tom, who never paid him anything for his years of hard work; if Clovis wanted any kind of future-his own home and family-he would have to make it happen on his own. He couldn't count on Tom's help. Jake meant well enough, but he wouldn't be around forever and Clovis' younger brothers and sisters could benefit from Jake's help now. Clovis would prove to Tom that he could make it on his own.

The freight wagon Clovis upgraded to was quite impressive. Its wheels were six feet high and he intended to pull it with eight teams of young, big and strong mules.

At the end of a trip, a new load of freight was available and as soon as it was loaded into his wagon he would depart once again. Most of the teamsters he knew spent what earnings they made on each trip in the saloons and brothels and then went back to work. Clovis averaged about three trips for every two his competitors made, and his good equipment could haul larger loads than most of theirs. By buying extra mules some could be left to rest between trips. The investment paid off, as faster time was made with fresh and well-fed stock. Before long, Clovis acquired a reputation as a reliable fast freighter. Instead of wasting his money on whiskey and whores, Clovis saved it to purchase more wagons and mules to expand his business.

Clovis looked into hiring teamsters to drive his new wagons and mules; however, most of them wanted to go spend their money after one freight trip and didn't like the long hours. They were unwilling to make back to back hauls the way Clovis did. He found that new teamsters had to be hired after every run, and this was a great frustration to him. He had never gotten away with such laziness back home on his pa's spread. Finally, his luck changed one day when an elderly Mexican who needed a job approached him. Clovis had his doubts when he met the man and almost didn't hire him because of his age. But something about the man's determination inspired confidence. "My name is Poncho Garza and I work hard. I'm a good cook too," he said. Clovis agreed to hire him.

Clovis hired him and found him to be his best teamster, as he also took on the responsibility of cooking for the other drivers. A big pot of beans was always available and cornbread was made in an iron Dutch oven. Poncho's coffee was hot and strong. The first day new teamsters hired on, they usually griped about having to work with a Mexican, but Clovis didn't give in to anyone's complaints. In his abrupt way he told them, "Poncho stays." And as usual, grumbling ceased once they started eating Ponchos' good cooking. A good cook on freight runs was hard to find, and it wasn't long before word got around about the darn good cook Clovis had. Clovis contributed to this reputation by keeping the camp provided with the fresh meat of wild longhorn cows and deer.

Poncho proved to be a valuable asset in that he knew routes to and from the coast that Clovis had no knowledge of. Even though Poncho was old, he had a wealth of experience and seemed to enjoy working as hard as Clovis did. Clovis learned early to consult him when needed.

One of the many hazards freighters faced out on the road were the outlaws who often tried to rob them. Another real danger was that in some regions there were aggressive Indians. For this reason, Clovis rode a horse with his wagons and was armed with two pistols, a rifle, and a ten-gauge shotgun. The pistols were Walker Colts, which he carried in saddle holsters, the rifle was an 1843 United States Carbine, and he slept with the shotgun loaded by his side. Clovis didn't intend to give up anything without a fight. One night while on a return trip from Indianola, two thieves approached their campfire with drawn guns and demanded the money Clovis had earned from the delivery of his load. Without a moment's hesitation, Clovis shot one of them with the ten-gauge shotgun so badly he almost severed his body. The other one fled, wounded by Poncho, and word spread quickly that Clovis Williams was dangerous to fool with. The biggest loss was Tip, the dog brought from home. One of the bandits shot him when he started barking, and Clovis and Poncho immediately opened fire. Despite the incident, the William's Freight Company continued to develop a reputation for being fast and efficient, and was in demand.

Clovis often thought of Claude and thought he would probably like to join him. Finally he wrote a letter to Claude and his mother inside his letter to Jake so his father wouldn't see it.

> *Dear Grandpa,*
>
> *For obvious reasons I'm enclosing a letter to Mama and to Claude. I'm asking Claude to join me because I've got a great opportunity here with more business than I can take care of on my own. I now have   three big freight wagons and sixty big healthy mules.*
>
> *I hope all is well there, and if Claude should decide to join me, please sell all of my stock and send the money by him.*
> *Love and respect,*
> *Clovis*

> *Dear Mama,*
> *I'm well and healthy and I hope you and the family are the same. I'm writing Claude asking him to join me. My freight business is doing well and I've rented a small farm outside Jefferson to headquarter from. Now is the time to prosper in this business but I need help I can trust and I hope Claude will come.*
>
> *Please write me at general delivery, Jefferson, and let me know what goes on.*
> *Love to all,*
> *Clovis*

> *Dear Claude,*
>
> *I've done well for myself since I left home*

and now have three large freight wagons and sixty young healthy mules. I need someone I can trust to help and would like for you to come and join me. If you decide to come, bring with you any saddle stock or anything else you have to put in the pot and I'll make you a full partner in the freight hauling business.

This is hard and dangerous work, and yet quiet profitable for those who will work diligently and not waste their profit in bars and brothels. There is still some danger from Indians, and bandits always present a threat. We were recently attacked by bandits but were successful in fighting them off.

I've asked Grandpa to sell any stock I have left and to send the money by you if you come. If you decide to come, do so as soon as possible and be sure you are well armed. Grandpa can tell you what to bring.

I haven't met any fetching girls here because I haven't had the time. As soon as I get back from a freight run I immediately leave again with fresh mules. I've had numerous offers to haul freight going to different places but couldn't take the business because I don't have anyone I can trust. Please come.
Clovis

Clovis' spare mules were left in the care of Poncho's son Lupe and his wife, Anna, who lived at the farm he had rented. Lupe had a crippled leg but was still able to take good care of the mules. He had been thrown from a horse when he was a young boy, and his leg was broken in the accident. It hadn't been set properly, leaving it crooked and a bit shorter than the other. Lupe seemed to do all right, though, working in short spurts but without much stamina. Clovis headquartered his business out of the farm, and usually slept in the tack room when he was in town. The farm also had a smaller house in which the Garza family lived.

By the fall of 1856, the mares that Jake had given Claude had reproduced and he now owned about twenty head of good horses. Years of hard field work and his mother's good country cooking had made Claude big and strong—six feet tall and all muscle. He had the same coloring as his father, even down to his reddish blonde hair. At sixteen years of age he didn't yet have a full beard, but between shaves his scruff showed bright red.

Although Clovis had mailed his letter in mid-summer, Jake didn't receive it until he went to Clarksville for supplies in early September. The letter had been delivered two weeks prior, but no member of the family had been to town during that time. Despite the recent growth in Clarksville, mail service between Jefferson and Clarksville had not improved.

Claude was so pleased with his letter from Clovis, he nearly shouted with excitement. Claude had reached the point where he almost hated his father and welcomed a chance to get away for good. Claude's horses would have to be gathered and Jake needed a little time to sell off Clovis' stock.

For the past few months, Claude had been trying to get his friend Peter Gault to join him in leaving Indian Springs, but Pete wasn't interested. Because of his work schedule, about the only time he saw Pete was an occasional Sunday. With or without Pete, Claude was serious about getting out of Indian Springs and away from his father.

Effie's letter from Clovis both excited her and brought her to tears. She had missed him terribly and this was the first time she had heard from her son since he left home. She cried even harder when she read the part about his inviting Claude to join him.

Effie knew Claude would want to go and she couldn't blame him. She had worried about Claude's increasingly dark moods and could sense the resentment he held in his heart toward his father.

She believed that God had heard her countless prayers for Tom, but he sure was a long time in answering. She would have to resign herself to the fact that Claude's leaving was imminent and ultimately for the best. Effie made him promise to write more often than his brother had done but wondered whether he would follow through.

Claude's sister Sophie was attending school in Clarksville and so he made a trip out to see her to tell her goodbye. Before leaving, Jake briefed him in detail about the route to take. Claude listened intently to Jake because he had never been further away from home than Clarksville. Claude was as ready as he'd ever be, and was now determined to get to Jefferson as soon as possible.

Tom was furious when he learned that Claude was gone. "How long have you known about this? Why didn't you tell me?" he railed at Effie. "I would have stopped him."

"Maybe that's why I didn't tell you," she snapped back. "I warned you, Tom Williams, if you didn't ease up on that boy, he'd be gone."

"There is absolutely no excuse for his leaving-or for Clovis to have left in the first place. I'm very disappointed in my sons, I provided for them their entire lives, and this is how they show their gratitude?"

"You're disappointed in them?" asked Effie, shaking her head in disbelief. "Your sons are more than disappointed in you, Tom. All you ever did was order them around without ever showing respect or appreciation."

"I'm their father, Effie. All I've done is seeing they carry their share of the work."

"Exactly; that's all you've done. I've never once heard the words 'thank you' leave your lips. And it's too late for them now. So that leaves Wash, and I hope you appreciate all he does for us or else he'll be gone, too. Then where will we be?"

Tom didn't seem to be listening to her. "They should never have left," he muttered as he paced the room. "The boys should be helping us build for the future! I thought they were smart enough to know what we build here will belong to them some day."

"Too bad you never made that clear to either of them. All they ever wanted was to gain your love and approval; they just wanted you for once to say you were proud of them. They never asked for anything more. But you worked them too hard and never showed them any love or appreciation, and they got fed up with it. I wish to God it weren't so; but I fear we may never see those boys again. I love you, Tom but I've had to pray mighty hard to not harbor resentful feeling against you for the way you've treated our sons. If they ever do come home to visit, I sure hope you make amends with them. Meanwhile, we'll just have to hire some help. And that's the best we can do. A lot of the newcomers don't have land, so it shouldn't be a problem to hire someone. You just better be reasonable with them though, or before long you won't have any help at all."

At that, Tom stormed out of the house and didn't mention the boys again.

CHAPTER 11

Clovis and Claude
1856-1857

Claude was a bit anxious on his way to Jefferson, being his first long journey alone, but much to his relief the trip turned out to be relatively uneventful. When it became too dark to see at night he got off the beaten path, hobbled the horses, and slept with a loaded shotgun at his side. Claude had sent word ahead to Clovis accepting his invitation to join up with him; however, when Claude arrived in Jefferson, he discovered that Clovis was out on a freight run. Fortunately for Claude it was not hard to get directions to the company's headquarters since Clovis' reputation was so well known in Jefferson. After taking a quick look around Jefferson, Claude found the small farmhouse his brother rented on the outskirts of town. Lupe met him in the yard of the farmhouse, and after Claude introduced himself, he helped him release the horses to pasture. The Garza family fed him a large meal of stewed beef, beans, rice, and Anna's handmade corn tortillas. Claude hadn't eaten so heartily for some time. Claude retired to the tackle room and slept in Clovis' bed.

This would do just fine until his brother returned.

Lupe and Anna happily brought Claude up to speed with the working of the farm. They were very hospitable, and Claude appreciated their loyalty to his brother even in Clovis absence. Clovis had met with good fortune in finding such a hardworking couple to man his headquarters while he was away. Claude spent the next several days working with the horses. Although the horses were saddle-broke, time on the open range made them more than frisky. Claude rode each of them numerous times, getting to know them better than before he left home. One day a horse trader came out from Jefferson and wanted to buy some or all of the horses. Claude decided to wait for Clovis to return. "I'm a friend of Clovis and helped him find his mules," said the trader. Claude declined the trader's offer, feeling it would be best to wait for Clovis to return. The horse trader's name was Shorty Spence, a name Claude thought was appropriate since the man stood only a little over five feet tall.

Although they had never been close, the two brothers were certainly glad to see each other when Clovis got back from his run. They realized that their family blood provided them with an especially strong bond. Together, the brothers fixed another bunk in the tackle room for Claude's use. That evening, they sat in silence eating Anna's cooking. Anna had made a favorite Mexican dish of beef that she cooked in red chili sauce, rolled in cornmeal, and baked in cornhusks. She explained to Clovis that they were called "tamales," and she had made them in honor of the reunion of the brothers. Claude and Clovis didn't seem to feel the need to talk much over the tasty meal; their feelings of resentment toward their father were still raw and better left alone. They trusted and respected each other, and that was what mattered for now.

The next morning, they looked Claude's horses over and decided to keep ten of the best and sell the rest. Clovis knew just where to sell them and so he and Claude could both travel on horseback; this gave them spares when they returned with tired horses. Once they were on the trail, Clovis was the first to speak.

"With the money we get from your horses and what we'll make on a few more freight runs, I'd like to buy more mules and another wagon. Then that will give us two wagons each if we need to take our loads in different directions."

"Alright," Claude said, careful not to miss something important. He was determined not to let his big brother down.

"My first friend here is a freighter named Doyle. He advised us to get a partnership agreement drawn, so in case something happens to one of us, the other can keep going. I'd like for us to jointly own everything I've made up to now and all that we'll make in the future. So what do you say, Claude?"

Claude replied, "Well, I don't know anything about business, but I'll work hard and help build the company every way possible."

Clovis clapped him on the back. "Sounds good to me."

Having discussed the business details, Claude moved to other pressing questions. "How about girls, Clovis? Have you met any of the local girls since you've been here?"

"No, not really; but look, right now we don't have time to think about that. Maybe later," as he knowingly shook his head and chuckled to himself. Claude was right; they would have to make time for some socializing in town.

The two brothers rode into Jefferson and found the lawyer that Mr. Doyle recommended. The lawyer, Charles Fletcher, drew up a simple partnership agreement and suggested that they make a will, each leaving the business to the other. Fletcher had been representing people in the freight business for a long time and knew it was dangerous work. On leaving the lawyer's office they were approached by a man with three loads of lumber that he needed to be transported to Galveston. Clovis and Claude discussed plans to make the run and left early the next morning.

As he worked with Clovis, Claude learned that it was important to set up their evening campsite near water whenever possible. At night, they pulled the wagons together closely, watered and fed the mules, and ate their evening meals prepared by Poncho. Each teamster was responsible for taking care of his own mules. Claude also found that they could almost always find wild longhorn cows or deer for fresh meat when needed. The leftovers from what Poncho cooked at night were often served as lunch the next day. Claude slept under the front wagon while Clovis slept under the rear one, both with loaded ten-gauge shotguns at the ready. At daybreak the next morning, Clovis had everyone up and moving.

For the first few days, Claude and Clovis mostly rode together. They often rode a short distance ahead of the drivers so they could warn them of dangers in advance. The brothers enjoyed riding ahead, because this gave them a chance to talk. They were already getting better acquainted than they had ever been before. On one occasion, Clovis told Claude about the time he had to kill a man who was trying to rob him of a trip's earnings. "I never thought I could kill a man, but that thief wanted to take away what we had worked so hard for without turning a hand. He was armed, and I figured it was either him or me. One blast with the ten-gauge stopped him."

Claude was awestruck. "Do you regret it?" he asked.

"Nope; I'd do it again if necessary. Hell, we have the right to protect what we've worked for. My best advice to you is to keep your shotgun handy and loaded and try not to let anyone make us work for free."

I'm gonna give you one of my pistols and we should also get you a carbine because they're pretty handy to hunt with. You'll find that using the same ammunition is convenient."

"So how did you manage to do so well in such a short time?" asked Claude.

"It's simple," said Clovis. "I've just outworked the other teamsters and saved my money instead of spending it in saloons and brothels. Plus, there's been plenty of business available. Some of the freighters make a little and then slow down. For some reason, they just don't think about the weather and other factors that could reduce their income. Like Jake used to say, 'we got to make hay while the sun is shinin'. It's the same for freightin'; we've got to work hard while there's work to be got. For example, before you came, if I got sick my income would stop dead. That's one reason why I'm so glad to have your partnership. We can get twice the work done before big rains and big snows keep freight from moving. We need to be mindful that business won't always be this good. Right now, we have plenty of business between Jefferson, the coast, and back. So I say, let's make the best of it while we can."

Most of the other local freighters relied on two oxen to haul large quantities of freight, as they were cheaper and didn't eat as much as mules. The big wooden wheels of the carts could be heard squeaking from almost a mile away. But Claude used four-wheeled wagons with two to four teams of strong mules, depending on the weight of the load. It proved to be much more efficient than the method of his competitors, Clovis had invested his savings well, and profits were beginning to show.

By the spring of 1857, Clovis and Claude purchased themselves a fourth wagon with some money they had stored in the bank. One of their lumber clients wanted two loads of lumber hauled to San Antonio, and this was the first trip Claude made without Clovis. He missed Poncho's cooking, but they got by. San Antonio was now a booming town, with countless shipments coming from the coast. Claude soon realized that two-wheeled Mexican carts were hauling most of these shipments. While Claude was in San Antonio, he was approached by a man with two loads of cotton that he needed delivered to Galveston. Claude took the job.

About half way to Galveston, they came upon a Mexican freighter lying unconscious beside his cart. The man had been beaten badly and his load and both oxen stolen. Claude cleaned the man's wounds as he had seen his mother do, and loaded him on one of his own wagons. The Mexican was feeling better the next day, but still unable to walk from being so viciously beaten. Claude guessed him to be around twenty-five years old and about five and a half feet tall. Despite his injuries, Claude heard no complaining, and the Mexican seemed grateful for the care and food they provided him.

Claude planned on purchasing some first aid supplies to take with the wagons the next time he had an opportunity. He remembered how his mother always used her homemade lye soap to wash and clean wounds; he would have to buy some to have on hand. And he could not remember his mother's other remedies. He wished Poncho and Clovis were with him so he could have their advice.

The Mexican could speak only a little English. He introduced himself as Vicente Gutierrez, which was too much Spanish for Claude; he decided to call the man Pete. In the same manner, the name "Claude Williams" presented a challenge for Vicente, and so he called Claude, "Señor Colorado" which proved to be appropriate since "Colorado" meant "red" and Claude's hair shined unmistakable red in the noonday sun. By the time they reached Galveston, Pete was able to limp around, and helped out in every way he could. Pete found one of his friends who could speak English, and with his friend's help explained what had happened to him. "Two gringos rode up and knocked me in the head from behind, and when I fell to the ground they hit me many times with the butt of their rifles and kicked me with their boots and spurs. They stole my oxen and my freight and left me for dead. I might have died if you hadn't stopped to help me."

While they stood talking, one of Claude's teamsters came up and announced that he wasn't going back to San Antonio. Without hesitation, Pete asked for the man's job, and Claude agreed to give it to him.

Claude made an additional trip to Galveston before returning to Jefferson. Although he made more money on those trips than he could have between Jefferson and the coast, by the end of it, his mules were spent. So once a load for Jefferson became available, Claude and his teamsters headed home for fresh mules.

The other gringo driver quit in San Antonio. Fortunately for Claude, Pete had a cousin there who wanted a job. In the end, Claude was pleased; he found that his Mexican drivers complained much less and had better dispositions than the men they replaced.

Eventually, Pete wanted to learn more English and Claude wanted to learn Spanish, and so they got together in the evenings for mutual language lessons. Their methods were rather haphazard, one man pointing at objects and naming them, while the other gave the name in his native language.

The day before he left San Antonio, he sat down and wrote his mother a letter.

> *Dear Mama,*
>
> *I'm sorry I haven't written but time seems to fly by. Clovis and I are both doing real good. We now have four wagons, about eighty mules and all the business we can take care of.*
>
> *Please write to us in care of General Delivery at Jefferson. Tell everyone howdy for us.*
> *Love,*
> *Claude and Clovis*

This was the first letter Claude had ever written, and he knew it didn't amount to much. Claude missed his family and really didn't know how to tell them in words.

As it turned out, Effie knew more about the boys than they could imagine. Tom had made trips to Jefferson, but each time the boys were on the road with loads of freight. Effie got more information when Jake went to Jefferson. The boys were gone again, but he had learned second-hand that they were doing well and had a place near town where they headquartered.

In response to Claude's letter, Effie wrote:

Dear Clovis and Claude,

Both your father and grandfather have been to Jefferson and so I have had some word about you. That is no excuse for your not writing.

You have made quite a reputation for yourselves in the freight business. Jake is sorry to have missed you on his trips to Jefferson, as you are of on trips of your own. If you are so busy, things must be going well for you. Your father is getting feeble and forgetful but he still goes to work every day. There are plenty of people in town who don't own land and want to work so getting enough hands to do what needs to be done isn't a problem. Thank goodness for Wash. He brought your father home today around noon with a high fever, and I have him in bed. He is coughing and rattles when he breathes. Probably not pneumonia but I hope this doesn't get worse.

Your grandfather is in good shape physically, and I depend on him a great deal. Sophie finished school in Clarksville and married John Gault. Hannah is tired and Sophie is going to take over the school this fall. The other children are all in school, helping with chores and overall doing well.

We have a lot of new people in town. I miss you and wish you were here but understand that you are better off there. Please write.

Love,

Mama

Clovis arrived in Jefferson just before Claude, and was very pleased about the money Claude brought in. They began discussing San Antonio at length. Being that there were no big freight companies working out of San Antonio, they discussed the possibility of moving their headquarters there, but made no immediate decision.

The brothers spent a few days doctoring mules, repairing harnesses, and replenishing needed supplies. They also purchased groceries for their next trips. Clovis felt it'd be wise to have a blacksmith come and check every mule and reshod those that needed it. Due to the fact that San Antonio was growing quite rapidly, there was a large demand for lumber. Their next job was four wagons worth of lumber for San Antonio. On the first night of their trip, the brothers made the decision to move their business to the newly booming city. It seemed clear that more money could be made in less time in San Antonio than in Jefferson.

Clovis rode on ahead to rent a place. By the time Claude got there, he had found lodgings southeast of town on the San Antonio River. It was larger than the one in Jefferson, with a big barn and a bigger house. The owner wanted to sell it but Clovis wanted to talk to Claude before buying, so only arranged to rent it temporarily.

When the brothers regrouped in San Antonio, Clovis told Claude what he had found. His words seemed to tumble out of him with a feverish intensity. "Claude. I almost bought it. The place I found, I mean. But I thought I'd—"

"Whoa! Clovis, slow down there," Claude said. He had never seen his brother that animated before, as in the throes of a delirium.

"What? Yeah—anyway, it's a lot bigger than we had in Jefferson and also has a big barn and a bigger house. I made arrangements for us to use it until you see it and we decide…"

"All right, now settle down, Clovis, you're making me nervous," He felt his brother's forehead. "You have a high fever."

"Yeah, I guess I'll go back now because I do feel terrible. But if you agree, I think we should buy it."

Claude got the wagons unloaded, settled for the shipment, and headed south as Clovis had instructed. When he arrived at the property he found Clovis violently ill with diarrhea, and so sick he was unable to move. Claude stayed up throughout the night, taking care of him. When Clovis wasn't unconscious he was delirious, and so Claude didn't bother him with attempts at conversation.

Early the next morning, Clovis died. His skin began to turn dark almost immediately and Poncho, who had seen this happen before, told Claude it was cholera. He and Poncho dug a grave for Clovis under a big cottonwood tree on a little rise about a hundred yards from the house. Claude had no experience with death or funerals. As he and the Mexicans stood around the grave, he gave an impromptu eulogy: "Clovis was a good brother and a good man. Lord, please forgive him his sins." He then quoted the first half of the Twenty-third Psalm and the Lord's Prayer. The Mexicans all crossed themselves. After the burial, Claude determined that he would purchase both a Bible and a gravestone the next time he went into town.

That evening for Claude was as sleepless as the night before. He was only seventeen and couldn't believe their dreams had been shattered in the one night's passing. He had only just begun to get acquainted with his older brother. Disappointment and anger churned inside him, but his eyes remained dry. He had never seen his father cry in all the years he could remember-in fact, he couldn't even imagine his father showing any sorrow or expressions of tenderness. Maybe men weren't supposed to show such things.

Claude spent most of that night down by the river, gazing at the moon's reflection on the water, which seemed to look as lonesome as he felt. It would be left for him to write his mother with the news of his brother's sudden death. She would cry for sure; she would weep.

The fence that marked the parameter of the whole place needed repair, but there was still a small fenced in pasture near the house where they could keep the livestock.

"Pete, I need you to pick four of the best mules and hitch them to one of the wagons. We are going to leave for Jefferson right after breakfast. I'm gonna leave you in charge of the wagon so I can ride on ahead to Jefferson."

Once in Jefferson, Claude broke the news too Lupe and Anna. He told them about Clovis' death and announced the company's relocation. "We have to get everything ready; we're moving to Sam Antonio."

Learning of Clovis' death, Lupe's eyes filled with tears and his head hung in sorrow; he put his arm around Anna as she wept about Claude's brother. Lupe reacted in shock to Claude's plans to move the business o San Antonio.

"Listen Lupe, we've got a bigger and better place there, and Pete will soon be here with a wagon to haul all our equipment to San Antonio. San Antonio is booming right now, and our freight company can boom right along with it. So we need to get packed right away."

Together, they loaded all of the harness and supplies into the big wagon and drove the herd of mules. He talked to Mr. Fletcher, the lawyer, who took statements from Claude and Pete before he started the processing of the will. Mr. Fletcher assured Claude that it was okay to proceed with his business. Saddened by the thoughts of what could have been with Clovis and him working together, Claude led the caravan towards San Antonio. He was more determined than ever to fulfill his brother's dreams to build up the freight business in that booming town. After all, his brother had real business smarts, and if Clovis had seen a bright future for their business in San Antonio, then Claude was resolute in his desire to do all he could to make it happen. Clovis' hard work wouldn't die with him, but would continue on as a memorial to him, for Claude could see to that.

CHAPTER 12

Claude
1857-1859

As they traveled to San Antonio, Claude had Pete ride horseback with him so they could discuss plans for the future. "Listen, we're going to need two more drivers once we get to San Antonio," he told Pete.

"Don't worry, Señor Colorado; I have many cousins. Besides, you treat us like men and not like slaves, so we will have no problem getting workers. Also, Señor, you should be riding one of the mules instead of a horse. The ride is much easier and the mules have more stamina."

Claude had never thought of riding a mule but the idea kind of interested him and he certainly owned his share of mules. "Well alright, Pete; pick out one of the mules for me and I'll try it."

The next morning Pete brought Claude a big brown mare mule saddled and ready to ride. The mule looked to be sixteen hands high, with black stockings and a white nose. "This mule has never been ridden, Señor, but she is very gentle and easy to catch and saddle. I don't think she will buck, but you never know for sure. As far as I can tell, she is about six years old."

"Where did you learn so much about mules?" asked Claude.

"When I was a boy, I worked for a mule trader in Brownsville for four or five years. He worked me hard and treated me like I was stupid, but I learned a lot about mules," replied Pete.

Claude rode the mule for the duration of the day; she had a gait that was fast and smooth and she seemed eager to go. Claude talked to her and petted her and that night he fed her by hand. He named her Maggie and resolved to ride her every day that week. After a few days, she learned to turn with the pull of the reins and moved forward with the touch of his boot heel.

After the run, Claude returned to his farmhouse and told Pete that he and the hired hands should work on fixing the property fence. In the meantime, Claude rode Maggie into San Antonio and bought the land they had been renting and using for the company headquarters. After the workers finished repairing the fence, Pete returned with him into San Antonio. There Pete found two more drivers and Claude contracted three loads of cotton and a load of hides-all needing to be transported to Galveston. But before he headed off with his new freight, Claude wrote a letter to his mother and another to his grandfather.

Dear Grandpa,

    This letter bears tragic news. Clovis and I had decided to move the freight company to San Antonio, but when we got here, Clovis fell ill with cholera and died. I'm growing up kind of fast and most of the time I don't know what I should do.

    Fortunately, before he passed, Clovis had hired an old Mexican who drives and also does the cooking. Whenever I'm at a loss, I ask him and a newer teamster for advice and both have been a lot of help.

With no choice except to keep going I've purchased a place on the southeast side of San Antonio, on the river, to use as a headquarters.

I hope everything is fine at home. Please write to General Delivery San Antonio.
Love and respect,
Claude

Dear Mama,

I regret to write you with such tragic news, but I have no choice. Clovis and I had decided to move the freight company to San Antonio but before we got settled, Clovis caught a sickness and died soon after. I have purchased the place where he is buried.

I really miss him and of course have little experience. Clovis told me a lot about his freighting business. He told me he did well because he out-worked his competitors; I intend to carry on his legacy.

Please write me at General Delivery San Antonio.

I hope all is well at home.
Love,
Claude

The next morning, Claude and his drivers, loaded everything and departed for Galveston with all four wagons. Claude was pleased with the way Maggie rode. He spent some of his evenings with Pete practicing his Spanish and often tried it out whenever he talked to any of the Mexicans. The Mexican teamsters laughed and found humor in some of the mistakes he made.

Once they arrived in Galveston, Claude found a client with

enough barrels of flour, coffee, sugar and salt to load all four wagons on their return trip to San Antonio. The roundtrip to and from the coast from San Antonio was shorter and faster and made more money than any of the longer trips to and from Jefferson. While on the road, he still managed to kill enough game to keep him and his teamsters fed with fresh meat, and Poncho always purchased fresh tortillas for them in Galveston and San Antonio. Unsurprisingly, the Mexican freighters preferred tortillas to Poncho's cornbread. When speaking directly to him or amongst each other, Claude was El Jefe, but to everyone else he was Señor Colorado.

At first, Claude had relied on both Clovis' reputation and his clients, but with time, Claude made new contacts of his own. He looked much older than he actually was, and because he kept his mouth shut and followed through on everything he said he would do, Claude's respectability as a businessman grew. He earned his own reputation as reliable and trustworthy, which led to success.

Claude was pleased with the way Maggie rode; her back was narrower, flatter, and her shoulders were narrower and slimmer than a horse. Consequently the saddle had a tendency to slide forward. Annoyed by the constant sliding, Claude put an extra pad underneath it and fastened a wide strap to the rear of the saddle encircling the mule's hindquarters. This kept the saddle from moving forward. Claude was gradually becoming more and more attached to Maggie; he curried and brushed her nearly every night. When she was out in the pasture, she would come to Claude when he whistled to her. Claude had fallen into the habit of talking to her as if she understood what he was saying. Being his father's son Claude didn't expect he would ever be able to share his feelings with another human being.

Business was good and Claude's reputation was growing steadily. The U.S. Army had now contracted him to haul their supplies as they came into Indianola or Galveston. Because of those jobs, he met a Major White and they eventually became friends.

After several brief roundtrips, Claude would usually break

for a week to let his married teamsters see their wives. He'd spend that time repairing harness, equipment and getting ready for the next run. Claude used some of the company funds to purchase warm coats and raingear for all hands and armed each of his teamsters with a shotgun. He later had a bunkhouse built for the men and a small house for his own use. Pete, Poncho and his family lived in the bigger house. The Mexican teamsters seemed to be as loyal as they were fond of Señor Colorado.

Claude had grown two inches and was now six feet two inches tall; and with his red beard, he cut an imposing figure astride his big brown mule. Everywhere he traveled Señor Colorado was well respected.

Most of Claude's daily interaction was with his Mexican employees and soon he spoke Spanish more than English. His thoughts were now in Spanish—he even dreamed in Spanish.

One day, Claude finally received a letter from his mother.

Dear Claude,

We are all very shocked and saddened to hear the news about Clovis. And I would have liked it if he could have been buried here in the family cemetery instead of way off down there. But I suppose you did the best you could under the circumstances; it must have been hard for you.

My only solace is the thought that at least he didn't suffer a long time. We have to remember that all of us are going to one day pass into glory, though it doesn't make it any easier.

We all miss you terribly. Your grandfather wants to know how much you've grown and how you are doing in the freight business. Share with us more details in your letters so we will know more about your life. Clovis hardly ever wrote, but I hope you can do better on that score. We so appreciate your letters. Please write to us whenever you can.

Your father got over that relentless high fever but really isn't doing much better. He just sits in his chair all day and acts like he sees nothing. Tom was feeble before getting sick, but now he is almost completely helpless. I'm spending most of my time taking care of him. Thank goodness the children are now old enough that they don't require constant care. The rest of the family is doing fine and send their greetings.

Your grandfather and Wash are taking care of the farming. We aren't having any trouble getting more hands; many of the new comers need the work.

I know we are a long way from San Antonio but I wish you would try to come home for a visit, even if it's just for a day or two. I miss you real bad.
Love,
Mama

As time passed, Pete went from being a mere employee to becoming a trusted friend, and Claude spent the majority of his time with him and his other Mexican workers.

Early in 1859, three thieves attacked Claude and his teamsters after they left Indianola; it was not far from where Pete had been robbed years earlier. Pete had killed one of the bandits and Claude got another. The third thief fled, wounded from a shotgun blast. Fortunately, all the teamsters had their shotguns out and were ready to help when the bandits ambushed them. They hoped that the word would get around and the outlaws would learn to leave them to make their runs in peace.

More business was available than Claude and his teams could handle, so Claude bought more mules and two more wagons. Pete became the official "Segundo," or second in command no longer driving a wagon but riding a mule, checking the route and making sure everything was running smoothly and safely.

In early winter of 1859, a letter from his mother brought news that shocked him:

Dear Claude,

We have expected it for some time, but it still comes as a shock. Last Tuesday morning at dawn, your father was dead in our bed. He died in his sleep. As far as we could tell, Tom never did suffer but kind of wasted away.

We've gotten along without his help or company for so long, his passing is almost a relief; caring for him day and night was certainly taking its toll on me. Your grandfather is suffering from rheumatism and is also getting feeble. Now I will have time to help him in his final years. Thank God for Nell and Wash; Nell takes care of so much of the house and the family, while Wash oversees the farming.

They are having some trouble with their oldest son, T.C., who is now ten years old and rebellious. T.C. has run away twice but someone brought him back each time. Your brother and sisters are doing fine. Elizabeth is helping Sophie while she teaches, and Jake Thompson and Edna Mae are a big help after school.

I do wish you would try to come for a visit. We are glad you are doing well but still want to see you. Your Grandfather has said that he wants to see you before he goes.
Love from all of us,
Mama

CHAPTER 13

Claude and T.C.
1860-1861

In the early spring of 1860, Claude was still hauling freight from Galveston to Jefferson and loads of lumber to San Antonio. His mother's letter had been weighing on him a great deal and so one day he decided to leave the wagons with Pete so that he could make the trip north to see his family. He had no idea what they might want him to bring so he took a pack mule loaded with bolts of cloth and household things he thought might be needed. He also took a sack of gold coins to give to his mother; there was nothing he would hesitate to give her.

His mother and sisters all cried because they were so glad to see him.

"Claude, you've grown into a handsome man, so grown up! You look a lot like your father did when I first met him except you might be a bit taller. Why, I'm surprised some pretty girl hasn't caught you yet," exclaimed Effie.

Later when they were alone, Claude gave his mother the sack of gold coins and said, "I'd like for you to hide these and keep them for a rainy day."

"I don't need them, son; your father and grandfather have seen to our needs; we really have everything we need; but if it will make you feel better and help you not to worry about us, I'll put them away for safe keeping," replied Effie with a grateful smile.

Claude spent a good part of the afternoon with his grandfather, who wanted to hear everything about his freight operation. When they had exhausted the topic, Claude brought up something that had been on his mind for some time. "Grandpa, do you think I should come home and help Mama?"

"Lord, no. Son, I think you should stay right where you are. You're making more there than you ever could here. But I tell you what, if and when you are needed here, I'll be sure to write you or have your mother write to let you know."

Effie reminded Claude that he should stop in and visit with Wash and his family; in fact Wash had asked if he would do just that. So that night Claude went to see Wash and Nell. They now had four children, two of which Claude had never seen.

"Mistah Claude, would yuh be willin' to take T.C. wid yuh when yuh leave? The boy's been very unhappy here an' keeps runnin' away an' ah'm 'fraid he'll come to no good. He's too young an' don't have a lick of good sense," pleaded Wash.

"Wash, I don't know if it would be wise for me to do that. I'm almost always on the move and freighting is a dangerous business. I spend most all of my time with my Mexican employees and that would be difficult for T.C. since he doesn't speak Spanish," replied Claude.

Claude couldn't help but not notice the hurt look in Wash's eyes, as much as Wash tied to hide it. "Well, that's all right, Mistah Claude. It don't sound like work for a boy with no sense. Just forget ah asked—"

Claude cut him off mid-sentence and turned to the boy.

"T.C., do you want to go with me? Is that something you'd really like to do?"

"Yes sir, Mistah Claude!" T.C. had been sulking in the background, hanging on every word, and now he leaped at Claude's invitation.

"Ah'll sho'lly do anything yuh tell meh and won't cause no trouble. Ah promise ah won't run like ah done here. Ah'd do mah best to learn that language them Mexicans talk," said the boy, reassuringly.

"You need to understand that if you go with me there will be several days of hard riding before we get to San Antonio, and from there we go with my wagons. I spend most of my days working and supervising the freight business. You can ride the mule I brought with me. My headquarters is in San Antonio, but I'm rarely there more than a few days at a time. If you go, you will have to ride a mule and stay with me day and night. You may think what I do is fun, but I tell you it's work. Very boring work sometimes and you'll miss out on school. Can you read and do your numbers?"

"Yes sir, ah can read a little an' ah do numbers pretty good. Miss Hannah, she made meh learn. Please take meh, Mistah. Claude!"

"There will be no more home cooking and washing. I won't have time to bring you back and neither will anyone else. If you go with me, you'll have to be prepared to stay and act like a man, whatever happens."

"Whatever yuh say, Mistah Claude," T.C. said, nodding all the while. "Ah wants to go."

Claude kept a stern face, but patted the boy on the back. "Nell, get him ready to go tomorrow morning. I'm probably going to regret this but I'll give it a try." Claude paused for a moment. "I want you to know I'm doing it because I'm mighty grateful for everything you both have done for my family." Turning back to T.C. he said in low voice, "T.C., you better enjoy eating your mama's cooking and sleeping in a bed because it's the last time you will be able to do either for a long time."

Claude made his way back to the house to tell his grandfather and Hannah goodbye. He told his mother and the rest of the family that he was leaving in the morning and would return when he could. The next morning when he was packed and ready to depart, Effie gave him a sack of food and began to cry. It was harder for her to say goodbye to him than he thought it would be. Only God knew when he would be coming back for a visit. His mother sensed that, and could not hold back the tears. She never had the chance to say goodbye to his brother Clovis before his passing, and she wondered how much time she had left and if she would see Claude again.

Claude had fitted the pack mule with an old saddle he found in the barn and two saddle blankets. Although T.C. was tall for his age, Claude had to help him to the back of the mule. Nell had fixed T.C. a sack of food and a couple of quilts and a piece of canvas for a ground sheet. Claude reminded T.C. that they wouldn't be eating this good again soon.

Claude and T.C. rode over twenty miles the first day. Claude would have gone for another four or five miles except T.C. was obviously very tired. Although T.C. didn't complain, he walked funny, like he was sore, and Claude saw him rubbing his backside more than once. Claude chuckled quietly to himself for he knew this trip to San Antonio would toughen T.C. up for the longer freight trips that lay ahead of them. The next day they rode another twenty miles. T.C. gradually got accustomed to the strain of long-distance riding and began to move less stiffly after being in the saddle for so long.

Lupe and his wife Anna were still taking care of the mules and the headquarters. This kind and loyal couple had no children of their own and so Anna beamed when Claude showed up with T.C. He told T.C. to sleep in the bunkhouse, and Anna made sure he was comfortable there. From speaking with Lupe, Claude learned that the wagons were on a trip to Indianola and were due back shortly.

The men who worked for Claude respected him, and most of them followed his example when they could. When he was young, Effie had taught all of her children that taking a bath was healthy and so he bathed whenever he had the opportunity. He had placed some flat rocks in the water at the edge of the San Antonio River and whenever they got back he went to the river and took a bath with the homemade lye soap he purchased at the general store in town. This time when he finished at the river he gave T.C. the bar of soap and sent him to take a bath. T.C. wasn't too excited about bathing in the cold river water, but did as he was told. He figured that his new privileges, living and working with Claude, were worth such inconveniences. Claude's drivers had observed his habits over the months, and most of them began bathing more often. Poncho, the cook, set up a pan and water and began requiring the drivers to wash their hands before eating.

While spending some time in town waiting for the wagons to return, Claude began to hear talk. What he heard in town was quite a few rumors and whisperings about seceding from the Union. Claude wasn't too concerned because he and his family had always thought highly of Sam Houston and he figured that if that ever happened, the Governor would probably take care of any problem the state might face.

One of the men he met in town was Capt. Richard King, who owned a ranch south of the Nueces River. Captain King seemed to like Claude and hired him to haul two wagonloads of supplies from San Antonio to his ranch. As soon as Pete got back with the wagons, Claude took the trip to the King Ranch himself, but left T.C. with Pete, saying, "I'm responsible for this boy, so please take care of him and see he doesn't get into trouble."

He had a long visit at the ranch with Captain King. King liked the fact that Claude used Mexican drivers, spoke Spanish, and was well armed. He told Claude, "On occasion, I will probably need someone to take freight to and from Brownsville. It's rough country between here and there, so I'm looking for someone who has plenty of gun power and is not afraid to use it. I'm not willing to let my hard work and profits be stolen by thieves out on the trail."

Claude assured King that his freight would be safe because his teamsters were reliable, well-armed at all times, and had been effective in warding off thieves on several occasions. Having heard of Claude's reputation, King agreed to commission Claude's company to haul his freight. King's business, added to the rest of his regular clients, put Claude's company in the ranks of the top freight companies, especially those based out of San Antonio.

When he wasn't on one of the wagons, T.C. rode a mule with either Pete or Claude. The Mexicans all seemed to appreciate T.C. and began to grow fond of the boy in their own way.

T.C. grew a full inch over the summer and his pants now stopped above his ankles. Claude took him into San Antonio and bought him all new clothes, including a heavy coat and rain gear. He also started paying T.C. half as much as the teamsters and asked that he help Poncho, who was getting older and slower and needed help with the cooking. The boy's Spanish was also improving; actually, he really had no choice since everyone he was with spoke Spanish. Even Claude reached a point where he stopped speaking English to T.C. as soon as he was sure T.C. understood him. Like everyone else, T.C. got into the habit of calling Claude "El Jefe."

The U.S. national election was held November 6, 1860. For several days after the election, businessmen in Indianola told Claude that even if it wasn't final; Abraham Lincoln was going to be the next President of the United States. There was still a lot of talk of secession in Indianola, Galveston, and San Antonio. Claude was determined not to get involved in politics, as his freight business took all the energy he had.

T.C. heard a lot of the talk too. He asked Claude, "What's this 'Black Republicans' ah keep hearing about?"

"Well T.C. that's what people who don't like the Republicans call them. They want to remind people that the Republicans want to free the slaves and that if Lincoln wins the election, it'll lead to slave rebellion and what-not. Unfortunately this has stirred up a lot of bad feelings about Negroes. When we're in town or around people we don't usually work with, stay close to me and don't get involved in any political conversation. You do this and I'll look out for you."

"Yes sir."

"In fact, I'm gonna give you a letter to keep in your pocket. If you have any trouble, just show the letter and get to me or Pete as soon as possible."

Claude wrote the letter that night.

> *This letter is to verify that T.C. Hill was born free in 1849 and is employed by Claude Williams of the Williams Freight Company, San Antonio, Texas.*
> *Signed,*
> *Claude Williams*

Pete came to Claude one day and told him he was worried about his family. Pete's home was south of the Nueces River and just north of the Rio Grande. "I've heard word that Mexican Bandito raiders killed my father and I'm concerned about my mother and two younger sisters being by themselves."

"I'm really sorry to hear about your father." replied Claude. "I want you to know that your mother and sisters are welcome to move here so they can be near to you."

Pete breathed a deep sigh of relief. "That's just what I've been thinking, El Jefe."

When Pete returned with his family, Claude and some of the men built a small house on his property for Pete and his family, who moved in soon after. Before long, several of the married drivers asked to move their families to the headquarters, as well. After Claude gave them his consent, and the men quickly began constructing the traditional huts called *jacales*, which were made of mud, sticks and straw. They were much happier with their families together, although they still came to Claude with their personal problems and disputes.

Maria, the eldest of Pete's sisters was eighteen years old and the most beautiful woman Claude had ever seen. He couldn't help but take notice of her right away—her skin was lighter than most Mexicans, her shapely form, large brown eyes, and long shiny black hair made his heart race fast every time he was near her. He eventually came up with the idea of offering to teach her English, which delighted Maria and so he spent as much time with her as possible. He often found himself getting lost in Maria's big brown eyes— which he realized had flecks of gold in them when the light hit them just so—in the middle of an English lesson, and forgetting what he had been saying. He was aware that he was more than slightly infatuated with her, but tried not to make it obvious to her or to anyone else.

Claude might as well have not even tried concealing his feelings because just about everyone could see he was love-smitten. Certainly, Pete knew exactly what was going on between Claude and Maria and, to Claude's great relief, approved. Besides, Maria's younger sister, Juana, who was only sixteen, was having enough trouble keeping the unmarried drivers from hanging around their house all hours of the day. Pete knew that Maria would be well cared for if things worked out with Claude, as he suspected they would. He really couldn't think of a better match for his sister.

In generally every community across Texas, the big topic of conversation those days continued to be the talk of secession. Committees were sent to Governor Houston from Indianola and other parts of the state asking him to call a special session of the legislature, or a convention, to facilitate secession from the United States. Sam Houston, being strongly opposed to the idea of secession, was certain the North would prevail over the South and this view branded him a traitor in the eyes of many Texans. Houston eventually resigned from office when it became clear that a majority of his people were against him. It was then left to Lt. Governor Clark to call the convention that the people of Texas demanded. On February 1, 1861, the legislature voted, almost unanimously, in favor of leaving the Union. The question was put to a general vote of the Texas population on February 23, and nearly seventy-five percent of Texans voted in favor of secession. Dire consequences followed. The most devastating blow came by midsummer; Galveston and the other ports on the upper Texas coast were blockaded by Northern Yankee ships, as other Southern ports had already been.

Claude took T.C. with him to King's Ranch and there Captain King advised him, "I'd recommend you invest in cotton. Buy all the cotton you can afford and start freighting it to Brownsville. From now on, it'd be a good idea to take all of your wagons and crew to travel together in order to increase your firepower. Banditos are a never-ending problem and we will possibly have to put up with Union troops sometime in the future. I'll advise you how to handle trade in Brownsville.

Make no mistake, cotton is going to get more and more expensive. I think the Mexican part of the Rio Grande entrance will stay unblocked."

T.C. was most impressed with the King Ranch and the people he met there. On the way back to San Antonio, he said, "When I get older, I might like to be a cowboy."

Claude grinned at him. "That right? I think you might make a good one, T.C."

Claude had begun taking T.C. with him almost everywhere he went. T.C. seemed to love it.

Taking Capt. King's advice, Claude quietly started buying up cotton as soon as they returned to San Antonio. He and T.C. rode on to Jefferson and purchased ten wagonloads. They stored the cotton at his headquarters in San Antonio while Pete was sent with all the wagons to pick up the cotton in Jefferson. Claude joined them in San Antonio and they began their first trip caravanning through the wild horse desert to Brownsville.

Back on the trail, when T.C. wasn't helping Poncho, Claude spent time teaching him to ride and shoot.

On Claude and his teamster's first trip to Brownsville, Captain King sent along one of his *Kineños*, (as "King's Men" called themselves), to show Claude where to find water and warn him of where the most dangerous areas were. As it turned out, they were attacked on their first evening. Claude and his men were ambushed and attacked by six outlaws. Three of the bandits were shot dead and the others, who escaped, left behind a bloody trail. The outcome might have been different if the teamsters hadn't been sleeping with shotguns at their side.

Pete had been particularly alert because bandits had killed his father several weeks earlier. Fortunately, they made the rest of the trip without incident and sold the cotton in Brownsville for a good profit. It was well worth the trouble he had gone through in taking Captain King's advice. In town, Claude found sugar, coffee, and other commodities to take back to his headquarters in San Antonio, as these luxuries were going to become increasingly difficult to come by. When he returned home, he hired a cotton buyer to take over finding and purchasing loads of cotton so that he could spend could spend his time with the wagons.

Every time Claude got close to San Antonio, he went home to visit Maria. His employees knew their boundaries well enough not to pry into his private affairs, but T.C. didn't. "El Jefe," he asked, "when yuh goin' tuh get married tuh Maria?"

"That doesn't have anything to do with you, so mind your own business," he replied defensively. Claude didn't have time to think about marriage for that was too consuming a commitment. He had his hands full with building up his freight business. It would be foolish of him to burden himself with a wife and the family that would follow; he needed to invest all of his effort into the company. The impending war would not wait for him.

Claude told himself he had to stack hay, so to speak, while

the hay was ready for stacking, and that there was no hurry; there would be time for a wife and family later.

Claude hauled his own cotton when he had it, as well as State-owned, and any other cotton he could get his hands on. He brought back flour and other sundries. Some military supplies, guns, and gunpowder were boxed and labeled as farm equipment. Bandits, as he had hoped, generally left them alone. There was no doubt word had passed around that Claude and his men would kill if attacked. They hauled cargo to landings on the Rio Grande from Laredo to Brownsville. Pete ran the operation as well as Claude and was both respected and paid accordingly.

CHAPTER 14

Claude, T.C., and Dr. Fuqua
1863

The delivery of mail to and from San Antonio was haphazard at best; letters were often slow in arriving, and sometimes never reached their intended destinations. Nonetheless, Claude was becoming concerned because he hadn't received letter or word from his family in nearly a year. In the spring of 1863, Claude decided he had to find out how his mother and family were doing. He couldn't wait any longer.

Claude loaded two big pack mules with salt, sugar, coffee, nails, medicine, and other things he knew to be in short supply. He also told T.C. of his plans to travel up to Indian Springs and suggested that T.C. ready his mule if he wanted to go along on the trip to visit his own folks. Before leaving San Antonio, Claude went to see Maria and tell her goodbye. By this time, Maria had learned enough English so that it was not necessary for Claude to speak Spanish to her; they were now able to freely converse in English. Claude confessed to Maria, "I'm going to North Texas and I might possibly buy some land there. Some day, when I'm older, I may want to go back to that part of the country to live out my days"

Maria made no reply as she placed her hand on his arm and smiled. She knew she would willingly follow him anywhere and in his heart he must have known it too, because without saying a word he returned her smile, kissed her gently on the forehead, and said good-bye.

That evening, Claude and T.C. headed north. They traveled hard and fast, and mostly under the cover of darkness. At daybreak, they would get off the road and sleep in thickets or some other place where they could hide themselves and their mules.

"Remember T.C., a big war is going on and slavery is one of the things that brought it about. If anyone stops us, promise me you'll say nothing and let me do the talking. There's also a chance authorities might question why I'm not in the army. I have money that I've been saving with me and don't intend to give it up to anyone. So keep your shotgun loaded and near at hand; watch my lead, and hopefully we won't have to use our guns," Claude ordered gruffly.

Now fourteen years old, T.C. no longer looked like the same boy he was when he first left home to work for Claude. At five foot ten, he towered over the Mexicans in the freight company and didn't have to crane his neck to look Claude in the eye anymore. He was also muscular, his body strong and wiry from the years of hard work and riding. Claude knew T.C. was looking forward to seeing his folks and he remembered to put extra supplies on the pack mules to give to Wash and Nell. Claude, despite himself, couldn't help but grudgingly admit that this once troubled young boy was now one of his best and most trusted men.

"I'm gonna be glad when we get there," said Claude. "I'm tired of jerky and old biscuits; I'll sure welcome some of my mother's and Nell's good home-cookin'."

"Ah think my mama is the best cook in the world," replied T.C. quietly. Claude agreed that both their mothers were better cooks than most.

They arrived in Indian Springs at the crack of dawn. The first thing Claude did was to escort T.C. to his parents' home. "Now go in and see your ma and pa. I'm going straight to the main house to see my mama and the rest of the family. I'll be back later with some of the stuff that we put on the pack mules for your folks. So tell them I'll see them later on today. And T.C., it's your choice whether or not you want to stay home or go back with me to San Antonio. Either way, I'll be here for a few days so you have some time to decide," said Claude, urging his mule on while he waved goodbye.

When Claude rode up to his mother's house, there was a man sitting in a rocker on the front porch with a quilt around his shoulders. Effie heard Claude arrive and ran to meet him with tears and hugs. His mother then introduced Claude to the man who was sitting on the porch. "Claude, this is Dr. Ross Fuqua. He was discharged from the Confederate army and made it as far as Indian Springs before collapsing with consumption; I've been trying to help him get better. But come on in the house. You can't imagine how glad I am to see you."

"Mama, you look wonderful. I've really missed you and the rest of the family. I haven't received a letter in a year and I had to know what's going on with you all. How are Grandpa and Hannah and my brother and sisters? I'm going to be here for several days and I want to hear the details about everything."

"Son, I'm so sorry that I haven't been so good at writing, but I've got my hands full here. I kept meaning to write, but I prayed for you every day, and now you are here! Your visit is so much better than a letter. Oh thank you for coming, son; we all missed you so!" exclaimed Effie, who seemed startled by her own burst of emotion, smiling sheepishly at Claude.

She continued, "Grandpa is having a little trouble getting around, but once he gets on horseback, he can ride all over." She laughed. "Hannah is in better shape than he is, but spends almost all her time taking care of him and their home. You need to go have a nice long visit with them while you're here."

"Oh, I will," promised Claude.

"Let's see—your sister Sophie is still teaching school. Sophie and John still haven't had any children together and John has been gone at war for two years now. Elizabeth is nineteen and beautiful and is still in school in Clarksville. It's funny; she seems to like all the boys there, but no one special boy so far," Effie laughed. "And your little brother Jake Thompson is sixteen and is into too much. Fortunately, he spends most of his time with either your grandfather or with Wash. I'm praying they will help him find direction in his life, the way they helped you boys, and in a way that a mother just can't do."

"The time I spent with Grandpa and Wash sure did make a difference in my life and I'm sure it will in Jake's, too," said Claude.

Effie smiled. "Come to think of it, he does remind me of you when you were his age. Maybe you might consider taking him with you when he matures a little. Ask your grandfather and see what he thinks about it. It would give Jake a chance to learn something outside of the homestead here—and maybe that would be good for him. And you could teach him about your business like Clovis taught you. Jake's even mentioned that he would like to go to San Antonio someday, and I wouldn't worry so much if he were with you." Effie smiled softly and returned to her narrative. "Who else, now? Oh, our little Edna Mae is fourteen and she's also going to school in Clarksville. All in all, everyone is doing well. But like I said, Jake Thompson has too much time on his hands and has been itching to go to war. Nearly all of the young men and a good many of the older ones are gone; they all went to join the army. We've had serious trouble finding help, but Wash manages somehow."

"He always did, didn't he? Good old Wash."

"Luke Gault died last year, and all of the Gault boys are gone to the war. Sophie Gault has had a hard time not only missing Luke and her boys, but just surviving and keeping her homestead—not to mention the livestock. Actually, she has had to sell most of it off. We try to help her when we can." Effie's voice trailed off a bit. She reached over and touched Claude's hand as she said, "Your friend Peter Gault was killed somewhere in Virginia."

Claude nodded dumbly, staring at Effie's hand resting on his as he took in the news. It was Pete who had the more temperate nature, who always ran tail when they faced a boar or a swarm of yellow jackets; Pete never did the foolhardy things Claude did. But he had joined the army and now he was dead. Claude suddenly felt ashamed he hadn't thought about Pete Gault in such a long time.

Finally Effie broke the silence. "Well, enough about us. I'll try to give you more details as we go along if you want me to. I want you to tell me about you. When are you going to get married and give me some grandchildren?"

Claude grinned sheepishly. "Well mama, there is a special girl in San Antonio, but I'll tell you about her later. Right now, I have to unload the pack mules. Maybe we can find a few surprises for you," he said with a grin.

"I do hope you brought us some salt and coffee! We haven't had either since we used up what you brought for us last time. Coffee, sugar, and salt haven't been available to anyone since the war began."

"Hang on, then," said Claude as he left the house.

As Claude made his way over to unload the mules, Effie followed close behind to see what he brought. T.C. was waiting outside for Claude and when Effie saw T.C., she gushed over how big and strong he'd become. T.C. beamed at hearing such praise and fumbled a bit while helping Claude unload the supplies they had brought for Effie. There were also some things for Nell and Wash, as well as for Jake and Sophie, which Claude left on the mules. Effie was thrilled and hurried back into the house with an armful of bundles.

Once Effie was back in the house, T.C. said in a breathless rush, "El Jefe, Ah'm glad tuh see my folks and will sho'lly spend more time with 'em, but Ah want tuh stay wid yuh. If yuh go any-where, please let me come wid yuh; A jus' feel like ah don't belong here anymore."

Claude took his time answering T.C. as he handed him the lead rope of the mule that carried supplies for Nell and Wash. "Take these things home for your folks. I'm going to be passing back and forth between here and my grandfather's for the next two days. I plan on visiting with your folks in the meantime. Keep in mind that if you're coming with me, you'll need to be ready to ride at the end of two days. I'm going to look at some land, but I don't want it dis-cussed with anyone. Understand? I'd like you to take both our rid-ing mules to the barn, rub them down good, and be sure they're well fed. I'll turn this mule into the corral once I get it unloaded. See to it that all of our mules are cared for; they've had a long and hard trip," instructed Claude.

"Yes sir. Ah'll take care of 'em," replied T.C.

When Effie got through unpacking all of the things Claude brought into the house, she was crying. "This war has created terri-ble shortages. And all these young men being killed; the whole thing is horrible. I hope it's over soon for everyone's sake." Effie paused to dab her eyes dry with her apron. "Let me make us a pot of coffee and I want to hear about this young lady of yours. Have you had any breakfast? We have eggs and ham; I'll fix you some. Just sit down and don't run off!"

It didn't take long for Effie to fix Claude a big breakfast of scrambled eggs, fried ham, hot biscuits and gravy. Claude declared it to be the best meal he'd had since he was last home. "And this coffee is great," he added. "I'd like another cup, but I want to take the things I brought over to Grandpa's and then I'll be back so we can have a long talk."

Effie gave him a mischievous smile. "I still haven't heard about that girl of yours," she reminded him.

"And I still haven't heard about that doctor sitting on your front porch. I won't be very long, Ma," he promised.

Grandpa Jake and Hannah were almost as glad to see Claude as his mother had been, His younger brother Jake was there too and he helped unload and carry in the bundles Claude had brought. The coffee and salt were especially welcome gifts. "Oh Claude, we've been out of both since using up the supply from your last visit," said Hannah with a grateful smile. "And sugar! We've been using honey as a substitute, but there's nothing like real sugar."

Claude sized up Jake Thompson, who had grown to nearly six feet and appeared to weigh at least 185 pounds. "Brother, I swear you're looking taller and fitter than I am. How about taking the pack mule over to rest in Mama's corral. T.C. is going to take care of it," said Claude.

As for Grandpa Jake, he now walked with a cane, but Hannah seemed to still be in pretty good shape. She moved a little slower than Claude remembered and her wrinkles ran deeper, but she was pleasant as always and seemed genuinely happy.

As soon as his brother left to take the pack mule to Effie's corral, Claude told his grandpa that he had something he wanted to discuss. Jake patted him on the back and led him out to the barn. Claude remembered when the neighbors had come to help his grandpa build this barn. It was still in pretty good condition. Claude explained to his grandpa, "I want to buy land and I don't think I can get it done in the little time I have here; I wouldn't want to rush into anything. I'd like to take a look at the land around the Cuthand area and along Sulphur River. I'm also thinking about purchasing some prairie black land. Now, if it's all right by you, I'll leave money with you and you can pay for it and get the deed put in my name. All of that takes time, which I can't spend here right now. But I trust you, Grandpa, to handle the transaction for me. You are well established here and better acquainted with the townsfolk than I am."

Grandpa Jake nodded. "Claude, you know I'll help you any way I can. So how much property are you talking about; did you bring that much money with you?"

"I have it all with me here, and I'll leave it with you." Claude drew several leather bags out of the saddlebag he had brought inside. There were gold Mexican coins worth over $1,500, $1,500 in Confederate bills, and $2,500 in U.S. bills. Old Jake whistled. "I also plan to leave some gold coins with Mama." Claude went on, "If you need any of it, she'll have it for you."

"So it's fair to say your freight company has been mighty profitable," said Grandpa Jake.

"Yes, sir; my mules are young and strong, my equipment is in good shape, my crew is all Mexican and loyal to a fault. Knowing that hard money is scarce, I figured maybe we can get some good buys," replied Claude.

"You figure right," said old Jake. "There are thousands of acres of oak, hickory, gum, pecan, and other huge hardwood trees out there. Someday, when this war is over, they'll be worth a lot of money."

Claude then asked Grandpa Jake if he would ride with him the day after next. "I'd like to do some looking around. T.C. wants to go with us and I'm hoping Jake Thompson will join us, too. I don't mind if they know about my interest in the land, but I'd prefer not to discuss money in front of them," said Claude.

"Understood," said Grandpa Jake. "If we're going as far as the Sulphur River bottom, we should probably leave early."

When Jake Thompson returned, Claude asked his brother to walk with him to their mother's house. The two brothers made their goodbyes to Jake and Hannah, and headed towards Effie's house. Claude took advantage of this time alone with young Jake to invite him, "Day after tomorrow, we plan to go to the Cuthand and Sulphur River areas," said Claude to his little brother.

"Grandpa and I are gonna ride out to look at some land. T.C. is planning to go along and I thought you might like to come, too." After a moment's pause, Claude decided to go ahead and bring up San Antonio.

"T.C. is also planning to return with me to work in my freighting business in San Antonio. I know you two have been friends all your life and I wanted you to know that if you want to go back with us, you're more than welcome."

Young Jake was silent as he considered the offer carefully. "You can include me when you go to look at land, but I don't want to go with you to South Texas. I want to go to war when I'm eighteen. If it was up to me, I'd go now; but I promised Mama I'd wait until after my eighteenth birthday," Jake responded, lighting up as he spoke about going to battle, and obviously frustrated about having given Effie his word.

"If you wait a couple of years, the war might be over." Claude paused once more before resuming. "Jake, I'm glad you're here with Mama, but I also understand why you might want to do what everyone else is doing."

"Well, how come you're not in the army, Claude?" asked young Jake.

Claude shrugged. "I'm exempt because the cotton I'm hauling to the Rio Grande is vital to the Confederacy, and its dangerous work."

When the two brothers reached Effie's, Nell was there waiting for them. She cried, her voice wracked with emotion, "Mr. Claude, Wash and I are forever grateful for what you've done for T.C. and for the things you have brought us. T.C. speaks of you like a god among men, and says he wants to be with you wherever you go."

"I'm glad to have both his company and his help," said Claude softly. "Where's Wash?"

"Oh, working on the corral fence, as usual. T.C. went with him," replied Nell.

Claude left the house shortly and went to visit with Wash. Claude told Wash how much he appreciated the help Wash and Nell had been to his mother. Wash nodded and said, "Yuh know yur mama is uh angel of a woman and Nell luvs her more'n da wheat luvs da sunshine. We will always do wha' we kin fer her. Sides all that, T.C. is happier than he has ever been an' we truly 'preciate your takin' an interest in him. We love him very much and wan' him tuh be happy."

"Yuh're talkin' 'bout me, aren't yuh?" hollered T.C. from inside his parents' house. Wash and Claude laughed as T.C. came out the front door, eating one of Nell's homemade muffins. "Yuh don't know how much Ah missed Mama's home cookin', Pa," he said to Wash.

By this time, Claude was feeling tired and so he got up to leave. "And I'm sure you're tired too, T.C; thanks for taking care of the stock. I intend to take it easy tomorrow. We need our rest and so does the stock. I may ride out on the prairie a little way, but not for long. Tonight I plan to spend a good twelve hours sleeping in a real bed. Come around in the morning if you want to ride with me," offered Claude.

Nell and Effie were hard at work in the kitchen, preparing chicken and dumplings, fresh beans, cabbage, and potatoes for lunch. Dr. Fuqua joined them as they sat down to eat and regaled them with the story of his travels. "I was riding west to reach a higher elevation and a drier climate for my consumption," he told them, "and I collapsed here. Your mother has taken care of me and I'm feeling better than I've been in two years. Rest, good food, and no war have helped restore my health. If I was healthy and could provide for her, I would ask Effie to marry me. She is the greatest woman I've ever met and she saved my life."

Claude spoke in a measured voice, "You're a doctor. It shouldn't be too hard for a man like you to make a living."

"That's true, there isn't a doctor here and as soon as I get a little stronger, I hope to start practicing medicine again. I might add that your mother's a pretty good doctor herself; she uses good common sense. I've tried to help her with her patients when I could. I hope that you don't resent me or my presence," replied Dr. Fuqua.

Claude gave Dr. Fuqua a friendly smile, but made no reply. He still wanted to visit more with his mother before becoming too friendly with Dr. Fuqua.

After lunch, Claude talked to Effie for nearly two hours. Over the course of the conversation, his mother told him that she liked and respected Dr. Fuqua, but had no marriage plans at the present time. "Now if you don't mind, I'd like you to tell me about your girl," she said.

Claude told his mother that he really cared for Maria and that she was the sweetest and most beautiful woman he knew, but hadn't asked her to marry him yet. He hesitated a moment, and said, "She's Mexican, Ma. Do you think she'd be accepted in Indian Springs?"

"I think you should ask her to marry you if you're sure she's the one you love. I'll love her and accept her and if you two come back here to settle, I don't think she will have a problem. There aren't any other Mexicans in the area, but I'm sure she'll find contentment with you and a family. Overall, the people in Indian Springs are kind and friendly folks. Most of them have embraced Wash and Nell. While at first there was hesitancy, once they saw how honest and hard working they both are, people warmed up to them. And I'm sure if Maria is as sweet as you say, people will take a liking to her, too," replied Effie.

Claude nodded; tiredness had begun to settle in. He had been on horseback all night and had been busy every moment since he'd arrived in Indian Springs. About four o'clock that afternoon, Claude crawled into bed and did not stir until the next morning.

Effie fed Claude another heaping breakfast of eggs, sausage, hot biscuits, gravy, and honey. Claude ate like he hadn't had a decent meal in ages, and with a smile, told his mother that such was the case. They didn't even dare cook on the trail to Indian Springs, but had kept a real low profile to avoid any problems or draw any attention to them. Being on the open trail with the war in full swing made travel all the more dangerous. Truthfully, Claude's biggest concern had been for T.C.'s safety. There was no hiding T.C.'s race—his skin was blacker than coal—and you never knew who you'd run into, renegade or otherwise. After breakfast, he saddled his mule and rode back over to his grandfather's cabin. Together, they decided to look at the prairie land that lay west and north of town and from there ride on to Clarksville and hire a lawyer to draw up the deeds and handle the paperwork for the property they intended to purchase. Just as Claude and Grandpa Jake were about to leave, T.C. rode up and pleaded, "Please don't leave wid'out me. Ah'm suppose' tuh go wid El Jefe when he rides!"

The three of them rode out west of town, and then headed north. All of the land they surveyed was prairie with grass that came belly-high to the horses and mules. A portion of the land was under cultivation, but most remained untouched. "It might be best for us to purchase the uncultivated land," said Claude, "because I don't know when I'll get around to doing something with it; that, and it'll probably be a little cheaper." They had discussed going to Clarksville when they finished surveying the land, but decided to leave it for the next day and instead headed for home.

The next morning, Claude, Jake Senior, and T.C. left at day-break with Claude's brother, Young Jake, now joining them. First, they rode out to Sulphur River, and then cut across to Cuthand.

"I haven't yet changed my mind; I would still like to own some river bottom land, but I'm most interested in the little rolling hills around the Cuthand area. With the good grass, the water sources, and the abundance of rain, I think it'd be the ideal ranching country," said Claude to the others.

It was almost dark when the four of them returned home. They were exhausted and their stock was as well.

When he awoke the following morning, Claude wrote a letter to his grandfather, authorizing him to hire a lawyer to handle the paperwork, as well as purchasing land with the money Claude had provided. Claude gave the letter to his grandfather, paid Nell and Wash one final visit, and then made preparations to leave the next day. It was hard for him to say goodbye to Effie; without his father there she was more vulnerable. Luckily, she had good neighbors who loved her and would look out for her. And of course there were Grandpa and Hannah, Wash and Nell, and now Dr. Fuqua. The doctor seemed like a nice and honest fellow, but time would tell. Claude asked his grandpa to keep an eye out for Dr. Fuqua and to make sure the doctor's behavior towards Effie remained above board and proper. Jake assured him that he would, and so Claude and T.C. departed shortly after noon because they intended to do most of their traveling under the cover of night—just as they had on their journey to Indian Springs.

CHAPTER 15

Claude and Maria
1863-1864

Claude and T.C. arrived at their headquarters outside San Antonio just before daybreak. Exhausted from the long night of riding, the two kicked off their boots and went directly to bed.

Early that afternoon, Pete and the wagons came in from Brownsville. In fact, during Claude's absence Pete made multiple trips to Brownsville. Claude awoke to the sound of their arrival and staggered out to meet them. He greeted Claude with a weary smile and told him that the men and the teams were tired and needed some rest. Claude nodded his head understandingly. "Alright. Well, when the mules are taken care of, come inside and let's visit a few minutes," he said.

Pete came in about an hour later with a handful of paperwork. "Here are the records and the money we collected while you were gone. I'd say we did well except for the last trip—bandits attacked us. Luckily, we were able to drive the outlaws away, but

Pancho was wounded. If you ask me, I think we should retire Pancho; he's getting feeble and needs more help than we can give him on the road. But right now, he just needs rest; in fact, we all need to rest."

Pete paused a moment and then resumed speaking. "Before we get into anything else, I would like to have a few days off to get married. My bride's a young woman who I've known for a long time. Actually, I've known her most of our lives. We haven't seen each other regularly, but I've tried to visit her when I could. If it's alright with you, my plan is to build an addition to the house where my family lives."

"Well, sure, it's fine with me. When do you plan to get married, Pete?" asked Claude.

"Right away," he replied.

Claude smiled and cleared his throat. "While we're on the subject, I'm planning to ask your sister Maria to marry me and I'd like your permission to do so. I know she loves me and I think she'll say yes. So what do you think about our having a double wedding?" asked Claude.

"You know that I'd be honored to have you marry my sister, and I'm sure Maria will accept your proposal. We've all known for some time how sweet she is on you. I was just wondering how long it was gonna take you to get around to asking. As for a double wedding, I think it's a good idea. Do you think we could get a priest to come out here for the ceremony? It's more likely he'd come if he knows there's more than one wedding needing his blessing," added Pete.

"I tell you what, I'll propose to Maria tonight—I'm dying to see her—and if she agrees, I'll go to San Antonio tomorrow and find a priest. I'm sure our men, and their families, would be glad to have a priest come here. I'm sure there's more than one baby needing to be baptized. I'll put Pancho, Lupe, and Anna in charge of preparations and we'll have a big party for all. I'd like to arrange for the ceremonies as soon as possible; I don't know why I've waited this long either," replied Claude.

"As far as my bride and I are concerned, the sooner, the better," Pete agreed.

That night when Claude went to see Maria, she met him at the door and almost leaped into his arms, crying. Claude liked the embrace but was puzzled by her tears. "Well I'm glad to see you and I'm glad you're glad to see me, but why the tears?" he asked.

"I feared you were never going to want me. I've been crying with happiness ever since my brother told me you were going to ask," replied Maria between sobs.

"Your brother should have waited and let me speak for myself. I've been practicing what I was going to say. Maria, I love you and want to care for you for the rest of your life. Will you be my wife?" asked Claude.

"Claude, I love you and want nothing more than to be your wife. How soon do you want to get married? My brother said you both want to have the ceremony as soon as possible," replied Maria.

"Your brother has told me that he plans to enlarge and remodel the house your family is living in; I intend to do the same for my home. It will take a while, but I want to tend to it myself. I want to make sure it's going to be nice for you and the children we might have".

Claude liked the rosiness that appeared in Maria's cheeks when he spoke of having children. *She will be a wonderful mother,* he thought. *Pete was right; I don't know why I waited so long.*

"Pete says he and his bride are ready to be married, and so if you're ready, I'll go to San Antonio and find us a priest. We can have a double wedding, if you're alright with the idea. And after the wedding, I want to take you to San Antonio for a few days and stay in the new Menger Hotel. Would you like that?" asked Claude with excitement.

Maria responded by throwing her arms around Claude's neck and kissing him on the cheek, but then she recovered from her excitement, blushing again. "Well, I'll take that as a 'yes,'" said

Claude with a smile.

That evening, Claude and Maria walked hand in hand along the river together. Maria was quiet, and yet very ardent, glancing flirtatiously at Claude every so often. "I wish we could be married tonight, Maria, but it won't be long now. But I don't think it would be right for me not to make you aware of my plans—plans for us and our future together. So here's what I'm thinking: in a few years—when we've been married for a time—I'd like for us to move to Northeast Texas, where I was raised. My grandpa and I are in the process of purchasing some land in that area," explained Claude.

Maria was obviously startled by the news, but it only took her a split-second to confirm that she would be happy anywhere, as long as they were together. Claude had hoped for such a response.

The next morning, Claude and Pete discussed wedding plans and decided to have the double ceremony the following Wednesday. However, their plans still pended on whether Claude could get a priest to come out. He and Pete figured that a week would give the women enough time to get ready. They also assumed Pancho and his family needed the week to gather supplies for the wedding feast. Pete told Claude that they should expect a crowd because of all the relatives and friends who would want to attend the ceremony.

"Well Pete, I don't have any experience with Catholic weddings, or any other kind, for that matter. I guess what I'm trying to say is that I would appreciate your overseeing the preparations of the ceremonies and festivities. So I'll provide the money for the weddings, and you'll provide the direction. How does that sound?" offered Claude.

"Sure sounds better than the other way around," replied Pete with a grin.

Later that day, Claude went into town and found a priest named Father Ricardo Lopez who agreed to come out the next Tuesday to perform the infant baptisms and to conduct the double wedding ceremony the following day. Claude didn't know what was expected of him, so he made a generous donation to Father Lopez's parish church and told the priest, "A buggy will be sent for you Tuesday morning."

Having finished making arrangements with the priest, Claude went about to find a buggy for the occasion. Up until now, a buggy was the one mode of transportation that Claude had never seen a need for. Once he was married, however, he was sure his wife would appreciate a buggy as opposed to horseback or one of his large freight wagons. But due to the war, there were no new buggies to be found in town. Fortunately, Claude was able to find a wheelwright who sold him a used one that was still in good condition. Claude's mule, Maggie, didn't like pulling the buggy, but Claude gently insisted she pull them back to headquarters without further delay.

When he returned, Claude went to talk to Pancho and his wife about all that he and Pete were planning. It seemed that Pete had already filled them in on the news, and they were happy to assist. *Pete isn't wasting any time. He must be real anxious to marry his girl*, Claude chuckled to himself.

Claude then gave Pancho some money and suggested he enlist T.C. and Lupe to help him get all the supplies that would be needed. "Now, if you need more money, just tell me. This is the only wedding I've ever been part of and ever plan to have and I don't know what's expected or needing to be done. You might be better off talking with Pete because he probably knows more than I do," admitted Claude. "As for the priest, I've just come from speaking with him in San Antonio. We need to go get him on Tuesday. I've just bought a buggy that we can use to pick him up, and after the wedding, Maria and I will drive it back up to San Antonio and stay for a few days."

Pancho nodded and shifted the subject. "I'm sure you'll want to have a big spread after the weddings," he grinned. "After all, it's not every day that "El Jefe" gets married. We will have a big party that everyone will talk about for a long time! Don't worry; just leave it to us. And T.C. can help out as well."

"Sounds good. T.C. can go early Tuesday morning to pick up the priest," said Claude as his mind spun with all the pending details. *It's a good thing we're making this a double wedding and Pete has an interest invested in it as well. I wouldn't want to be responsible for all this myself,* Claude thought to himself as he headed home.

Claude was both surprised and a bit frustrated that he was not able to see Maria over the next several days. Nevertheless, Pete assured him that everything was fine. It was just that the women were all caught up in their preparations for the big day; they were even making new dresses. Fortunately, the rest of the week did seem to fly by as Claude was busy getting the business in order before the few days he had set aside to spend with Maria in San Antonio. There were always details and things to tend to in order to keep things running smoothly. There was equipment to repair, animals to care for, contracts to be arranged; his freighting business had grown into quite an enterprise.

Just before noon on Tuesday, T.C. drove in from town with Father Lopez. A crowd of Claude's employees and their families welcomed Father Lopez and he soon set up to hear confessions from the Catholics who were present. That, along with christenings, kept the priest busy into the night. It had been quite a long time since most of Claude's Catholic workers and their families had seen one. Most of the men could ride into town, but transporting their families was not as easy. Claude realized he should arrange for wagons to make regular runs into town to take the women and children so that their needs could be met. He would see to that when he returned from San Antonio.

Claude didn't sleep well that night as he tossed and turned in his bed. The new responsibility of being a husband made him anxious. He had tried to see Maria earlier in the evening, but her mother would not hear of it. "You will see her at ten o'clock in the morning. Don't you know that seeing her tonight would be bad luck?" asked Maria's mother sternly.

That particular wedding superstition was new to Claude, and it rankled him a bit because he hoped a visit with Maria would put him at ease. Surprisingly, Claude awoke the next morning feeling somewhat well rested. He groomed himself carefully, trimmed his beard, and put on the only suit he owned, along with a new pair of boots he had ordered handmade. Pete came to see him, dressed in a black bolero jacket and black pants that fit him tight. The two of them laughed about how nervous they were.

"There's quite a crowd of people here," said Pete. "Some of our friends and even relatives of our drivers have come from as far away as the King Ranch; I suspect there are about a hundred people."

"A hundred? Do you think we're gonna be able to feed that many people? Have you talked to Pancho?" asked Claude nervously.

"Don't worry, El Jefe; everything's under control. We have plenty of food. Our culture always celebrates weddings in a big way and we count on all the relatives and friends—whether invited or not—to show up. Pancho had plenty of help, and most of the women have pitched in. And I told T.C. to be available to take Father Lopez back to San Antonio when he's ready. Then he will return with the buggy for you and Maria to use."

Pete gave Claude a friendly slap on the back. "It's almost ten o'clock. Let's go."

The men and the priest had set up a makeshift altar under a large oak tree. Some of the women had decorated it with wild flowers of all colors. Claude and Pete were directed to stand in front of the altar and wait for their brides to join them. Fortunately, the weather cooperated and it was a beautiful, clear morning with the sun shining high in the sky. There were not enough chairs for all the guests, so they stood on either side of the aisle. The brides finally approached the altar. Both wore white flamenco-style dresses decorated with colorful ribbons and embroidery. Claude swallowed hard. Maria was beautiful; her long dark hair was tied in thick braids wrapped under her mantilla lace veil.

Claude soon learned that a Catholic wedding included a full Mass, mostly in Latin. He didn't understand much of it and thought it would never finish. The rest of the ceremony, thankfully, was spoken in Spanish and Claude understood it all. He and Maria, and Pete and his bride, spoke their vows for everyone to hear. When the ceremony finally ended, Maria wept. She always cried when she was happy or sad; today she was ecstatic and the tears flowed. Claude had expected it and didn't mind. He respected the differences of womanhood and was all the more attracted to Maria for her feminine ways.

Despite his own happiness, Claude did wish that his mother and grandpa could have been there for the wedding. He determined that when he was in San Antonio, he would make the time to send them a short letter with the news of his marriage. And hopefully, Grandpa Jake would send news of the land purchase.

Makeshift tables had been set up using the lumber that Pete had ordered to enlarge his house. The tables were covered with spicy rice, beans, piles of tortillas, platters of chicken and beef, jugs of wine, and of course, tamales. After the priest blessed the food, everyone began eating and drinking while a mariachi band played loudly. Maria clung to Claude's arm as they mingled with their guests. And so the afternoon flew by with the festivities until finally Maria got on her tippy toes and whispered into Claude's ear, "When can we leave?"

"I was hoping you would ask," replied Claude. "I suppose the sooner, the better." Maria smiled at his suggestion.

T.C., all smiles, came to congratulate them. Claude quietly took the boy aside and asked him to get the buggy hooked up and parked on the other side of the house, where it would be out of sight. "Maria and I want to slip off soon," he told T.C.

Just then, Pete and his bride approached Claude with a request. "When T.C. comes back from San Antonio with the buggy, may we borrow it?" asked Pete.

"Sure," said Claude, "but I think we should try to get back to work early next week. Remember to have T.C. pick us up at the Menger Hotel Sunday evening."

When Claude and Maria reached the house, T.C. was dutifully waiting with the buggy. Maria had sent her overnight bag to Claude's house before the ceremony. Claude went into the house to get their bags, and then he and Maria headed off to San Antonio with T.C. at the reins. The trip was relatively short, and the couple said goodbye to T.C. at the hotel door.

"This is the first time I've stayed in a hotel," said Maria excitedly. "You may have to help me know what I'm supposed to do."

Claude gave her hand a reassuring squeeze. "Don't worry, Maria; there's nothing to it. I'll do all the talking if you want."

When the newlyweds got to their room, Claude picked Maria up and carried her over the threshold. Maria shrieked with laughter, "Claude, what are you doing?"

"This is one wedding tradition I do know about," he replied with a smile.

When Claude put Maria down, she became quiet and her mood turned somber. "Claude, all of this is so new to me. I love you and I'm glad we're here, but I need you to be gentle because I am scared," confessed Maria.

Claude took her in his arms and told her that he loved her and that he didn't want her to be afraid. "We'll take our time," he promised.

The two of them then changed clothes and went out for a leisurely walk down the streets of San Antonio. Maria asked about North Texas and Claude told her about the area where he was raised. "I left money with my grandfather to buy land along a river and one tract in a large prairie. The biggest difference I can see is that it rains a lot more there than it does here. And except on the prairie, North Texas has large trees and a lot more rivers and creeks than we have here in the South," he explained.

Maria nodded but fell silent for a moment. "How will it be

for me?" she asked.

Claude knew exactly what she meant and felt sympathetic to her concerns. "Please don't worry, Maria; I promise to always take care of you. I think I was the only Anglo at our wedding and we made it just fine. And even if you're the only Mexican in North Texas, we'll make it because I'll be with you and I have family and friends who will be our neighbors. They are very excited to meet you," replied Claude confidently.

When they went to bed that evening, Maria quivered in Claude's arms. Knowingly, he whispered gentle assurances and told her nothing would happen that she wouldn't want to happen. It was a promise he almost wished he hadn't made because upon hearing it, she soon fell asleep with her head on his shoulder.

Early the next morning, Maria woke Claude up with her hand on his chest, as she told him she wanted him. Though she was passive in the beginning, she warmed up to his kisses and caresses; Claude was as gentle as he could be and Maria responded. Later, Maria held him tightly and cried, "My mother told me this was a wife's unpleasant duty, but she was wrong. Did I do things right? Please understand that this is all new to me. I want to please you."

"Maria, it's just as new to me; you are the only woman I've ever been with and you were wonderful. I'm glad it was good for you, too," he replied.

Claude gently moved his hand over Maria's body. She responded to his touch; her nipples became hard and when she reached for him he was ready again. This time, her actions were anything but passive and they climaxed together. Through happy tears she said, "Claude that was wonderful. No one ever told me being with my husband would be like this. I love you and I want to have your children."

When they weren't in their hotel room, the couple spent the rest of their time walking around San Antonio. They went to the Mexican market and Claude gave Maria some money and told her to buy anything she wanted. Claude then took time to write and post a short letter to his mother and grandfather sharing the news of his marriage. Maria sent her love too.

Sunday afternoon came too quickly, and soon, T.C. was there to take the honeymooners home. When they arrived at home, Claude left Maria to her unpacking and went off to find Pete. "Last week, you suggested we retire Poncho. I've been thinking about what you said and I think you're right; we need a full-time cook. When Poncho feels up to it, let's keep him on at half-pay so he can help train the new cook. While you're getting everything ready to go, I'll head back to San Antonio and purchase a small wagon that we can convert into a cooking wagon," said Claude.

Pete agreed that it was a good idea. "That should work better than hauling all our cooking supplies in one of the big wagons."

"If memory serves me right, the wheelwright that sold me the buggy also had a good wagon. I'm gonna see if I can find us a cook while I'm in town. And you might ask Poncho when you talk to him; he might know someone," suggested Claude.

In about a week's time, Claude and his teamsters were ready to roll again. They had a new chuck wagon, a full-time cook, and T.C. had been promoted to driver. On the road, T.C. was responsible for taking care of the mules, and at night he slept by Claude's side. Cotton was becoming both expensive and harder to find, so Claude decided to send his cotton buyer to East Texas. Most of the cotton for the Mexican trade was now coming by rail to Alleyton, Texas, which served as the terminal for the first and southernmost railroad in Texas. Here, Claude and his men could pick up cotton, haul it to Brownsville, and return with supplies for either Confederate Army or civilian use. Fortunately, Alleyton was roughly due east of San Antonio, allowing them to load there and then stop for a few days in San Antonio to stay with their families and rest the mules. Claude continued to haul for Captain King, picking up loads of cotton at his ranch and transporting it to various places along the river.

Throughout the rest of 1863 and early 1864, the only news

about the war that Claude was able to get was by word of mouth. Due to the shortage of newsprint and just about everything else, most newspapers in Texas were forced to halt production. When Claude heard any news, it was never good; it seemed pretty clear that the South was getting whipped.

Union forces had occupied Brownsville and most of Claude's trips were now confined to Laredo or other towns upriver from Brownsville. Worse still, the Mexican bandits were becoming bolder and often attacked the wagons in broad daylight. All Claude's drivers were good shots and the ten gauge shotguns they brandished were deadly. In their most recent encounter with bandits, two of Claude's drivers were killed and one was seriously wounded. Claude told the drivers' widows they were welcome to stay where they were until they wanted to move and he kept them on partial pay. Claude also brought a doctor from San Antonio to treat the wounded driver and kept him on full pay.

It was rumored that General Magruder, the Confederate commander of Texas, had ordered Colonel Rip Ford to recruit a group of cavalry to drive the Union forces from the lower Rio Grande Valley. When Claude read the recruitment signs, he stopped taking Confederate money and accepted only Mexican gold or U.S. dollars. Confederate money had depreciated to about one-quarter of its worth, if you could find anyone to take it. Claude carefully saved all the gold and U.S. money he could. It was 1864 and the future seemed nothing short of uncertain.

While visiting with T.C. one day, Claude told him that he hadn't heard any news from home and was planning to make another trip to Indian Springs toward the end of summer. Naturally, the boy asked if he could go along. Though he was only fifteen years old, T.C. had been doing a grown man's job and making a grown man's salary for some time now. "I wouldn't think of leaving you behind," replied Claude.

Claude liked being married. Maria was always pleasant to be with, and her only complaint was that she wasn't pregnant. She really wanted a baby, and seeing Pete's wife abundantly pregnant didn't make it easier. "Time will take care of it, Maria, just you wait and see," Claude told her reassuringly.

One day, Claude finally learned some news from a man in Alleyton who wanted a ride to San Antonio. The man had lost an arm at Gettysburg and was trying to get back to his home in San Antonio. Around the campfire each night, the man told Claude and his teamsters just how bloody and horrible the war had been. When everyone listening had fallen quiet and had bowed their heads in memory of the fallen, the soldier bucked them up.

"A funny thing happened at the Union hospital I was in. A Confederate soldier lyin' in the bed next to mine lost his foot—or part of it anyway—on the second day of the battle. He asked the surgeon not to cut off too much of it and to leave him something for walkin'. Well, he got his wish, and so I asked the surgeon to save me somethin' for playin' the piano. And the surgeon just looked at me and said, 'Unless you play with your toes, soldier, you're out of luck,'" said the soldier with a loud cackle.

When no one laughed at his story, the armless veteran murmured, "I guess you had to be there to 'preciate it."

Although the war had an effect on everything, there were still other problems. The area between the Nueces and the Rio Grande was suffering a terrible drought. Most water holes had dried up and the only available water was from a few wells. Water for Claude's men and the animals now had to be stored in barrels tied to the sides of the wagon and swirling dust was a plague to all.

Before the weather turned cold for the winter, Claude turned everything over to Pete, so that he and T.C. could head up north again. Together, the two of them led three pack mules loaded down with calico, thread, buttons, salt, sugar, wheat flour, nails, quinine, calomel, laudanum, coffee, blankets, and anything else Claude and T.C. could think of that was not available in North Texas. Claude had no intention of taking Maria on this trip, for it was arduous, but worse than that, it was very dangerous. He wanted her safe in their home at the headquarters. Maria reluctantly complied. He promised that one of these days—once the war ended—he would take her up for a visit. Maria knew Claude was right; she too had heard stories of the dangers even the men faced on the road. When would this brutal war ever end? The most she could do was pray for Claude's safe return.

CHAPTER 16

Ezra Spence and Gettysburg
1863-1864

A cannonball hit Sergeant Tom Baker's head, throwing him full force into Corporal Ezra Spence and sending the corporal to the ground. But before Ezra could move, a rifle shot blasted his right foot, causing him to pass out. When he finally came to, he realized two things: first that his good friend, Tom Baker, lay dead in a heap next to him, and he himself was probably going to be dead soon too, if he didn't do something to stop the blood flow from his foot. Laboriously, he was somehow able to struggle out of his shirt and wrap it tightly around his foot. However, the pain was so terrible that he kept slipping in and out of consciousness. When he awoke again, the shirt that wrapped his foot was saturated with blood, but the pressure and coagulation had thankfully stopped most of the bleeding.

Ezra's foot throbbed with pain, his head ached, and he suffered from dehydration. In his mind, he tried to reconstruct what had happened. It began to come back to him slowly, like a long-forgotten dream. Early that morning, the Confederate troops—including Sergeant Baker's squad and Corporal Ezra Spence—had launched an assault against the Union soldiers near Gettysburg, Pennsylvania. The Confederate volley appeared effective to Ezra, although he could only see part of the battle that was taking place directly in front of him. Despite heavy losses and stubborn opposition, Sergeant Baker continued to lead the squad forward. The Union troops had fought fiercely and Ezra was the only soldier from the squadron still alive.

Ezra was six feet tall and rawboned, with big hands, wide shoulders, and a trim waist. Shell-shocked and traumatized, he had completely forgotten that today—July 2, 1863—was his eighteenth birthday. The youngest of nine brothers and sisters, he was the only child still living at home when his mother and father died of fever early in 1862.

After their death, he packed up and rode a mule northeast from Kentucky. Ezra then enlisted after encountering his first group of Confederate troops in Pennsylvania and now, here he was.

As buzzards circled above in the late that afternoon sky, Ezra was picked up and placed in a wagon carrying both Confederate and Union wounded. He was conscious, though only briefly, when the Yankees who were gathering the wounded found him, but he soon passed out in the wagon from the excruciating pain in his foot. Union troops had retaken the territory the Confederates had only just secured that morning.

When Ezra awoke, he looked up to see a Union doctor with a bone saw in his hand, preparing to amputate his foot. "Ifen you jus' cut off what you need to, doc, and leave me somethin' to walk on, I'll be much obliged," he said between measured breaths. The last thing he remembered before passing out again was the look on the doctor's face. It was a look that said, "Consider yourself lucky to be alive."

Ezra did not regain consciousness until the next morning.

Fortunate for him, the Union doctor had been generous enough to heed his plea and remove only the mangled mess that had once been his toes. The doctor checked in on Ezra later in the day and told him that if he didn't develop blood poisoning, he would be able to walk again. The surgeon had pulled the skin together behind Ezra's toes and sewed the skin from the top of his foot to the sole.

"What will happen if I git blood poisoning?" asked Ezra.

The doctor shrugged. "We might have to amputate your foot, or even your leg," he replied.

"Well, I'm much obliged to you for takin' care of me, but you ain't gonna git to cut off nothin' else. I'm gonna git well and git out of here," Ezra told him.

After a brief pause, the doctor looked up at him. "I hope you do. And that was spoken like a true Scot-Irishman."

Funny, Ezra thought as the doctor moved on to the next cot and amputation. His father had once told him they were Scot-Irish. And when young Ezra asked what that meant, his father had explained that their ancestors emigrated from Scotland to Ireland and then came to this country. After they arrived, Ezra's progenitors made their way over the mountains to Kentucky with Daniel Boone nearly a hundred years earlier. Ezra couldn't imagine how anyone outside of their immediate family could understand anything his father said, with that thick Scot-Irish blend accent.

Ezra decided death was better than undergoing another amputation and becoming a complete cripple. Then his thoughts turned to escape. He knew that in order to escape, his wound would have to heal and he would have to regain his strength. As soon as he was able, Ezra sat on the side of his cot, and when no one was watching, he practiced hopping around, balancing most of his weight on his left foot and just the heel of his right. And although the food they gave him was terrible, he ate every bite. As the weeks passed, he began to regain his strength, all the while being careful not to let on.

The hospital was a scattered series of worn tents crammed full with cots. There was no need for guards, on account of the reality that the Rebel soldiers were all too wounded, crippled, or sick to attempt an escape. With no sanitation and gangrene spreading like a rash throughout the entire camp, the smell was putrid and sickening. Two or three times a day, the Yankees moved out the dead only to bring in more wounded. Ezra began to realize that if he could manage to escape, they might not even miss him. He had already been there over a month. The latest rumor was that the next day, the wounded Confederate soldiers were being transferred to a prisoner of war camp. If he was going to escape, he had to make his move today.

About mid-afternoon, Ezra heard a horse approach the entrance of his tent. A Union captain dismounted and entered the tent in search of a man named Sergeant Schmidt. When the captain came to Ezra's cot, Ezra shook his head, so the captain turned to other cots. With the captain's back now turned, Ezra realized that this was the chance he had been waiting for. He suddenly bolted up from his cot and hopped toward the entrance of the tent. Fortunately, the captain's horse was tied to a tent rope just a few feet from the entrance.

Ezra felt his body revolt against the burst of activity he had imposed upon it. He almost fainted as he attempted to mount the horse but somehow still made the mount. Once he was in the saddle, Ezra walked the horse slowly for a few yards and then began to increase his pace. Miraculously, no one stopped him until he reached the edge of camp. A Union guard yelled for him to halt, but Ezra used his good foot to kick the horse into a full gallop.

Lucky for him, the guard was a poor shot and his bullet missed Ezra. And so, by the time the guard found another Union soldier with a mount to follow the escaped prisoner, he was already a good distance from the hospital camp. Ezra followed the woods along a creek and didn't slow his pace until after dark. He could no longer see to ride fast, but he figured the Union troops weren't trying very hard to find him anyway, with his being wounded and un-armed.

By nightfall, the horse was limping badly. Ezra didn't know what was wrong and didn't dare get off to see for fear that he wouldn't have the strength to remount. From the direction the sun had set, Ezra could tell that the creek he trailed ran roughly south-west. At a place where the creek turned suddenly east, there was a little rise and a persimmon thicket with a small clearing in the middle. He figured it a decent place to stop and rest, so as not to faint and fall from the horse. Nevertheless, while dismounting, he clumsily bumped his right foot on the saddle and immediately passed out from the pain. When he awoke, he found that the rein was still wrapped around his hand and had held his mount. Ezra could not remember ever being so exhausted. Removing the bit from the horse's mouth but leaving the bridle on, he allowed the horse to graze. With the reins wrapped around his hand, sleep came instantly. When he awoke again, it was morning. The horse was gone and all he had was the bridle and the reins he had been holding in his sleep.

Ezra was in dire need of water, so he pulled himself up to a wobbly stand with the help of a persimmon sprout. He fell twice to the ground as he hobbled toward the creek. After drinking all he could, he looked around for a stick of some kind to use as a crutch. He found a large dead limb under a nearby oak tree, and although its twisted shape made movement awkward, it was better than no crutch at all.

His foot and leg ached all the way to his knee, and red hot flares shot up his leg. Ezra had nothing to eat, no way to treat his foot, no horse, no weapon, and he was probably still in Union terri-tory. He figured he would die right there by the creek. If the Yan-kees caught him, he might be better off dead.

Ezra didn't have the strength to crawl back to the thicket. Once more, he drank his fill of water and then submerged his bandaged foot in the creek. The hot red streaks running up his leg irritated him and his foot ached fiercely. But after soaking his foot for a good while, he felt some relief. Ezra was finally able to unwind the bandage from his foot, only to discover that it had swelled to twice its normal size. The hours of hard riding had broken the skin that had been sewn together, and the wound was draining. The smell of it reeked terribly and Ezra feared that he was developing gangrene or blood poisoning.

His clothes were all but rags. He had on the same Confederate pants he was wearing when wounded on the battlefield, and his shirt was a Yankee cast off. He stripped, tied his clothes to a limb, and put them in the creek to soak. As he sat on the creek bank, he began thinking that he needed a soaking about as bad as his clothes.

After crawling out of the creek, Ezra spread his pants and shirt over bushes to dry and laid down on the grass to rest. At one point, he thought he heard movement; but looking around, he didn't see anything. Since it was warm and he was tired, he slept until the sun rose directly above him.

When they felt dry to the touch, Ezra put his clothes back on. A thick, gray fluid was draining from his foot, so he soaked it again to make it feel better.

When he tried to stop thinking about the pain in his foot, he realized that he was starving. He knew there were some small fish in the creek and fat frogs on the opposite bank. There was even a bird's nest in a tree above his head, but he had no way of getting to any of this potential food. Ezra began to wonder if his fate would be to starve to death. At least he had water, and he drank as much of it as he could to stave off the pangs of hunger.

Ezra slept on and off for the next three or four days, although he had no idea how much time had passed. The high fever and chills caused delirium, and he dreamed that he was in Clarksville, Texas. His friend, Sergeant Baker, had been from Clarksville. On their long hike to Gettysburg, and during their longer wait on the edge of the battlefield, Baker had tortured him with descriptions of the dishes his mother would prepare for his homecoming after the war. Ezra now dreamed of Mrs. Baker's fried chicken and chocolate cake. It was even more delicious than—

He awoke, ravenous. He wondered if this was how blood poisoning killed you—with hunger cramps and visions of food you would never have. His foot oozed with foul-smelling infection, and the unmitigated streaks that ran the length of his leg burned red.

Several times he had a feeling someone was watching him, but he decided it was his own imagination because the birds kept flying and the usual sounds of the woods continued uninterrupted.

His foot still drained when he soaked it in the creek, but the fluid didn't seem quite as thick or smell as bad as when he first came to the thicket. One morning, after soaking his foot in the creek, Ezra crawled back to the softer grass to find that someone had left some jerked deer meat wrapped in homespun cloth. *Who could it have been?* Tearing into the meat, he was at the same time grateful and dumbfounded. He chewed the dried meal throughout the morning and as he did so, he began to feel a little better. His temperature went down a bit, and he now slept less fitfully.

The next morning, he was surprised to see more jerky had been left for him, along with an old crutch. The crutch, though a little short, was certainly better than the heavy tree limb he had been using. This newfound crutch was made from an oak limb, with one strong branch that fit under the arm and another for a handhold. It was old, well-worn, and yet sound. The top support and the handhold had been carefully carved.

He entertained himself with thoughts of his benefactor and what his motives might be for helping him to recover. Each morning, he found something different: cold cooked turnip and greens, bacon, cornbread, and more jerky. Within a few days, Ezra was beginning to gain some strength, and he hobbled all over the area with the aid of his crutch. He had all but lost track of time, but he was sure a month or more had passed. His foot had finally stopped draining, and the red streaks on his leg had faded. Even though his clothes were tattered, he washed them frequently in the creek. Ezra couldn't quite see his reflection in the swift waters of the creek, but he could imagine how unkempt he looked. His hair had grown down to his shoulders, and he hadn't shaved his beard for several months.

Then one morning he awoke to find his benefactor—a girl—leaving behind a deerskin shirt at the edge of the little clearing. Although he only caught a glimpse of the back of her, he figured that she was only a little over five feet tall and of a very thin and petite build. She was wearing a long, colorless homespun dress and moccasins, her long blond hair rippling down her back as she walked away.

Ezra picked up the shirt, pulling it over his bare chest. Although it was tight in the shoulders, the deerskin fit him well. It had obviously seen a lot of wear and was stiff and creased where it had been folded, but with the colder and rainier weather setting in, he welcomed the extra warmth.

Upon leaving the shirt, the girl had run down a slightly beaten path toward the southwest—a path that Ezra had never noticed before. The sticker bushes in the area had hidden it well, and he had stayed clear of them, not wanting to chance falling into the brambles when hobbling on his crutch. Wanting to thank her for her kindness, Ezra hobbled upstream and picked all the wild flowers he could hold in his free hand. He then tied the yellow and blue flowers into a bouquet with a torn strip of his old shirt. Ezra placed the makeshift bouquet in the middle of the beaten path where she would see it next time. If prayers helped, there would be a next time.

The next morning the flowers were gone and had been replaced with three cold baked sweet potatoes, cold fried chicken, and a pair of deerskin pants. Since the pants had belonged to someone shorter than he, extensions made of deer hide had been crudely sewn onto the end of each pant leg.

Around noon that day, Ezra awoke from a nap to find that

the girl was sitting on the grass where she had been leaving him food. She had straw-colored hair that was tied up in a knot atop her head. Her skin was fair, her nose and cheeks were sprinkled with freckles, and her light blue eyes gave her a haunted look that captivated him. Ezra was struck with wonder.

The girl was staring at him and knew he was awake. For nearly five minutes, neither spoke a word. Finally, Ezra broke the silence. "Much obliged for everythin'. You saved my life."

His speaking startled her. She jumped up from where she was sitting and ran down the beaten path. Ezra felt sore with himself for scaring her way; but how was he to know that she would take flight when spoken to?

The next morning, when Ezra awoke, the girl was sitting on the same patch of grass, only this time she was accompanied by a small mule. When he stood to his feet, she led the mule over and indicated for him to get on its back. She held his right knee as he boosted himself up. Then she handed him his crutch and the bridle and reins from the lost horse and slowly led the mule southwest.

Ezra was astonished, but didn't dare speak out and make conversation. Up to this point, she had only shown him kindness, so he had decided to trust her and let her lead the way. She never uttered a word but kept walking as she led the mule. After several miles, they came to a log cabin in a wooded valley, with a small creek running nearby. The girl helped him off the mule and escorted him inside where he sat on a bench at the table. She set about adding wood to the fireplace, prepared a meal of scrambled eggs, and then joined him at the table.

She asked him what his name was, speaking in a quiet voice and never looking him in the eye. "I'm Ezra Spence. What's yore name?" he asked.

"I'm Abby Simpson."

They said nothing else for a while. Ezra was afraid to say very much because he didn't want her to run off again. It warmed his spirits just to have her sitting across from him at the table. To him, she was beautiful. He reiterated what he had told her the day before. "You saved my life. My foot was shot, and I was in a Yankee hospital camp until I escaped. I would've starved to death if you hadn't helped me."

That night, Abby fried a chicken and served it with turnips and turnip greens from her small garden. She also gave Ezra milk to drink. "My Ma, Pa, and three kid brothers died last year with fever and I'm the onliest member of my family left. I can't plow or do thangs a man can, but I'm still here, nowhere else to go. When you git stronger, I'll show you aroun' the place. The cow is about dry and I don't know what to do about it. I have chickens and pigs and I can kill and clean the chickens, but I don't know nothin' about killin' pigs."

That night, Ezra went to sleep with a full belly on a make-shift bed with a straw mattress; it was his first night of sound sleep in what seemed like forever. With a roof overhead, it was the warmest night he'd had since fall set in. The next morning, Ezra felt stronger. Abby fed him cold fried chicken and eggs for breakfast. "Abby, I'm much stronger this morning. I'm gittin' better and shore would like to look around, ifen it's all right with you," he said.

The cabin had two rooms with a dog run in between. A pasture behind the house held the cow and three mules. The small barn had a corncrib about a third full. "I let the cow and the mules out to graze the hillside, but they always come back at night 'cause I always feed 'em a little," Abby explained. "I let the old sow out from the pen, but she comes back now and then and has some piglets with her. I always feed 'em somethin' so maybe they'll come back. It's been lonesome since my family died, and livin' in these hills ain't a good place fer a woman alone. No one has been here since they died, but I've been afraid that Yankee solders might come. I wish we wus further away from the war."

A muzzle-loading rifle hung above the door, and a sack with lead and a powder horn full of powder hung nearby. Ezra thought how handy that gun might be. Abby noticed his interest and told him there was a large jug of powder in the barn.

After a few days, Ezra was limping around without his crutch and was feeling much stronger. While he would have liked to hunt deer, and missed the gamey taste of venison, he feared that shooting in the wilderness might draw the unwanted attention of any Yankee who might be in the area.

One night, Abby came and crawled into bed with Ezra. The unexpectedness of this both surprised and delighted him. As he drew their bodies close together, he recalled a fleeting thought he had after being shot—that he would never know the true touch and love of a woman. It brought back the fear, sorrow, and pain of the battlefield, and he trembled with emotion. Abby accepted it without comment, and after that night, her shyness disappeared. She had obviously never been with a man, but her grief and loneliness spurred her to reach out to Ezra; and he was happy to return her kindness and love. Although he hadn't been with a woman before either, it didn't take long for their forlorn hearts to mentor their bodies into responding to each other. Ezra would have thought that he had dreamt it all, except that when he awoke to the morning light, she was still cradled in his arms.

Ezra lured one of the pigs into the pen and closed the gate. "Let's feed 'em a little corn and all our table leavins. When the weather gits cold enough, I'll slaughter 'em and we'll have fresh hog sausage, ham, and bacon. You know how to make good jerky, so we can have plenty. You said yourself that you'd like to git away from the war. If and when we leave here, we'll need jerky and anything else we can take to eat. A friend of mine, killed at Gettysburg, was from Clarksville, a town in Texas, and the stories he told about that land shore sounded good."

As fall rapidly progressed, Ezra set out to cut enough wood to get them through the winter. He would chop down a tree, trim it, and use a mule to drag it to the house. Before the first frost, he had succeeded in cutting enough wood to last the winter. In November, he killed the pig they had penned and fattened up. By spring, they had cured ham, bacon, and plenty of jerky.

In the spring Ezra led the cow over the mountains to the nearest farm and traded it for another mule. He and Abby loaded two mules with essentials, rode the other two, and headed out for Ezra's home in Kentucky. "My family buried some gold coins in a jar under the stoop," Ezra told her. "That'll help git us to Texas."

As Ezra and Abby traveled, they avoided towns and made their camp near a stream whenever possible. Although the nights were still cool, the pair made good time and subsisted on the preserved pork meat as well as any game Ezra was able to kill along the way.

When they got close to his home in Kentucky, they met a man who owned the next property down the valley. The man had just returned home, discharged because he lost his right leg just below the knee. "There's a mess of fightin' goin' on in Tennessee and the South. So if you're set on getting' to Texas, I recommend you go through southern Missouri and take the Texas Road," he advised Ezra and Abby.

They stayed in Ezra's old home for several days and exchanged the old pack mule for a younger, bigger one owned by Ezra's family. Ezra found cured meat and clothes that fit him better than the ones Abby had given him. Likewise, Abby came upon some clothes that had belonged to Ezra's mother and now fit Abby comfortably, as well as more ammunition and another muzzle-loading rifle.

The two of them traveled in a westerly direction, skirting southern Missouri into Kansas. Then they moved southwest across Indian territory, and finally down to Colbert's Ferry into Texas. From Colbert's Ferry they headed east to Clarksville, arriving in early November. The leaves on the hardwood trees were falling and the nights were getting nippy. Ezra and Abby kept each other warm that first night in Clarksville. Each tender movement and kiss, each sigh and rustle of the tall, cool grass under their bodies seemed to whisper, "We're home."

CHAPTER 17

Claude, Effie, and Dr. Fuqua
1864

Claude and T.C. arrived in Indian Springs about midnight. After helping Claude unload the pack mules, T.C. went straight to his parents' home. Claude went into the Williams' house and gently woke up his mother.

As always, Effie was so glad to see him that she cried. Now wide-awake, she began spilling her news before she even had a foot on the floor. "Oh Claude, what a surprise! It's so good to see you, son!" she said as she wrapped her arms around his neck and wept with joy. "I've prayed that you would come home; I've missed you so. Much has happened since you were last here. Your grandfather died about six months ago and Hannah isn't doing well. I've moved her here so that I can take better care of her. Dr. Fuqua says she really doesn't have a lot wrong with her except for her arthritis. It may just be that she's depressed with Grandpa Jake's passing and I don't know if she will ever recover from that."

"Seems like we have a lot of catching up to do. Would you mind fixing me a cup of coffee? I have a feeling this will take a while," said Claude.

Effie continued on unabated as she followed Claude into the kitchen. "Oh! I almost forgot what I most wanted to tell you. Your brother Jake left for the war. He and a friend named Jim Latimer in Clarksville wanted to join together and he just wouldn't let up about it and so I finally gave in. The two of them left before last Christmas and I haven't heard a word from your brother since. The boys had heard that a man named Ford was putting together a group of cavalrymen in San Antonio, and so I gave Jake money to buy guns and he left on a fine black horse. I thought maybe he came to see you because he said they were going to San Antonio."

"I'm afraid not, Mama," replied Claude.

"That's too bad." Effie maintained a brave smile while she prepared Claude's coffee. It was obvious she was deeply disappointed that he had no news of his younger brother. "Well, don't have much else to tell. Your sisters are all doing well. So tell me about yourself; are you married yet? I'm dying to have grandchildren."

"Yes, I married Maria not long after I was here last. I hadn't realized how much I loved her until I was away from her on that trip. And so I proposed to her when I got back and we were married a few weeks after. I love her very much and we are happier than I ever imagined. She's a fine woman, Mama; I know you'll love her too. But she hasn't been able to get pregnant yet. Now, how about you and that Dr. Fuqua? Is he still here? Are you two going to get married?" Claude inquired.

Effie blushed. "I love him. He's proposed several times and I want to marry him. It's taken me a while to work up the courage. After all these years since your father passed, I'm no spring chicken. But Ross is a good man; I'm lonesome and so is he. Maybe we can work it out while you're here."

"I'm glad for you both. Being alone isn't good—I finally learned that. I'd be happy to help you out while I'm here, but let's finish this in the morning, Mama. I've ridden some thirty miles today and I sure could use a good night's sleep," said Claude.

"You're right, Claude. The bed in the spare room is made up, and so you go on and get some sleep now. We'll talk more in the morning," said Effie as she bent down and kissed his cheek. "It sure is nice to have you home again, son."

The next morning, Claude sat down to breakfast with Dr. Fuqua while Effie served them hot griddle cakes and bacon. Claude wasted no time in getting straight to the point. "My mother tells me you two want to get married. What can I do to help?" asked Claude.

The doctor looked very relieved to hear this. "Thank goodness. I've been trying to get Effie to say yes for some time now. I had a feeling she was waiting to talk with you before giving me an answer. You bet you can help! As soon as she can get ready, let's go to Clarksville, get a license and do it before she changes her mind. Why, we could even go today. I've got a good buggy and a fast horse," he said impatiently.

Effie approached the table after listening to their conversation. "Hold on there! Let's not get in such a rush, Ross; we aren't sixteen-year-old kids. We'll go when Claude's able to go with us."

"I can go any time, but how's about tomorrow?" Claude offered. Effie was taken aback.

"Well?" inquired Dr. Fuqua.

Effie looked at the men and then realized that the time had come. "I guess so," she stammered. "Yes, that will be fine." Her head began to spin with all the preparations she would need to do between then and tomorrow. "Whatever will I wear?" she thought aloud.

Claude interrupted his mother's thoughts. "I brought three pack mules loaded with things from Mexico, including some medicine. I'd wager that both of you would be surprised to see what I was able to bring across the border," he said.

Effie and the doctor followed as Claude led them outside.

T.C. was out there waiting for them.

"T.C., would you bring the loaded pack mules over here?" asked Claude. He and T.C. proceeded to unload the pack mules and they all carried the bundles indoors.

"Claude, I've never had a Christmas that was this good. You've always brought us useful things, but this time you've brought things that no one in these parts has been able to get since the war. However did you come by all these things?" exclaimed Effie.

"Well, being in the freight business and traveling to so many parts enables me to find things that simply can't be found in the local stores these days. The business is going well, and so money is not a problem. I'm just happy you like what I brought." Claude smiled as his mother ruffled his hair endearingly and kissed him on the forehead.

Later on, Claude and T.C. went to see Nell and Wash. They were waiting on their front porch and Nell cried just as Effie had.

"I'll have you know, T.C. has been doing a man's job and drawing a man's pay for some time now and I'm proud of him just as I know you are, too," Claude told them.

"Our boy's jus' told us he aimin' tuh buy some land," said Nell in amazement.

"Well now I was thinking," Claude said, "that if we can find some property near to his, I'll buy it and deed it over to you, if you'll agree to stay here and help my Mama out."

This time even Wash had tears in his eyes. He never dreamt he'd have land of his own.

Later that day, T.C. came to Claude saying he had found some land that he wanted to buy. He then went on to ask Claude if he would help him make the purchase. T.C. didn't know how exactly to go about it and he needed guidance.

"Sure I'll help you, but let's wait until after tomorrow. We may have some complications because you aren't of age yet. And besides, Mama and Dr. Ross Fuqua are going to Clarksville to get married tomorrow—"

"No!" T.C. exclaimed in surprise and delight.

"—and after that, I'll have time to look around and help you find what you want," promised Claude.

"El Jefe, can ah go and drive the buggy for 'em? Ah don't want yuh runnin' off somewheres wid'out meh," said T.C.

Claude laughed. "I haven't abandoned you yet, have I? Be at Mama's early in the morning and we'll see what we can do."

The next day, T.C. arrived early to do some chores. He washed the buggy, polished the harness, and brushed Dr. Fuqua's horse until it shined. He then went home, got cleaned up, and drove Nell over to Effie's to help her get ready. T.C. parked the buggy in front of Effie's home and waited until they came out dressed in their Sunday best.

"What a beautiful autumn day! And my, T.C., the buggy looks so nice!" exclaimed Effie. T.C. beamed with pride.

Claude thought he had never seen his mother look so happy. She was in a pretty, deep blue dress that Claude vaguely remembered her wearing before, her shoulders were draped with a soft, cream colored shawl, and her hair was done up in a soft bun. Nell had weaved a matching deep blue ribbon through Effie's hair that shone in the sunlight. Claude was surprised at how young and carefree his mother looked, and it was a sight that pleased him. They helped Effie into her seat and then headed for Clarksville with Claude on his mule and T.C. driving the buggy.

Once in Clarksville, they went directly to the courthouse. After attaining a license, they went to the First Methodist Church and found Brother Porter, the pastor, who said he would be happy to marry Effie and Dr. Fuqua.

Claude stood with his mother and Dr. Fuqua in the pastor's parlor and pretended patience as Brother Porter preached for a while. Thirty minutes later, the pastor pronounced Effie and Dr. Ross Fuqua man and wife. Claude slipped the pastor a fifty dollar gold piece and wondered why on earth it took so long to get two people hitched.

As they stepped outside into the sunshine, Claude asked the newlyweds if they had any plans and the two of them said they wanted to go home. Nell had said that she was going to prepare a special meal for them upon their return; she was determined to have a celebration for the newlyweds. The rest of the family would be there, too. So while T.C. drove them back in the buggy, Claude went off to see Mr. Canterbury, the lawyer who had handled his land purchases, promising to be back in time for the celebration.

There was a tall, lanky young man speaking with Mr. Canterbury when Claude stepped into the lawyer's office. Mr. Canterbury introduced him to Claude as Ezra Spence. "Mr. Spence here has just come to Texas from the war in the east," Mr. Canterbury told Claude. "He found six hundred acres of land adjoining yours in the Cuthand area, but he can only afford to purchase two hundred acres. Would you be interested in purchasing the other four hundred? The seller won't split it and Mr. Spence can't handle all of it."

"I might," said Claude. "Let's discuss it."

In less time than it took for his mother and Dr. Fuqua to get married, Claude agreed to purchase the six hundred acres, sell two hundred outright to Ezra, and another hundred which Claude would finance and Ezra would pay off by working on Claude's property.

Claude paid the money to the lawyer and as he and Ezra were leaving, Claude asked him where he was staying. "We're camped in the Cuthand area," Ezra told him. "We plan to move onto our new property tomorrow, ifen it's all right by you."

Claude agreed and then said, "I need to talk to Mr. Canterbury about some other property, but I'm sure I'll see you again in a day or two."

Back in the lawyer's office, Claude asked Canterbury to have all of the land he had just purchased surveyed and to look out for more land within thirty minutes riding distance of Indian Springs. Claude thought for a moment and then said, "Maybe I'd better tell you why I want it."

Intrigued, Mr. Canterbury raised his eyebrows. "Well have a seat," he said.

Claude took a seat and then went on to explain that he wanted the extra tract of land for Wash, Nell, and their son, T.C. "All free Negroes," Claude added. "Wash and Nell have been free for years and T.C. was born free, but he's only fifteen years old."

"I see." The lawyer drummed his fingers on his desktop for a moment and then said, "You had best purchase the land yourself and secretly deed it to them later. There could be serious objections, so the transaction should be done quietly. Now, I'm not sure about the fifteen-year-old boy, but it can probably be worked some way." Mr. Canterbury went on to say that several tracts of land around Indian Springs were currently for sale. "So, the next time you're here, I'll have something lined up for you to look at."

Pleased with the business he was able to accomplish, Claude mounted his mule and headed for home. Nell was an excellent cook and the celebration dinner would be something that Claude wouldn't want to miss. Earlier, T.C. mentioned that his mama had already begun preparations the day before and hinted that they were all in for a real treat. Claude and T.C. returned to Indian Springs in time for the reception for his mother and Dr. Fuqua. It was the first time in ages that Claude had seen his sisters and many old neighbors of the community. Everyone was tickled to see Effie and Dr. Fuqua acting like courting teenagers. Claude smiled to himself, grateful that he could be there for this happy occasion in his mother's life.

The following day, Claude was putting the saddle on his mule when T.C. joined him. Together they sat on the top rail of the corral fence as Claude explained what he thought would be the best way to procure land for T.C. and his family. T.C. thought having property near to his parents was a good idea and understood why it had to be done quietly.

"This war is still going on and some people will object to your owning land," Claude told him. "The lawyer said he would have some tracts for us to look at the next time we go into town and I'll be sure to buy it for you and your folks. In the meantime, try to explain the process to Wash and Nell and if they don't understand, I'll come and talk to them about it. I'm planning to ride out to the Cuthand area today. So if you want to go, saddle up."

Later that day, when they stopped to let their mounts rest, Claude told T.C. about the man he had met in the lawyer's office. "His name is Ezra Spence. He's buying land in the Cuthand area near to the tract I purchased some years ago for ranching. So here's my idea: I'm selling him an extra hundred acres on credit, while he works on my land next door. Even though I don't know anything about the man, I have a good feeling about him and I want to meet his family. I'll explain to him who you are, so you just stay with me and let's see how it all works out. Alright?"

Claude and T.C. found Ezra busy erecting a shelter with small trees and a wagon sheet on the bank of a small creek. His wife, Abby, was pregnant but that didn't keep her from running about and helping with the task at hand. She was bashful and never once uttered a word during Claude and T.C.'s visit, keeping her eyes on the ground and blushing all the while.

Claude told Ezra that a surveyor would be coming by to take measure of their property lines. "Please help him in any way you can and don't run him off," he said jokingly.

"Well you know, I might have if you hadn't mentioned it," replied Ezra with a smile. "Now tell me what work you'd like me to do on your land."

"Don't bother worrying about that 'til you get a cabin built and a shelter for your animals. Besides, I don't know for sure when I'll get back to Indian Springs again. I freight cotton to the Rio Grande River for the Confederacy, but I'll try to get back by this time next year," said Claude.

"Sounds like dangerous work. That young man over there, does he travel with you?" Ezra gestured toward T.C, who was helping Abby Spence carry rocks from the stream to make a campfire circle.

"That's right. His name's T.C. Hill. He's a free man; he works for me and goes almost everywhere I do." Claude went on to explain that T.C.'s parents were free as well and had worked for his family in Indian Springs for longer than he could remember. "So if I can't come for any reason and I have to send T.C. in my place, I'd appreciate you listening to him because he has both my respect and trust."

"Understood," said Ezra as he and Claude shook hands on it.

"Now I'm not trying to pry," said Claude, "but having paid for this land, do you have enough money to buy the supplies you'll need to get you through the winter?"

Ezra shrugged. "I ain't got no money left a'tall, but we'll make out. Abby and I have salt and coffee and I can kill enough game to get us by."

"I think you'll make it just fine, but to be sure, I'm gonna loan you another fifty dollars to see you through 'til spring when you can plant corn and a garden. If you find yourselves in serious trouble, I want you to go see my mother, Mrs. Fuqua. She's wife to Dr. Ross Fuqua and they're both well-known in the Indian Springs community," said Claude.

"Much obliged, Mr. Williams. I'll do my best to earn your trust," replied Ezra. Claude believed he would.

When resting their mounts on the way back, Claude told T.C., "I think it's time we head back to South Texas. With as much trouble as we're having down there, they probably need us. Boy, I sure hope it rained because the drought has made it even more difficult for us than usual." He was also anxious to get back to Maria; they hadn't been apart this many days at a time since they'd been married. Maria had a way of occupying his thoughts; visions of her often frequented his mind. She was so beautiful, so sweet, and soft—

"Well, let's get going," Claude said to T.C.

"Well ah'm ready when yuh're ready," answered T.C.

When he arrived at home, Claude took his mother aside and informed her that he and T.C. had plans to head back south early in the morning.

"My son, I don't know how many mornings we've had to say goodbye," said Effie with a forgiving smile. "Besides, I was beginning to wonder how long you were going to be able to stand being away from that lovely wife of yours. I'm sure she's just as anxious for your return."

"Mama, I want you to know I'm really happy for you and the doctor," said Claude warmly.

Tears misted in his mother's eyes, but only for an instant. Effie took Claude's face in her hands and kissed him on his forehead. Being a mother had its difficult moments, like saying goodbye to her grown children. She was grateful to now have a husband, a good man who was willing to stay by her side. Effie was surprised with herself for having taken so long to say "yes" to Ross. She told herself that she would be able to bear Claude's leaving a little more easily this time than she had at other times before. *God is good and He's taking care of my needs*, she thought to herself. Turning again to Claude she said, "I'll pack you and T.C. some food for your trip.

CHAPTER 18

Baby Clovis and the End of the War
1865

When Claude arrived home, Maria met him with tears of happiness. She not only missed him, but she was especially anxious for his return because she now had reason to believe that she might be pregnant. She and Claude had desired it so strongly that she was certain that he would be as excited as she was—and he was indeed. Claude picked her up by the waist and swung her around and around as they laughed like carefree children. In the end, however, they both decided it would be best to keep this news to themselves, at least until it was confirmed beyond a doubt.

Claude's wagons were out on a freight run and there was no word of when they would return, so he and T.C. spent a couple of days resting and eating good home-cooked food and then the two of them set out to find and rejoin the wagons. Their first destination was the King Ranch. Claude had been so consumed with his own affairs that he hadn't paid much attention to the war and what was going on. But once he got to the ranch, he got wind of the latest news.

Claude heard that Col. Rip Ford's Calvary of the West had left San Antonio in mid-March for Laredo. Earlier, Ford had sent a detachment to the King Ranch because Union troops had been there, looking for Captain King. When Ford arrived in Laredo he learned that Union troops had attempted to seize Laredo, but had been repelled by Col. Santos Benavides and a handful of Confederate Texans. He then moved down the river and occupied Brownsville, knowing well that the only Union troops left were south of the port.

Claude knew that Colonel Ford was in the area, but hadn't yet encountered him or his men. He had been well occupied with the matters of buying and freighting cotton, trying to defend his operation from banditos, handling the death and affairs of two employees and a wounded driver, and not to mention a new and possibly pregnant wife.

Claude asked his friends at the King Ranch if they had met or heard word from his brother, Jake, who was possibly with Colonel Ford. There was no sure reply and Claude was deeply disappointed. Before Claude was packed and ready to leave the ranch, Captain King stopped by to talk with him briefly and see if Claude was available to do some work for him.

"Yes sir, I'd be glad to as soon as I can track down my wagons. We've been riding along my usual trade routes, but I thought we'd stop here first." Claude then asked King if he had seen or heard anything about his brother.

"No, I can't say that I've met him or seen him, far as I know," said King. A lingering silence followed and Claude felt a cold chill in the pit of his stomach. He didn't want his mother to have to go through losing another son.

Claude excused himself and hurriedly went off to find T.C. The pair headed out west and met up with the wagons that were coming east. The teamsters seemed very tired and were driving a worn-out bunch of mules that needed water, feed, and a few days rest. Pete looked like he had lost twenty pounds and didn't have the weight to spare. He told Claude that they had a serious run-in with banditos and that one of the drivers was wounded. "He can ride, but that's about all he can do," Pete confided in him.

Claude gave Pete the mules that he and T.C. were riding and told him to go straight home and to take the wounded driver with him. "T.C. and I will bring the wagons home as we can. But for now, the men and the stock need rest," said Claude.

On the way home to San Antonio, Claude, T.C., and the others stopped for the night at the King Ranch. Claude left word for Captain King that his teams and crew were to the point of exhaustion and that the wagons needed minor repair. He promised that he would be back with fresh teams and drivers as soon as he could.

Claude came home to find that Pete had already hired two new drivers. And so after resting, they hitched the four wagons with rested mules and Claude, T.C., and the new men headed back to the King Ranch.

Captain King wanted Claude and his men to pickup and haul some cotton that he had hidden in the Wild Horse Desert, as he needed the revenues from the cotton so that he could purchase the necessary supplies for Rip Ford and his cavalry.

When Claude arrived in Brownsville with the first load of cotton, he went to see Colonel Ford and was amazed to see his brother standing at Ford's side, serving as his aide. The two brothers were as surprised as they were happy to see each other. "Jake, why didn't you come see me when you got to San Antonio?" asked Claude.

"I didn't have a chance! As soon as Jim and me got to San Antonio, we heard that Colonel Ford was almost through recruiting and was about to leave. We hurried to enlist and the colonel happened by and asked me who belonged to the black gelding I was riding. Well I told him it was mine. He asked my name and I said I was Jake Williams from Red River County and the colonel wanted to know if I knew you!"

"Well how about that," said Claude, laughing.

"So I told him I was your younger brother. Then the colonel asked my age; I told him I was seventeen and so was Jim Latimer and that we had ridden all the way from north Texas to join him. Colonel Ford told the recruiter to sign us up and to have me report to him in the morning. And ever since, I've been either at his side or doing his bidding."

"He's a fine man, the colonel," said Claude.

"Claude, he's that and more; I feel honored to serve with him. Jim Latimer, my friend from Clarksville who joined with me, is now one of the messengers between here and the King Ranch," said Jake.

"Well, the next time you're in my neck of the woods—"

"Look, I'm really sorry I didn't get to see you in San Antonio. I'm anxious to meet your wife and the next time I'm in that area I'll be sure to come by and visit," Jake promised.

Claude nodded. Jake gave him a half smile and then changed the subject. "You know, I've been thinking surely it's gonna rain sometime. I'm waiting to see what this country is like when it ain't so dry. Colonel Ford said that it's always the case that it's either too dry or too wet in this part of Texas."

"Wet is right," said Claude, rolling his eyes. "When it rains, we'll have mud up to our ears. But for now, we have to see it through this drought. I came from home not too long ago and from what I can see, all is well. Mama and Dr. Fuqua got married before I left and I'm glad for them. I think they'll be good for each other."

"Mama married?" Jake muttered, shaking his head.

"You know, you should write her because she's been very worried about you. Mail may be slow, but it's still getting through. Just remember, even later is better than never, Jake," said Claude.

Jake promised.

Claude and his teamsters made it back from their trip, wagons loaded full with scarce and profitable consumer goods. He and his men loaded all of the wagons with cotton and made it half way back to Brownsville when it started raining. The gray dust quickly turned to brown mud and Claude was glad he had good mules. The rain was welcome and the water holes filled and the river became navigable once again. Within days, a sea of little green shoots began popping up all over the desert.

For the next several months, Claude made a good profit because the price of cotton had increased to its highest price ever. Although the Confederacy was confiscating the cotton it needed, Claude was a good trader and made more money during this period than he made at any other time before. He continued his policy of refusing Confederate money and only accepted Mexican gold and U.S. currency as payment.

Meanwhile, Maria was having a difficult pregnancy and the midwife who delivered all the babies in their community advised her to stay in bed. As an extra precaution, Claude hired the wife of one of his drivers to stay with Maria around the clock. They had waited too long for a child to take any chances that she might miscarry. And worse yet, if something were to happen to Maria, Claude didn't think he would be able to live with himself. The love he had for her was the strongest emotion he had ever felt in his life. Sometimes it scared him; but the thought of carrying out a life without Maria provoked in him an even greater fear.

Eventually, Claude made a trip to East Texas to purchase cotton. He had done business with a man named Moss for several years and Claude could now offer him more than the local market would pay. Claude was able to purchase so much cotton that he had to send for three more wagons to come and haul it. There was a serious fever epidemic going around the area and Mr. Moss was selling out. His wife, his children, and his slaves had died from the fever. Moss had one slave remaining—a thirteen-year-old girl—and he told Claude if he wanted to purchase his cotton, he'd have to buy the girl, too. As it turned out, Mr. Moss had enough cotton to load all four wagons. Claude had a mind to buy it all and so he agreed to take the girl. He had considered purchasing a horse for her to ride, but she was not accustomed to the saddle. So he decided to let her ride along in one of the wagons. The girl's name was Maude and she was so scared she trembled every time Claude came near her. He tried to reassure her, telling her she had nothing to fear and that she would stay with his wife. Claude went on to tell her that if the government wouldn't set her free, he would make sure of it when she got a little older. But from the look in her eyes, he could see that she didn't believe him. He supposed she didn't have any reason to.

When they got home, Claude took Maude into the bedroom to meet Maria.

"Maude, this is my wife, Mrs. Williams," he said as he knelt beside the bed and took Maria's hand in his. "She's going to have a baby, but she's confined to bed for the duration. Your sole duty is to stay with Mrs. Williams and do anything she asks you to. You can come in, Maude; you don't need to hang in the doorway."

But the girl stood stock-still in the threshold, her eyes darting warily from Claude to Maria, who was propped up on her bed pillows.

"She's shy, I guess," Claude murmured.

"Scared, I'd say," replied Maria. Once more, Claude tried reassuring Maude that no one would harm her; Maria rolled her eyes. "Well when you put it like that, of course that's what she'll think. Come on over here, honey," she called to Maude, giving her a friendly smile. "I won't bite."

As the girl inched her way to the bed, Claude asked Maria, "How'd you do that?"

"Being a woman helps," she admitted. "Now leave us alone so we can get better acquainted."

Later that afternoon, Claude and T.C. closely inspected the wagons. Knowing well that faulty equipment was a leading cause in accidents, Claude always made it a point to keep his wagons in good repair. As he made comments to T.C. about a couple of wheels that needed tending to, T.C. nodded his head but made no reply. After a while, Claude realized that T.C. was intentionally being quiet and that something was definitely bothering the boy.

"What's eatin' you, T.C.?" Claude finally asked him. T.C. was genuinely upset. "El Jefe, Ah didn't think yuh believed in slavery. Ah can't understand yuh buyin' that gurl," he said.

Claude nodded slowly. "I suppose now I should have talked to you about it. I was wishing you'd been with me on the trip to East Texas; Mr. Moss had four wagon loads of cotton that I needed and he wouldn't sell it to me unless I bought Maude—"

"So yuh bought a slave 'cause yuh wanted tuh buy—"

"Don't interrupt me, boy. If I hadn't bought her when I did, she would have gone to the slave market. Her family died of the fever and Mr. Moss was selling out and leaving and I knew she'd be better off with us than going to the market. I'll free her just as soon as she's old enough to take care of herself—and that's if the government doesn't free her first. She's very scared and so if you want to help her, you'll reassure her that we're gonna do what's right for her. She's far away from the only home and family she's ever known," said Claude.

T.C. was silent for a length of time, his head bowed down over his crossed knees. "Ah'll go an' see hur jus' as soon as we get back," he said at last. "Ah shou'da known, El Jefe. Ah shou'da trusted yuh wouldn't buy yuh a slave for no good reason; ah shou'da known."

As the weeks passed, Claude continued to worry about Maria. Every time she tried to leave her bed, she'd start bleeding. But the bleeding would cease once she went back to lying down. Whenever he went out of town, Claude had two women stay with Maria, one during the daytime and the other at night. Maude was also there—which was helpful—although the older women were more experienced.

Maude was quickly picking up Spanish. It was unavoidable on account of her spending all her time with Maria and the Mexican women who were taking care of her. As it turned out, Maude proved to be a bright and pleasant child, and she and Maria became fond of each other. She still backed away a bit whenever Claude was a round; but she didn't tremble anymore. Claude hoped that Maude's fears would eventually leave her. But he also knew that Maria was a positive influence in the girl's life; although it was slow, Maude was beginning to blossom under Maria's tutelage.

In March of 1865, Union General Lewis Wallace arrived from Washington and succeeded in negotiating a truce between the Confederate and Union armies on the Rio Grande. Trade would continue as usual. The warring parties reached the conclusion that more bloodshed on the Rio Grande would have little to no effect on the outcome of the war.

On April 9th, General Lee surrendered and the Civil War officially ended. However, communication was still very slow and even news this momentous took its time getting to South Texas.

On May 1, 1865, a passenger aboard a steamer heading up the Rio Grande to Brownsville tossed a copy of a New Orleans newspaper to some Confederate troops. The newspaper told of the news of Lee's surrender and President Lincoln's assassination.

During the ten days that followed, a number of the Confederate troops left for home. Loyal to their commanders, the remaining troops stayed put until they were officially discharged.

On May 11th, the gentlemen's agreement to a ceasefire was broken. Union troops marched from Brazos Island toward Brownsville. The Union soldiers encountered some Texas cavalry at Palmetto Ranch, and after a sharp skirmish the Confederate troops fell back until reinforcement arrived a day later and they returned to Palmetto Ranch. In the afternoon, Colonel Ford arrived with mounted cavalry and artillery. Retreating, the Union infantry was forced back to Brazos Island; Colonel Ford's men pursued the enemy no further. Jake Williams had been at Colonel Ford's side throughout the battle and thus participated in the final battle of the Civil War.

Following his release from the Confederate army, Jake went to San Antonio to visit Claude and meet Maria. After spending two days with his brother, Jake was anxious to get home and so he set out for Northeast Texas on the third day.

With the war now over, the cotton market on the Rio Grande came to an abrupt standstill. Claude was left with no choice but to park all of his wagons at his San Antonio headquarters and call his men together for a meeting. Once everyone was gathered, he explained that for the present he was going to have to cease operations and if they wanted to leave to find other work, it was all right with him. Claude went on to say that if they chose to stay, he would furnish their food and other essentials until the future became clearer. Those choosing to stay would be responsible for repairing fences, wagons, harnesses, looking over each and every mule, and getting things ready in anticipation of business returning to normal. In private, Claude told Pete that he would keep him on the payroll.

Maria, having lain in bed for eight months, was now in the final stage of her pregnancy. Claude continued to worry about difficulties and unforeseen problems relating to Maria and their unborn child. One day, he even went as far as to ask the midwife if he should take Maria to a doctor in San Antonio.

"You could," replied the midwife with a smile, "but I think you're worrying too much over nothing. Everything will be all right; besides, the trip might not be good for her," she added.

Her smile did not convince Claude and he wasn't sure he could trust the midwife's judgment or honesty, for that matter. He wondered if she was more concerned about losing money if Maria went to see a doctor.

But at two o'clock in the morning of June 15, 1865, Maria went into labor and a fine six pound boy was delivered. Claude was bursting with pride. Maude, who was present at the delivery, jumped up and down excitedly and said, "I'm going to help take care of this pretty baby!"

Unlike his father, who had never been known to hold any of his children when they were infants, Claude held his little son for over an hour, all the while cooing over him and complimenting Maria for delivering such a fine and healthy son. And although the delivery had taken its toll on Maria, she still found the strength to smile and marvel at Claude's attention to their newborn baby. She had thought all along that Claude would make a fine father. Later that evening, Claude took the time to write his mother to tell her about her first grandson, whom they named Clovis.

CHAPTER 19

War Over
1866

When T.C. wasn't on the road, he spent nearly all his spare time visiting Maude. Finally Claude said, "T.C., don't take this the wrong way, but remember that Maude is only fourteen years old. I promised to protect her and that means from you as well as everything else."

T.C. replied, "I understand, but I do enjoy being with my own kind. She's a good girl, so you won't be ashamed of me, El Jefe."

When the U.S. Army came to San Antonio, Claude went to see them and after taking an oath of allegiance to the United States, was given a contract to transport government supplies from Galveston to San Antonio.

A gang of renegades from Galveston attacked them on their first night out. Most of the offenders were wearing remnants of Confederate uniforms, and one shouted an epithet about traitors working for Yankees. But his remark was left unfinished because he was almost cut into two parts by Claude's ten-gauge shotgun. Of the five who attacked, three were killed and the two who left were bleeding. The incident left Claude shaken, more so than any other highway robbery had. Being attacked by soldiers, Confederate or not, and most likely for reasons born of desperation—this was something different. He reported the incident to the army, but they made no comment. He had hoped that with the end of the war he wouldn't have to defend against bandits. The Mexican banditos were gone, but the Confederate and other renegades were plentiful and there was no effective law enforcement of any kind.

The boom of the war years was over, but the freight business gradually returned. Cotton and lumber went to the coast, whiskey and other manufactured goods went from Galveston to San Antonio. Army officers asked if he wanted to freight supplies to West Texas installations and he said he would go where needed. From what he had heard, he gathered that the army planned to open new posts in the western part of the state to defend against Indians.

Claude found himself worn down with exhaustion. So much had happened in the last year. The war had ended, Effie had her first grandson, and Claude's business had changed dramatically. He hadn't heard from Jake since he visited and was concerned about what was happening in Red River County now that the war was over. In early spring 1866, he had Pete replace T.C. as a driver and he and T.C. again headed north to Indian Springs with four pack mules loaded with things he thought would not be available there. This time, they traveled during the day, and Claude was heavily armed because he was afraid of lawless bandits. He told T.C. not to carry any visible weapons, but both slept with their guns at their side.

They arrived late in the afternoon and a light drizzle created a mist about them. It had been raining all day and looked like it would continue. They unloaded the pack mules in the barn, rubbed them down and gave them hay and corn and went to see their folks.

As always, Effie cried with joy to see him. She and Dr. Fuqua were just sitting down to supper and she quickly set another plate. There was always enough food on Effie's table to feed two or more in a pinch, especially when it was one of her boys.

Typically, she bombarded Claude with questions before he had a chance to sit down at the table. "When am I going to get to see my grandson? Tell me all about him and you have to figure a way to get Maria and little Clovis up here."

"That's all she talks about," Dr. Fuqua whispered to Claude.

Claude laughed. "Mama, that little boy is a character. I didn't know I could love anybody the way I love my son. I'm looking forward to the time when he is big enough for me to take him with me when I go somewhere."

"He's healthy, then? You wash and bathe him regularly, I hope."

"Yes ma'am," he said with a grin, "just like you taught us. He and Maria are both healthy and doing fine. Mama, you should hear him talk. He plays with the little Mexican kids and his words are a mixture of English and Spanish."

He reached over the table to help himself to seconds, but Effie beat him to the punch. "Pass me your plate."

"Lord, it's been over a year since I've been here and so much has happened. I want to hear what's been happening here since the end of the war. Have the federal boys taken over? What's happened in Clarksville? Where's Jake? And how's the rest of the family? Ross, you're looking good. You're health is fine, I hope?"

"Can't complain," Dr. Fuqua said." The truth was he never did complain. "I'm pretty good, thanks. My chest is much better. Thanks to your mother, her good food and lots of rest, my consumption is cured. She's a pretty good doctor in her own right and her advice has been invaluable. I'm happy and Effie is the greatest thing that ever happened to me." He reached over and put his hand on hers. Effie seemed to melt at his touch.

Claude suppressed a grin. "So, are you able to practice medicine?"

"Hmm? Oh yes, indeed. My practice is growing and I have about all the patients I can handle. I treat both black and white, whoever asks for me. I'm especially concerned with what is going on in the Negro community, Claude. Most of them are scared to death."

"With just cause," Effie murmured.

"Isn't that the truth?" Dr. Fuqua sighed. "Most of the Negroes I come in contact with are just looking for someone who doesn't cheat or threaten to kill them. The end of the war has left them in limbo and a lot are going hungry. We try to see the ones who work for us have enough to eat and we've allotted garden plots to those who want them. Wash and Nell and their kids seem to be happy and your sister Sophie has established a school for the Negro children whose families work for us."

"That's wonderful," Claude said.

"Unfortunately," Dr. Fuqua went on, "my Negro patients can't afford to pay for my services, but I plan to continue treating them anyway. They deserve it, with what they've had to put up with. Claude, we live in a completely lawless society. Some of the old slaveholders resent their being free and take advantage of them. Wash now has a bunch of ex-slaves working with him and so far the Freedman's Bureau hasn't bothered us. Of course, we treat them fairly. You do know about the Freedman's Bureau, don't you?"

Claude said he had read something about it in the San Antonio paper. "If I remember correctly, it's a bureau run by the army to make sure ex-slaves are treated as free men."

"That's correct. I understand we're supposed to execute some sort of work contract with the ex-slaves. We will when we find out what we are supposed to do, but it's going to be difficult to execute a contract with someone who can't read. We'll manage and do what we have to do. The bureau has caused some trouble in the Clarksville area, but so far they haven't bothered with us."

He fell silent and for the first time since they had sat down at the table, no one said a word. Claude felt completely at peace. He put down his fork and told them about his plan to move back to North Texas. It was just what Effie wanted to hear, and she hung on his every word.

"One of the pieces of land I bought on the prairie extends into the edge of the sandy land and into woods with big oak trees. I aim to build a house there. With no lumber available I may have to freight it in, as well as, windows, doors, et cetera, but I thought I'd look for a builder while I'm here."

"Well, you know Wash built this house," Effie reminded him.

"Mama, he doesn't have time to build one for me now. But he'll probably know a good builder, won't he? I've sketched out a house plan and I hope Wash can help me decide what to do. Ross, what do you hear about the price of land?"

"Well, I can't site you any figures precisely, but I hear that land prices have fallen since the war ended. There's a lot of land for sale, some priced less than half the price before the war. Some of the farmers just can't make it without slave labor."

When they got up from the table, Claude helped Effie with the dishes and Ross announced that he was going out to the porch.

"Well don't get wet, for heaven's sake," Effie said. "It's pouring out there." After he left the house, Effie shook her head. "Fair or foul weather, he always goes out to the porch after supper."

Claude smiled. "That's where I first saw him, remember?"

They cleaned the dinner dishes in silence. That was Effie's preference, Claude remembered. She always seemed to be in a meditative frame of mind whenever she worked. When they finished she said, "You have to go see your sister Sophie. Don't you remember? She married John Gault and then he had to leave for the war. He's home now, but he's not in good health. The poor man spent the last several months of the war as a prisoner and almost starved. And Sophie tells me he still has occasional bouts of severe diarrhea. Ross is treating him, and he seems to be getting better. Love, rest, and good food can do a lot for a patient. He's a good man but he doesn't have anything to do yet. Now that I think about it, Claude, he might be a good choice to oversee the construction of your house. You know he was raised right and will be honest."

Claude nodded.

"And Elizabeth—well, she's living with Sophie and John and helping Sophie in the schools. She seems to be very serious about a young man named Kyle Peyton, who just returned from the war. I don't think you knew him, but his father was a farmer and when he died, Kyle inherited some land that he's now farming. Your sister Edna Mae is seventeen and she's still in school in Clarksville."

"I keep forgetting what a big family we are," Claude said.

"And getting bigger," she said with a smile. "I can't wait to see my only grandchild and Maria. Who does he favor? Does he have your hair and fair complexion?"

"No, he isn't fair. His skin is dark and he has black hair. He isn't as dark as his mother and he's a good-looking boy, even if Maria thinks he looks like me. I'll get them up here when I can. First, I have to build a house and sell the freight business. These things get very complicated. I like your suggestion about John Gault, though. I'll go see him and Sophie tomorrow."

Before retiring for the night, Claude told Effie he brought four pack mules loaded with lots of things she probably needed. "I don't know what you've been able to buy, but I brought laudanum, quinine, coffee, and sugar and loads of other stuff. T.C. and I unloaded the packs in the barn. Shall I go out now and fetch it?"

"For heaven's sake, no, it hasn't stopped raining."

"We'll take a look tomorrow, then. I have a lot I want to do while I'm here and I'm tired. See you in the morning."

"Good night, Claude."

Just as she started for her bedroom, Claude remembered something. "Mama, you told me all about my sisters, but didn't mention Jake. What's going on?"

Effie stopped at the doorway. It was a moment before she answered, and when she did, her voice was low and tinged with sadness. "I'm very worried. He came home just after he visited you and stayed a few days. Jim Latimer, his friend from Clarksville, came over and they left to go to some place way down south of here to round up cattle. Something was said about capturing wild cattle and selling them. I haven't heard a word from him since he left. I just hope..."

Claude nodded in a way that told her he understood what she was thinking, and she left it unsaid. "Good night, Mama," he said.

The next morning Claude and T.C. unpacked what they brought and after distributing it to Effie, and then to Wash and Nell, they headed for the Cuthand area. There they found that Ezra and Abby had finished building a house as well as a barn. They had a nice plot for a garden and had cleared a field for corn and cotton, too. They also had a baby boy. They named him Tom, after Ezra's sergeant during the war. Claude thought they seemed to be happy, healthy, and thriving.

Claude took Ezra to his land, about a mile from Ezra's property, and showed him where he would like to have a cabin built. "See that rise to the left of the big oak trees? I was thinking that would be a good spot."

"That's a perfect spot," Ezra agreed, "right next to the creek, too."

"By the way, did the surveyor come by and did he give you a copy of the survey?"

"Yes sir, he come and no sir, we ain't got no copy, but I shore would like to have one."

Claude nodded. "The next time you're in Clarksville, go see the lawyer that drew our papers. I'll tell him to be sure to give you a copy."

A short while later, Claude and T.C. headed for home. When they stopped to rest their mounts, Claude explained the Freedman's Bureau and suggested that they go to Clarksville the next day and see what the lawyer had found for Wash and T.C. "I told you what kind of prejudice you're up against. We may have to leave the land in my name for awhile, but it will be yours."

Once they arrived in Clarksville, Claude went straight to Mr. Canterbury's office. "Your timing couldn't be better," the lawyer told him. There's a lot of land for sale and some is selling cheap. Claude snapped up two twenty-five-acre tracts south of Indian Springs and five hundred acres more of black prairie land that adjoined what he already owned. He also left enough money with Canterbury to keep the taxes paid on all of his property.

He spent the next day visiting his family and took his brother-in-law John Gault to where he planned to build his house, barn, and corral. "Nice spread," John said.

"Wash built my mother's house and did a great job, but he's too busy. I thought you might want the work."

John looked at him in surprise, his lips changing from a thin, solemn line to an enthusiastic grin. "You bet I would."

"Glad to hear it. You'll be construction supervisor, because I doubt I'll be back here before it's finished. I'll buy the lumber, doors, windows, and everything else needed for the house. I'll probably send T.C. with the wagons and you can show him where to unload." He also told him he wanted all the non-prairie land fenced in and a well dug. "The mail seems to be functioning pretty well again, so I'll mail you a set of plans. Shop around the area for a builder; Clarksville is probably your best bet. And don't hesitate to ask Wash for advice."

The next morning, Claude and T.C. left for Jefferson. When they arrived, Claude contacted the most experienced builder in town and asked him to draw a set of plans and make a list of materials needed to build the new house in North Texas. While they were waiting for the plans to be drawn, Claude was talking to a horse trader named Carl Winters. The man asked if he was related to Tom Williams.

"He was my father," Claude said.

"Well, I'll be. Son, I just came in from Kentucky and while I was there I bought the finest Morgan stallion I've seen recently. I thought of your father, because I once sold him a stallion every bit as fine as this one. Sold him a big black jack as well, I seem to recall."

Claude recalled it only too well. His foolish attempt to mate the two animals, and Tom's violent reaction, brought back bittersweet memories. His life had changed completely after that day—mostly for the good, he felt in retrospect, but it also inaugurated his loss of innocence and joy.

Suddenly, he became aware that Carl Winters was still talking about the stallion he had just bought in Kentucky and he snapped to.

"...he would have loved this horse, your pa would. Come with me and let me show you this fine animal."

"Yes sir," Claude said. He didn't have anything else to do, so he went along. It turned out Mr. Winters wasn't exaggerating; his Kentucky horse was the most beautiful animal Claude had ever seen. It was fifteen hands high, a reddish tan bay with black ears, mane, tail, and legs. Claude entered the corral and walked up to the horse. It was as tame as a puppy and seemed to like to be petted. Claude asked, "He's a beauty. Can I ride him? Has he been bred and have you seen his colts?"

"Sure, you can ride him. There's a saddle hanging by the gate. I don't know if he has any colts, though. I was so pleased to get him I didn't even ask! But he's three years old, so he probably has been bred. I'd like to keep him but I have to be careful and not fall in love with my stock because I want to keep every fine horse I buy."

The horse had a fast, flat-footed walk and a rapid single-foot gait that really covered ground. Claude rode him for about a mile and by then he knew he was going try to buy him. He had always been frugal and had tried to save every dollar he could, but this horse was the first thing he had ever truly wanted, except Maria, and he knew he was damn well going to try to have it.

"How much?" he asked as soon as he returned.

Mr. Winters laughed. "Not for sale. Sorry, son."

Claude looked him straight in the eye and didn't crack a smile. "Mr. Winters, I don't believe you'd show me this horse unless you thought I'd make you a good offer."

They negotiated for most of the rest of the day. Finally, Claude said, "I never thought I'd pay four times the price of a good mule for any horse, but we have a deal if you'll hold and board the horse until I'm ready to leave. Does he have a name?"

"None that I know of, so I guess you that'll be up to you."

When T.C. saw the horse he exclaimed, "What a beautiful horse. If I buy a mare can I have a colt?"

"You sure can, but I suggest you get your land paid for first. Right now I'll let you ride my mule because I think it's bigger and better than the one you've been riding."

Claude contracted with a lumber dealer for everything he needed for the house. "When you get it all together, contact me and I'll send wagons to haul it to the building site. We have wagons in and out of here so transporting it won't be a problem."

Claude named his new horse Rusty and the trip back to San Antonio only confirmed his feeling that his purchase had been worth every penny. When they stopped for the night, he hobbled him close by because he didn't intend to let someone steal him.

When he got home, Maria and the baby were fine. Pete and the wagons were on a trip and Claude enjoyed several days of rest and playing with his son and getting spoiled by Maria.

He told her what he was planning and she said, "Claude I'll go anywhere and do anything you want me to do, but I'm scared. You will have to show me what to do and I'll try to do as you tell me, but I'll need your help."

"Don't worry. I'll be right with you. I think everything will be fine. You'll be moving into a brand new house and my mother and her friends will help you in every way."

The next thing to be done was unload his business. Claude

approached the other freight companies in San Antonio and found that all of them were broke. Williams Freight Company had gotten so big that his competitors couldn't afford to buy him out.

"Ask my brother," Maria suggested. "I bet he's got money saved up."

He took her advice and asked Pete when he next saw him. Pete had saved about a third of his salary but didn't have enough to buy the company. Claude considered selling him part of it, but decided not make a decision right away. After all, he needed to get his house built first; maybe he could make enough to pay moving expenses plus extra during the next year.

A few weeks later, his brother Jake showed up at Claude's with Jim Latimer, both stinking to high heaven. They had been killing and skinning wild cattle and selling the hides through Brownsville. "Brings us about two dollars each," Jake told him with a big grin.

"Before you boys get too comfortable," Claude said, wrinkling his nose, "grab that bar of lye soap in the kitchen and head down to the river for a bath. Maria will pitch a fit if she catches you smelling up the house. I got some clean clothes you can change into."

When they came back from the river, their hair still dripping and their borrowed clothes clinging wet to their bodies, Claude asked Jake if he had written their mother.

"Not yet," Jake mumbled sheepishly, "but I intend to."

"How about right now? She worries about you like crazy, and I'm tired of hearing about it. I'll get you some writing paper."

Jake followed Claude to the kitchen as Jim Latimer teased him. Maria was glad to see him and Jim again and got an endless stream of compliments over dinner. "Best we've had in months," Jim told her.

Maria beamed, but Claude warned her dryly, "Keep it up and we'll never be rid of them. Meaning to ask you, how come you've been killing the cows? Surely there must be a market for them somewhere."

Jake shook his head. "Friend of ours shipped cattle to New Orleans and lost two dollars per head. We don't have the money to gamble on a sale."

"Tell you what," Claude said after thinking it over a bit. "Round up two hundred very young heifer cows or calves and deliver them to my property at Cuthand. I'll pay three dollars per head. I'll need some bulls, too, about two years old. If you can round up ten, I'll pay five dollars per head for the bulls."

Jake looked across the table at Jim. "What do you think?"

"Sounds good to me," Jim said without hesitation. "This could give us enough money to really get in the cattle business."

"Fine," Claude said. "How many horses did you bring with you?"

"Six," Jim said.

"You'll need more. I'll send T.C. with three good horses, extra rope and anything else you think you'll need. He'll know where to release them. And when Jake is satisfied with the quality of the cattle delivered, go see my lawyer in Clarksville, Mr. Canterbury, and he'll pay you. I'll write him today."

"You want them old enough to breed," Jake said, "so we'll get the bulls in a different area from the cows. Less chance of inbreeding."

Claude nodded. "Where've you been doing this cow hunting?"

"In Live Oak County, mostly," Jim said.

"I want true mavericks. Jake knows what I mean."

"There's plenty of wild cattle never been handled before all over the brush country," Jake said. "With three of us working, I think we can get at least ten a day. It could be more, but these have to be branded, marked, and penned in some way to keep them from going back into the brush. You got a brand?"

"CCW," Claude said. "It's recorded in Red River County, along with my earmark. Half-crop on each ear." He got up from the table. "I guess that pretty much covers it."

Jake glanced at Claude thoughtfully, "T.C. worked with cattle before?"

"No, but you'll find him a fast learner. And eager, too."

T.C. grinned. He had wanted to learn to be a cowboy since the first time Claude took him to the King Ranch. Claude told him to go to San Antonio and buy three horses. "It might be a good idea to ask Jake or Jim to go with you because they know what is needed from the horses, and also, well..."

"They're white," T.C. finished for him.

Claude nodded somberly. "I know you understand. Come by in the morning and I'll give you enough money to buy the horses and anything else they think might be needed. Go to the blacksmith we use and have three cattle brands made to take with you. He knows my brand—it's CCW. These cattle are going to be mine, so I'll keep you on the payroll while you're gone."

"Thanks, El Jefe."

Claude patted him on the back. "I told Jake you're a quick learner, and I know you'll do just fine. Show them where the cabin is being built and release the cattle in this area. The grass is waist-high and there's plenty of water so I don't think they'll stray, but please stay for a while after they're settled to be sure they don't drift south toward where they came from. I'm going to have the lumber for the house in Indian Springs delivered as soon as I have wagons in the Jefferson area and you can show them where to unload if you're available. I may even bring the wagons myself."

Jake, Jim, and T.C. ran into more problems than they expected. Culling the older cows, and then keeping the young cows after they were captured, created real problems. Jake had thought they would have all of the cattle Claude had ordered in two months' time, but they were still short a few young cows and three or four young bulls by the end of January. They were tired and their horses were worn-out, so they started moving the stock north, planning to pick up the rest on the road. By the end of March, they were glad to be finished with the job. They went to Clarksville to pick up their money, and afterwards headed home; Jim Latimer to see his people in Clarksville and Jake home to see his family.

The three had gotten very thin after eating their own camp cooking all these months. "I don't know about you," Jim said, "but I'm plenty ready to put my feet under a dining table and eat home cooking."

"I'm hungry enough to eat a bear and truly crave my mama's cooking," Jake said.

"Amen," whispered T.C., and they all laughed.

The cabin on the Cuthand property was newly finished and T.C. moved in as Claude had suggested. He stayed there a month to make sure the cattle settled down and didn't drift south, and only then went to see his folks.

Claude arrived with three wagons loaded with building materials and a few pieces of furniture. T.C. showed up to help unload the wagons, and afterwards they took the mules to the prairie and hobbled them. The prairie grass was young, tender and knee-high. Claude's drivers made camp and he told them he was going to Clarksville in the morning to see if he could get a load to haul to Jefferson or somewhere else south.

T.C. asked him, "When are you going to leave? I'd like go with you."

"What? I thought you liked being a cowboy."

"I do, but it gets lonesome out at the ranch alone."

Claude had dinner with his mother and Dr. Fuqua and told them this was going to be a short trip; he wanted to get freight back to Jefferson. He also wanted to get his lumber and supplies unloaded and wanted to go to Cuthand to see the cattle he bought.

They left just after daylight. As soon as they got to Clarksville, Claude went to see his lawyer, Mr. Canterbury, and told him what he was looking for.

"I have a client named Tom Clarkson, an older man, who owns a sawmill located near Sulphur River. As a favor to you, I'll ask him if he still has lumber that he needs hauled to Jefferson," Mr.

Canterbury offered.

Claude thanked him for his help and as the two shook hands, the lawyer promised he would send word as soon as he made contact with Mr. Clarkson.

Claude and T.C. left immediately for Cuthand and arrived just before nightfall. They slept in the cabin and got up at sunrise to look at the cattle. Claude was pleased to see they seemed to be totally contented, fat, and happy. "I know you want to go to Jefferson with me, but I'd like you to stay here until I find someone to live here to look after the cattle." T.C. reluctantly agreed, and moped the whole way back to the cabin.

When they got there, a messenger was waiting with a letter from Mr. Clarkson, the sawmill owner his lawyer had spoken about. He informed Claude that he had a lot of lumber he needed taken to Jefferson. "Change of plans," he told T.C. "We're going to Clarksville early tomorrow morning."

T.C. smiled for the first time since they left the cattle pasture.

The trip to Clarksville was a success. "You have good equipment and good stock, Mr. Williams. I have enough lumber already cut to keep your three wagons busy for a few months."

Claude nodded at Mr. Clarkson. This was the news he had wanted to hear.

"When you have time, I'd like you to look at my mill. I'm getting old and tired. It would be nice if someone would buy me out and let me quit."

Claude replied, "I've never thought of the lumber business, but I'll take a look. How much land with timber do you own—and will you sell it?"

"How much land...well, let me think a bit—"

Clarkson was a man with time on his hands, but Claude wasn't.

"Tell you what, Mr. Clarkson. If you could please give all the information to Mr. Canterbury, I'll stop by and visit with you on my next trip here," offered Claude.

Clarkson beamed. "I'll look forward to that," he said, and they shook hands.

"T.C., do you think you could run a freight company without me looking over your shoulder? Sooner or later you are going to have to get on your own. Think about it. You could headquarter at the ranch and Mr. Clarkson can keep you busy if what he says is true. When I come back we'll go see his operation. If our Mexican drivers don't want to come, we can hire Negro drivers here."

Early the next morning, Claude left with his wagons and went to Sulphur River. Mr. Clarkson had hauled the lumber out of the flood area to higher ground. They loaded the wagons and left for Jefferson. Once they arrived there, Claude turned the unloading and all details over to T.C. "All yours now," he told him as they parted.

"I'll do a good job, El Jefe," T.C. promised, although he was nervous with all the responsibility he had now acquired.

CHAPTER 20

Jake and Jim
1866-1867

Jake and Jim visited with their respective families for a few days longer and then set out for Live Oak County. Together, they planned to round up as many cattle as they could and take them up to Kansas to be sold; their backup plan was to join up with some others driving a big herd to a cattle market of their choosing. The two of them headed to Live Oak County because they knew the area and could reuse the pens they had previously built there. On the way they traded for fresh horses, but held on to two of their better roping horses.

After several days of hard riding, Jake and Jim arrived at their old camp to find it occupied by three Mexicans who had about a hundred head of cattle in the pens.

Bewildered, Jake and Jim sat on their horses and watched the camp for a few minutes while they thought it all out. All three Mexicans were in camp and Jake noted that they only had three horses between themselves. "The way I see it," said Jake, "we can round up a lot more cattle because we have six horses between the two of us. Let's see if we can make a deal with those Mexicans, maybe a partnership of some kind. What do you think?"

"We can try, anyway," replied Jim doubtfully. "After all, they're using our pens and it took us a long time to build them. So let's go down and see."

Surprisingly, the Mexicans seemed pleased to see the two strangers, and soon after meeting, a verbal agreement for a partnership was made between the two parties. The Mexicans had slaughtered a calf and were roasting it on a skewer over an open flame. The men invited Jake and Jim to join them for the meal in honor of the partnership they had just made. As it turned out, one of the Mexicans proved to be a good cook. In addition to the beef, he had stewed a pot of beans and made fresh tortillas on a large flat stone that was heated in the fire. It was a hearty meal and the deal between the men seemed promising. At daybreak the next morning, as Jake and Jim began rounding up cattle, an unspoken tension between the two of them and the Mexicans began to develop. Truth be told, neither group felt as if they could actually trust the other. Two of the Mexicans, as Jake noted, were experienced wild cattle catchers, but the one who was a good cook, wasn't good for much else. Nevertheless, the cook did speak English better than the other two men.

In a little over a month, Jake, Jim, and the Mexicans had rounded up and corralled about three hundred head of cattle. Eager to sell, the Mexicans were now ready to take the cattle to market. However, Jake and Jim were not as eager and thought it'd be best to stall a while longer.

Late one afternoon, Jake and Jim discussed the situation when they were about a mile from camp. "It just doesn't feel right," said Jim. "Whenever those Mexicans talk about it between themselves, it's always them going to San Antonio, not us. I don't think you and I are even in the picture."

"Hate to say it," said Jake, "but I've noticed that, too." Up until this point, Jim had been increasingly suspicious of the Mexicans' motives, while Jake had warned him not to jump to any conclusions. "Fact is, we can't put them off forever," said Jake as he noticed his friend's distracted behavior. "Jim? Are you listening to me?"

"What? Sorry, but I'm not liking the looks of that cloud," replied Jim.

Jake cast his gaze heavenward. A large and looming black cloud was rolling in rapidly from the west. "Me neither, Jim. We should head back to camp before the storm hits," said Jake. "The cattle are going to get restless and I don't enjoy riding in the rain."

When the two of them were about a half mile from camp, they rode across a little creek to a spot where there was a slight rise beside the water. Nature was beginning to call and Jake didn't think he could make it back to camp.

"Wait up, Jim I need you to hold my horse for a few minutes while I take a piss," said Jake.

Jake had only gone a few yards down into the creek bed when he heard the crack of thunder. A tremendous bolt of lightning struck down Jim and the two horses. The impact of the bolt was so strong that it knocked Jake off his feet as he scrambled in terror. He felt a bit addled as he got up, and looked back at the spot where Jim and the horses had stood only a moment before. They had been struck dead.

Jake blinked, as if in an attempt to dismiss the gruesome sight before his eyes. His knees buckled beneath him and he collapsed to his hands and knees, in an overwhelming state of shock. Since the war, he and Jim had been nearly inseparable and they had been closer than most brothers. But now there wasn't anything Jake could do. It was beginning to pour down rain so he quickly retrieved his slicker along with Jim's. After covering Jim with his slicker, Jake started walking the half-mile back to camp. When Jake finally reached the camp, he told the Mexicans what had happened and then spent the rest of that lonely night slumped by the fire with a tin cup of coffee. The tin went cold in his hands, but he never noticed.

When it finally stopped raining in the morning, Jake and the three Mexicans went out to the spot where Jim Latimer and the horses lay dead. Together, the four of them dug a grave a few feet from where Jim had been killed and then laid him to rest. Jake stood at the end of Jim's grave and prayed silently with tears for his dearest friend running down his face.

Next, they stripped the horses of their saddles, bridles, and other gear, and then left them where they had fallen.

That night, as Jake sat by the fire with his tin cup of coffee, the Mexicans stood in the shadows, carrying on a whispered conference. While Jake couldn't hear their words, he knew what they were discussing.

"We'll take 'em to San Antonio in the morning," Jake called out.

"*¿Qué?*" one of them asked.

"The cattle. We'll sell them all," replied Jake. With that, the Mexicans' mood seemed to lighten and Jake hoped his consent to take the cattle to San Antonio in the morning would be enough to keep them honest with him.

When the four of them got to San Antonio, they sold the cattle and split the money. Initially, the Mexicans wanted to take three-fourths of the money for themselves, but Jake balked angrily and said with determination that Jim's share was going to his mother and little sister in Northeast Texas. For a few minutes it looked like a gunfight might erupt between the men, but Jake refused to give an inch until the Mexicans yielded one half of the money.

With his own share of the money, Jake purchased all new clothes, including boots and a hat. He also got himself a haircut, shave, and bath. Jake then took his two horses, which he and Jim had taken as spares, and his new clothing, and set out for Claude's headquarters. He arrived to find that Claude wasn't there. When Jake asked Maria, she told him that Claude had gone to Jefferson. "But Claude's been gone long enough to be back now and I'm worried about him," said Maria.

"I bet he took a load of lumber and other supplies to work on the house in Indian Springs and something's now delayed him. You and I both know he's anxious to see that house finished. So don't worry, Maria; I'm sure he'll be back soon. In fact, if Claude isn't back in a few days, I'll head in his direction and meet him on the road," said Jake, reassuringly.

And that's what he did. After three days of rest and good food, Jake said goodbye to Maria and started out for Indian Springs by way of Jefferson. He rendezvoused with Claude about two day's ride from San Antonio and had a long talk with his brother about what happened to Jim and where that now left him. "I don't want to chase wild cattle alone, Claude. I think I'm about ready to settle down. So if you haven't hired anyone to take care of your cattle, how about letting me have the job? Most of the time, I'll be able to handle it alone if you can loan me T.C., or the hillbilly that lives nearby, or just someone to help with the round-up. Of course," Jake added with a slight grin, "I'd do even better if you'd loan me that beautiful stud you're riding."

"Forget the horse," said Claude, grinning back. "But I am concerned about not having anyone on my property in Cuthand. We have a cabin that Ezra Spence built; you can use that for the time being. Get yourself enough groceries to last you the next month or two and when I come back, we'll make some kind of deal that'll be satisfactory for both of us. Does that sound all right to you?"

"Sounds great," said Jake as he breathed a deep sigh of relief. At least now there was some semblance of a future he could look forward to.

When he arrived in Clarksville, Jake took Jim Latimer's share of the money that they had made on the cattle and gave it to

Jim's mother. He also took it upon himself to tell her what had happened. It was a very emotional meeting; Jim's mother wanted to know all of the details of her son's death and Jake didn't have to dress up the story to spare her feelings. There was a catch in his voice when he spoke and Jake had to pause a few times to collect himself. He finished by saying, "Jim enjoyed his life to the fullest and his death was mercifully quick. We buried him near the spot where he died and we prayed over his grave. I loved him like a brother."

While visiting with Jim's mother, Jake met Faye Latimer, Jim's little sister. Jim had talked about her on occasion. Jake was surprised to find that Faye was very pretty and already fifteen years old. The impression he had gotten from listening to Jim, had caused him to think of Faye as a little girl.

After visiting his own mother in Indian Springs, Jake purchased some supplies and then set off for Cuthand. He spent the first few days cleaning the abandoned cabin and organizing his living quarters. Although it was a small and simple structure, it was still more of a house than anything he and Jim had experienced out in the wilderness. Coincidently, Jake was now warming up to the idea of having a little place to call home.

Once he tidied up the inside of the cabin, he set to cutting firewood. Although he knew there was still some time before he had to worry about the cold, he still wanted make sure he had enough firewood to last the winter. The cattle he minded were fat, healthy, and every bit as wild as they were when he and Jim first caught them.

One day, Jake decided to ride over and visit with Ezra Spence. Ezra and his wife, who were just preparing to eat, invited Jake to join them for lunch and that day he enjoyed the best squirrel stew he had ever eaten. "Miss Abby, I think you're a very fine cook," said Jake.

Abby didn't reply; in fact, she said nothing at all. She just smiled as she offered him fresh corn, beans, and greens from their garden.

After the meal, Ezra showed Jake the land survey that Claude had given him. "Well, with your permission, I'd like to ride over your land and push out any of our cows," said Jake.

"If you'll give me a few minutes," replied Ezra, "I'll saddle a horse and come help you."

Jake and Ezra found about twenty head of cattle that had strayed over into Ezra's property and together they pushed the animals back over to the Williams' property. When Ezra started for home he said, "Any time you need, just ride on over and I'll be glad to help you out. Mr. Claude has been very good to me and I'll never forget it."

Jake couldn't get over how tasty Abby Spence's stew was, so he started carrying his rifle in his saddle holster with the hopes of killing a squirrel or a rabbit to bring her. Later on, when he was in the woods along Cuthand creek, he came upon a young hog, which he shot on sight. The hog had no markings on it, so Jake figured it was fair game. He butchered the hog, kept a loin and a ham for himself, and then took the rest to the Spence family.

A few days later, T.C. came to see Jake. He had been hauling lumber from the Sulphur River mill to Jefferson and things had been going pretty well until the previous day, when all his Mexican drivers quit at once.

"We wur in Jefferson an' the men said they had been away from home fur too long," T.C. recounted. "El Jefe, ain't gonna be too happy when he hears what happened. Now ah is in a real pickle."

T.C. went on to explain how he went into Clarksville to hire Negro drivers because he was afraid to try in Jefferson. He assumed he was better known in Clarksville and didn't expect to have any trouble there. Nevertheless, a big white man came up to him and said, "No nigger is gonna hire people in Clarksville. You git out of town before you git beat or hung." After recounting the story, T.C. then asked if Jake could help.

"Tell you what, I'll saddle my horse and we'll go to Indian

Springs and talk to your daddy; he'll know what to do. In fact, I'll bet he knows of some good men who need work," said Jake.

Jake and T.C. took extra horses with them in case they hired help who needed something to ride. The two of them arrived in Indian Springs at twilight and found Wash at home; he had just come in from a long day in the fields.

Jake explained to Wash what had happened and asked if he knew of any good Negro drivers to work for T.C. "They'd be loading lumber and hauling it to Jefferson and sometimes to Clarksville."

"Got plenty of drivers fur yuh," said Wash with a wave of his hand. "Got more strong young men than ah got a job fur! Ah'll git 'em fur yuh in the mornin'; how many yuh want? Mr. Jake, ah think yuh best help this boy, an' by that ah mean that yuh should go wid him to Jefferson an' Clarksville an' let it be known that these Negroes are workin' for yuh, that yuh're the boss, an' that yuh want 'em lef' alone. Frankly, ah'm surprised T.C. hasn't had trouble before."

T.C. spent the night with Wash and Nell while Jake spent the night with his mother and Dr. Fuqua. When Jake told them about T.C.'s near-skirmish in Clarksville, Dr. Fuqua shook his head and said, "I'm also surprised that T.C. hasn't had trouble like that before now. It's hard to imagine that Claude didn't realize this type of thing would happen. I think you'd better help T.C., at least until Claude gets back. I wouldn't want to see any harm come to him."

The next morning, Wash had five young Negroes waiting for Jake and T.C. However, two of the men were married, so T.C. hired the three who were single. He explained to the married men that he preferred to hire single men because he wanted to keep a crew that could be out for long periods of time and it would be best if his drivers didn't have wives waiting for them in Indian Springs. Jake had two extra horses that the men could ride and they were able to borrow a third horse from Dr. Fuqua.

Before he and his new hires left for Jefferson, T.C. explained, "One or all of yuh will haf tuh do yuhr own cookin'; ah'll provide the food. An' when the mules need a rest from the heavy labor, yuh'll be allowed to go home for a short visit. Do any of yuh like to cook?"

The largest of the three Negroes, a man who stood at nearly six and a half feet tall and weighed well over 200 pounds, spoke up at once. "Yas sir, I's a pretty good cook. I cooks good beans, good stew, cornbread, and can fry fatback anytime. An' mah name's Joe, sir."

T.C. smiled. "Joe, yuh'll be the cook then. Ah'll bet yuh can get the others tuh help build a fire an' do whatever else needs doing'. Am ah right?" asked T.C. as he turned to the other two men. The men nodded their heads enthusiastically while T.C. continued on.

"We'll sleep on the ground under the wagons and ah'll haf blankets fur yuh. Remember, each man is tuh take care of his own mules; they do all the haulin' an' we need 'em to be well cared fer." he said.

When they arrived in Jefferson, Jake went with T.C. to buy the supplies. When they had finished, Jake slipped T.C. the cash and encouraged the boy to pay the merchant. T.C. gave him a look of uncertainty, but Jake was insistent. "Go on, now," he said.

The merchant looked at T.C.'s money as the boy slid it across the counter. It was exactly what both Jake and T.C. had expected: the merchant looked up at T.C. and then at Jake, as if awaiting Jake's approval.

After a moment of silence, Jake introduced himself and T.C. "I appreciate your selling to T.C.; if there's ever an occasion where he doesn't have enough money, please let him have what he needs and the Williams Freight Company will see you are paid." Jake then went on to explain that the Williams Freight Company had been hauling freight in and out of Jefferson for years. "I'd like you to spread the word that these Negroes are working for me and my brother and we want them left alone."

The merchant slowly nodded, but T.C. wasn't able to relax

until they had left the store.

"Yuh knew he'd do that, didn't yuh?" asked T.C.

Jake nodded. "Let's just say I overheard a few things in that store once. But I think the merchant and I have come to an understanding."

They had a lighter load going back to Clarksville. The Negro drivers talked to the mules like nothing Jake or T.C. had ever heard before. Instead of yelling and jerking the mules around, these men kind of sweet-talked them. In an effort to slow the pace of the others, T.C. moved Big Joe to the lead wagon. It was a good ninety miles from Jefferson to Clarksville and freighters with oxen were taking nine days to make the trip. "Unless it rains and the mud holes become worse than usual," said Jake to T.C., "you can make the trip in a week and not wear out your mules."

When they arrived in Clarksville, Jake went to see Claude's lawyer to tell him what had happened and to share his concern for the safety of T.C. and his drivers. Mr. Canterbury didn't appear to be surprised by the news.

"Don't worry about it, Jake. I'll spread the word that the wagons belong to the Williams Freight Company and that the Negro drivers are to be left alone. Just tell T.C. to come to see me if he has any more problems," said the lawyer reassuringly.

Having finished with his business, Jake met T.C. outside The lawyer's office. "Mr. Canterbury knows who you are now, so don't be shy about seeing him if you need to." Jake then informed T.C. that he was heading back to Cuthand. "Whenever you need to rest the teams, come out and see me. Claude should be back up here in early spring and you should be finished hauling about that time."

"Mr. Jake, what do yuh think Mr. Claude would want meh tuh do about some clothes fur these boys? Them are just about barefooted an' none haf coats. It's gettin' late an' it's goin' to get cold. Ah've been collectin' money for freightin' and ah think ah should buy them some clothes an' boots," said T.C.

"Well I don't think you have much of a choice if you want to keep hauling," said Jake. "You better get them some raingear, too," he added.

T.C. and his wagon crew made two more trips before they returned to the Cuthand ranch. "Ah believe all of us need a few days off an' the mules need their rest, too," said T.C. to his drivers.

T.C. put a bell on the mare he had been riding and then turned the mules and the mare out into the field together. He knew that the mules would stay near the mare. Besides, the grass and water were plentiful, so there wasn't any incentive for the animals to stray far from where he left them.

T.C. and the three Negro drivers all went to Indian Springs to see their loved ones and enjoy some home cooking.

When they regrouped a week later, the weather took a definite turn toward winter with icy rain and even a little snow. T.C. bought his drivers some winter clothes and extra blankets, which the men made full use of. They were now a happy, tightly knit group. The men treated T.C. with the same respect he showed them, and for the first time, T.C. felt a new self-confidence he never knew he had.

On the second return trip from Jefferson, T.C. and his wagons were ambushed and surrounded by men in white sheets and hooded heads. "You niggers better quit this business or we'll hang you. We'll have no more lumber hauled by a bunch of nigger bastards," said the men in white hoods. And without another word, they vanished from sight.

Instead of going for more lumber, T.C. took the wagons straight to the Cuthand ranch to see Jake. After he and the drivers told Jake what had happened on the road, Jake said, "Well, if any of you want to quit now, I don't blame you. But we still need to haul the two loads of lumber we have left, so I'm going with you this time. And I'm going to spread the word that anyone who bothers you will be shot. If you should decide to go, you'll be guarded by me and another war veteran."

That afternoon, Jake went to see Ezra. "I'm gonna need your

help," said Jake. "And bring your shotgun."

Ezra didn't hesitate for a moment; he disappeared from his doorway and returned ten seconds later with his shotgun, hat, and heavy coat. It was December and the air was bitter cold. Under Jake and Ezra's watchful eyes, T.C. and his men loaded the wagons with the lumber and then set out on their trip to Jefferson. Once in town, Jake went to see the same merchant they usually bought their supplies from and asked him to spread the word that anyone who interfered with the wagons and their Negro drivers would be shot. Jake made it clear that he and Ezra were Confederate veterans with shotguns and that they would tolerate no foolishness.

The wagons were empty on the way back from Jefferson, as they just had to make one more trip and all of the lumber they had been contracted to move would be delivered. Jake's warning must have circulated or it might have been the cold weather, but at any rate no one bothered them on the ride home. The following day, T.C. and his drivers loaded the last of the lumber and were not bothered on that final trip either.

CHAPTER 21

Move to Indian Springs
1868

It was only ten days until Christmas when T.C. and his drivers finished hauling all the lumber. He and the men parked the wagons at the Cuthand ranch, fed the mules, and then turned them loose with the mare. After paying them their wages, T.C. and the Negro drivers headed toward Indian Springs to see their families.

Soon after the holidays, T.C. returned to the Cuthand ranch with two of the drivers. With Jake's help, they built a brush windbreak to give the mules some protection from the bitter winter winds. After completing this task, they set about feeding the animals. Jake knew that with most of the ground covered with snow, the mules would have suffered otherwise. The cattle, too, seemed to be doing fine under his supervision. The longhorns knew instinctively to get out of the north wind in the storms and some used the shelter of the windbreak the men had made.

When Jake and the men went hunting for wild game, they were fortunate enough to find and kill a large deer and a few turkeys, which proved a great source of food during those freezing winter months. Assured that they had plenty, Jake took a generous amount of their meat to Ezra and Abby. The weather was cold and harsh during January of 1868, but by the end of the month and into early February, it began to warm up a bit, much to their relief.

Fortunately, the cattle survived and by the end of February, some of the older heifers began to drop calves. Although most of the cows tried to hide and shelter their offspring, Jake still caught glimpse of the calves' flailing limbs and faltering first steps from behind their protective mothers.

Around the first of March, Claude arrived at his mother's home riding Rusty. Effie, however, greeted his homecoming with a chastising. "You said on your last visit that you would bring your wife and my grandson, but now you show up alone. And here it's been all these months that I haven't had a single bit of news about my only grandson. When am I going to get to see your family? For pity's sake, Claude, you're the only one of my children to produce any grandchildren for me to spoil and I'm beside myself to even get to see little Clovis, let alone hold him while he's still young enough to be held."

"So it's all on me, is it?" replied Claude with a grin. "What's holding up Sophie and John Gault? They should have a baby by now."

Effie sighed as she put the coffee to boil. "Well, they're sick of me saying that, so you tell them."

"Well," said Claude as he kicked off his boots, "you won't have much longer to wait. Once my house is finished, I'll move my family up here where you can pester them full-time. Maria and Clovis are both doing fine and I'm just as anxious as you to make the move. The trip from here to San Antonio just seems to get longer and longer. And both Maria and I want little Clovis to grow up with his family around him. So, just as soon as the house is ready, Mama." He bent and gave Effie's cheek a kiss and she smiled, seeming placated for the time being.

Over a big stack of pancakes with syrup and several cups of hot coffee, Claude told Effie his itinerary. "I'm gonna ride out to see the house tomorrow and then I'll head over to the Cuthand ranch and probably spend the night with Jake. The day after next, I'll ride to Clarksville to see about purchasing a sawmill." Effie listened attentively as she poured him another cup of coffee.

"Do you know if T.C.'s at home?" he asked.

"Nell said he was going to the ranch," replied Effie, "so you'll probably find him there. A sawmill, Claude? Whatever for?"

Claude shrugged. "Well, we've been hauling the lumber they cut, so why not keep it in the family? But I'm going to check it out first." Effie smiled; she was impressed with that astute businessman her son had become.

Claude was glad to see that his house was indeed almost finished, so he left immediately for the Cuthand ranch. He arrived to find that Jake and T.C. were both there. Claude was pleased to see that T.C. had kept good records of his income and expenditures. Jake and the boy told him of their problems in Clarksville and the run-in they had with the Klan. Claude shook his head sadly. "I really appreciate all you've done, T.C." Then turning to Jake, "I had hoped they would leave him alone, but I guess I put too much faith in human nature. What kind of shape are the mules in? Are they ready to go to work?"

"The mules ate all of the feed ah had, but they seem tuh be doin' okay. The winter grass is bountiful enough that they haf somethin' tuh eat. But fur a full-fledged freight operation, ah'd suggest get more mules so we can let the teams rest after hard loads," replied T.C.

"I brought half my mules with me and I'll bring the others when I move my family here. How's the freight business going?" inquired Claude.

"Couldn't do much good gettin' loads from Jefferson tuh Clarksville," T.C. admitted. "Ah feel we could get more work if yuh wur here even part of the time."

Claude nodded. "Alright, let me see if I can't contract some loads for you to transport from Jefferson to San Antonio. Besides, I'd like to have these wagons there anyway to move all of my belongings. I've sold half of the business to Pete and I plan to move the other half here or somewhere else in North Texas."

That afternoon, Claude went over to the Spence's' where he found Abby very pregnant and Ezra sick with the flu. "I'm sorry you're ailing, Ezra. I just came by to thank you for helping us when we really needed it. By the way, your note to me is paid in full. I'm on my way to Clarksville now and I'll have the lawyer record a release of the note. You're a good neighbor and if you need us, you only have to ask," said Claude.

Still recovering from a recent heart attack, Mr. Clarkson was feeling ill and the mill was not in operation. Nevertheless, the poor man was as anxious as ever to sell his mill to Claude. "I want to be sure my wife is taken care of when I'm gone," he told Claude. "I've had a verbal agreement with the Hardwood Furniture Manufacturing Company in New Orleans to buy all of the number one hardwood I could deliver to them. If you buy me out, I suggest you go to New Orleans and confirm that they still want the lumber. I've received checks for the lumber you hauled to Jefferson, so I believe they're still interested."

"Good to know," replied Claude, "but don't bother yourself none; I'll just go have a look at the sawmill myself, if you don't mind."

"Go on right ahead," responded Mr. Clarkson. He was grateful that Claude was still interested in buying him out.

The sawyer, the man who actually operated the mill, gave Claude a tour. His name was Jeffie Hilley. "I'm very anxious to get back to work," he told Claude. "We can have a full crew here and be in operation in twenty-four hours." Claude nodded. The mill appeared to be in fine shape, so Claude decided to purchase it—with the addition of three thousand acres of timberland along the Sulphur River.

"You're getting a bargain, Mr. Williams. You'll earn your investment back in one year if the New Orleans people continue to buy all you can cut," said Mr. Clarkson.

"Guess I'd better head out to New Orleans then," replied Claude with a friendly chuckle.

When he returned to the Cuthand ranch, Claude asked Jake and T.C. to take the wagons to Jefferson. "Go see Joe Waters at the livery stable there. He'll have information regarding loads for you to take to San Antonio. Waters will also have my horse, Rusty, and I'd appreciate it if you would take him back to San Antonio with you. I'm going to catch a boat to New Orleans and when I'm finished with my business, I'll take a boat to Galveston and then get to San Antonio from there."

Claude paused as if he was going through a mental list in his head. After a moment, he resumed speaking. "Also, tell Maria that I need her to start packing; tell her the house is ready and that as soon as I get back, I want to load everything up in the wagons and move to Indian Springs. She's been expecting this and will be happy at the news. I'd also like for both of you to bring back the mules. You'll need drivers, so I suggest you hire the three Negroes you had before. We're going to need all three of them on the trip back. I've given T.C. enough money for any supplies you might need. Lastly, go to Ezra's and ask him to stop by the ranch occasionally and see that everything is all right here. I'll see you in San Antonio."

Claude rode the ninety miles to Jefferson in three and a half days. He found plenty of freight ready to be transported to San Antonio and left word and his horse, Rusty, with Joe Waters at the livery stable as planned. The following day, Claude caught a boat heading for New Orleans.

The trip down the river and Big Cypress Bayou was a new experience for Claude. He saw countryside and swampland that he had never seen before. When he arrived in New Orleans, he took a horse-driven cab to a hotel so he could rest for the night. Claude went to the furniture company early the next morning. The principal owner, Mr. Ladoux, seemed genuinely pleased to meet Claude. "I can use all the clear-cut hardwood you can ship, Mr. Williams. And truth be told, we can use a heck of a lot more than Mr. Clarkson shipped."

"Well then, I'd better get busy, Mr. Ladoux," replied Claude as he shook the man's hand, grinning.

"I look forward to doing business with you," said Mr. Ladoux.

Claude was able to catch a steamer heading to Galveston the following day. The steamer went downriver to the Gulf; the sea was so rough there that Claude felt seasick the entire time aboard. He decided then and there that the best he could do was to keep his feet on solid ground and he intended to do just that once he made it to Texas soil.

When he arrived in San Antonio, Claude purchased a tent, a fairly new stagecoach, and a pair of fast horses to pull it. Maria was fluttering with excitement as she packed all of their belongings; the long-awaited move was finally underway. Little Clovis could sense her excitement and readily joined in. In his enthusiasm, Clovis kept pulling at her skirt, saying, "Let's go! Let's go! Mama, when can we go?"

It appeared to Claude that Maude had—seemingly over-night—turned into a young woman. He knew it was time he had a talk with Maude about her future and her rights and freedom. After dinner, Claude went into the kitchen where she was finishing up the dishes and said, "Maude, you are a young woman now and you know you're free. If you want to go with us to help Maria, you will draw a salary and we will take care of you. Or you can take your freedom and go wherever you wish. The choice is up to you. Do you want to stay or go with us to Indian Springs?"

Maude seemed surprised that he had to ask. "Oh yes, Mista Claude. I love your family, and to my knowing, I don't got any other family of my own; why I feel like little Clovis is part mine. So please take me along!"

Claude nodded and afforded her a smile. "I'm glad to hear it and I know for sure that Maria and Clovis will feel the same."

Together, Claude, Jake, and T.C. loaded all of the wagons with the household goods as well as the harnesses and supplies for the extra mules. They brought all of Maria's belongings to the stagecoach and put the tent in the boot where it could be easily retrieved.

Their leaving was an unexpectedly emotional event. Pete, his family, and all of the Mexican families had gathered to bid them goodbye. Maria cried and Claude found himself making a little speech, which he had to cut short before the tightening in his throat got any worse. This had been a place of new beginnings for him so many years before and he didn't realize until now how hard it would be to leave.

After a final round of hugs and handshaking, they were off. Claude was glad to have Rusty back because he felt comfortable and at home astride him. T.C. and Jake took care of the mules, the three Negroes from Indian Springs drove the wagons, and Maude drove the stagecoach. Big Joe took charge of the cooking and each of the Negro men was Google-eyed around Maude. She, however, seemed to only have eyes for T.C. They often sat alone to eat at night, their faces leaning close as they whispered and laughed together.

Claude encouraged everyone to keep a steady pace because he wanted to get to Indian Springs before fall set in and it got too cold. At least once a day, he picked up little Clovis and let him ride with him on Rusty. At night, they set up the tent for Maria and Clovis. Maude shared the tent with them as well. She seemed quite content on the journey, never being too far from the attentions of T.C. and her beloved Clovis.

CHAPTER 22

Indian Springs
1869-1870

The caravan arrived in Indian Springs on November 15, 1869. It had taken longer than expected due to Claude's slowing the pace for the women and his young child. But upon arrival to Indian Springs, everyone's excitement soared as they set about unloading the wagons, especially the personal items that the women would need right away. Effie and Nell had already spent several afternoons cleaning Claude's new house and they happily offered to take little Clovis with them to keep him from falling under foot while everyone was unloading and settling in. T.C. and Jake went directly to the Cuthand ranch, taking all of the spare mules with them. Once they finished unloading, Claude had the three Negroes drive the wagons back to the ranch as well.

On Thanksgiving, there was a big welcome party for Claude and his family. Sophie and her husband John were present, as was Jake, and their other sisters, Elizabeth and Edna Mae. Although

Maria was a little overwhelmed, she seemed to glow in all of the attention.

Effie prepared the turkey and the dressing, and all the other women pitched in with side dishes and fresh baked pies. Dr. Fuqua visited with Maria and kindly shared that he, too, had been a stranger to the family once, but that they were a friendly bunch and not hard to warm up to. Maria seemed to gather reassurance from his words.

Over the next week, Jake branded nearly a hundred calves. He was planning to sell fifty steers once they reached maturity. After the roundup, Claude asked Jake to come work with him, offering Jake both payroll and considerable supervising responsibilities.

On the day after Thanksgiving, Claude rode out to see the sawmill. He had spent some time thinking about the location of the mill and decided that he needed to move it to higher ground. The mill was on a little rise of land near the river and while the water didn't flood the mill itself, after a heavy rain, it flooded all the grounds around it.

When Claude arrived at the mill, Mr. Hilley, the sawyer, was waiting there for him. Hilley explained that he and the other mill employees were in desperate need of work and that their families were hungry.

"I'm sorry I've been absent so long; it couldn't be helped. But I assure you that we're ready to go now. I'd like you to have all of the mill employees here tomorrow to help move the mill to higher ground. The place where we've been picking up the lumber seems as good a spot as any," said Claude.

"True, and the stream nearby can provide water for the boiler," replied Hilley, enthusiastically.

"And more importantly," continued Claude, "we won't be forced to shut down every time it rains. I'd like for us to get ahead with logs so we can keep sawing even when we can't get to the timber because of high water. I'm going to advance all of the workers a week's pay so they can get some groceries. I've sold all of the lumber we've cut, and my plan is for us to cut as much as we can, as quickly as we can." Mr. Hilley looked greatly relieved and promised to inform all the other workers.

After a few days of backbreaking labor, the mill was finally moved in its entirety. The engine was cranky and although Claude knew virtually nothing about steam engines, they eventually got it running smoothly with the help of some of the more experienced workers.

Although the mill's previous owner had been contracting for logs, he didn't have any logging equipment. As a consequence, Claude contacted the man who had been providing Mr. Clarkson's logs and hired him on. Claude's mill was only in operation a month before they ran out. Unfortunately, the river was in its flood stage and they were unable to get more logs until the water levels went down again.

Claude informed his log contractor that he wanted to double the amount of logs that were being cut and if the contractor couldn't provide them, he would need to get crews to assist him.

Fortunately, there was a dry spring and when the river went down, Claude and his workers resumed cutting trees in earnest. He also hired Ezra and put him in charge of a crew. When the logs were ready, Claude had T.C. and his mules transport them to the mill.

Claude soon busied himself spreading the word that he would purchase logs from anyone who had them and would deliver them to his mill. He was interested in buying logs cut from someone else's property in order to spare the trees on his own acreage. Word spread quickly as Claude stockpiled logs and put out about three times the amount of lumber Mr. Clarkson had ever produced. The milling business was proving profitable and eventually Claude began looking around for a new, larger mill and a more efficient steam engine.

1870 was a good year for Claude and his lumber operation. As the mill workers cut the lumber, T.C. and his crew hauled it to

Jefferson, where it was then shipped on to New Orleans. Claude made a few trips with them to remind the Jefferson merchants that the Negro drivers working for him were not to be threatened or harassed.

Claude was only home on weekends and sometimes not even then. Maria, by this time, was pregnant with their second child and Effie and Sophie both treated her like royalty. She tried to resist their constant attentions, but they were so excited about the new baby that they just couldn't do enough for her. After the first month, Maria started bleeding and Dr. Fuqua ordered her to bed rest.

Maude attended to her every need, which included keeping Clovis occupied and away from his mother so she could rest. Clovis adored Maude and usually did as she told him. From Claude's vantage point, it seemed as if everything was running smoothly at home, so he kept busy and tried not to worry too much about Maria. After all, he reasoned, what could he do?

Maria missed Claude and tried her best not to feel abandoned when he was away, but it wasn't easy because he seemed to be absent more than he was present. Nevertheless, she refrained from complaining, assuming that he would spend more time at home as her date of delivery drew ever nearer.

In February, Dr. Fuqua sent a rider to the mill with an urgent note: "Claude, Maria is seriously ill and I think you should come home as soon as you can."

Upon receiving the note, Claude turned everything over to Jake and rode home as fast as he could. *How could I have let this happen?* he chided himself.

He arrived home to find both Effie and Sophie keeping vigil at Maria's side. In hushed voices, they told him that Maria had been bleeding profusely for several days and was very weak. Maria managed a smile when Claude stepped into the bedroom and held the smile as he sat beside the bed and held her hand. Seeing Maria rest her pale, thin face on the pillow in their large bed made Claude's heart ache. He could hardly swallow; he felt as if someone was squeezing his throat shut. Later, he realized it was fear—the fear of losing his beloved wife. And he had reason to fear, for over the course of the evening, Maria slipped into a coma. And around ten o'clock the next morning, she passed on.

Claude could not believe what had happened. He had stayed at her bedside since his arrival the night before and would not leave her until Effie and Sophie pried Maria's lifeless hand from his. Then, without quite remembering how he got there, Claude found himself alone in the barn, weeping inconsolably. He cried for hours in the dark, wracking his guilt-ridden conscience with questions he couldn't answer: *Why didn't I come sooner? Why didn't I spend more time with her when I had the chance? Now it's too late!*

Claude finally rinsed his face in the water of the horse trough and told himself to buck up. *Maria's gone; there wasn't anything I could do for her.* Besides, if anyone needed worrying over, it was his son. Claude realized with a start that in his grief, he hadn't had a single thought about little Clovis and he berated himself for it. *Perhaps*, he reasoned miserably, *there wasn't any room for anyone else in my heart and mind but Maria.* Still, Clovis needed a father now more than ever and Claude wasn't about to pass on his duty. He took an oath that he would care for the son Maria had given him; he would make her proud.

The next day, Maria was laid to rest in the Williams' family section of the cemetery. Claude felt as if he was stuck in a dream and hoped that he would wake up from this awful scene and find Maria alive and well. But instead, a new wave of grief overtook him and he shook with emotion as his sisters' and mother's hands reached out to console him.

After the funeral, Claude and Effie had a long talk. "I know you're crushed, son, and these feelings are natural. Maria loved you and gave you a fine son. But now you have to get on with your life. Sophie's been keeping Clovis and I would suggest that you speak with her and see if she'd be willing to continue."

Claude gave her a shocked look.

However, she continued with determination. "I know it's hard, but this matter must be dealt with. I want you to think carefully about this, Claude. As you know, Sophie and John don't have children of their own and Clovis is too young to be following you around the mill or going on freight runs with you."

Claude left his mother's home and went directly to Sophie's house. Clovis was quietly taking a nap and so Claude and Sophie took advantage of the opportunity to openly discuss matters that involved Clovis and his future living arrangements. Claude said, "I know taking Clovis is a big responsibility, but I think Mama's right; it's best for all those concerned. She said you and John would be happy to have him; I know that you two will love him and take good care of him. Also, I'd like for you to move into my new house. And it will be yours to keep."

Sophie's jaw dropped; she had not been prepared for this discussion.

Claude pretended not to take notice and continued, "I won't take no for an answer; you'll need the extra space with a young boy to rear. I know Maria would agree. Besides, why do I need such a large home for anyway? It's the least I can do for you. I'll speak with Maude and I'll offer to pay her to stay with you. She and T.C. are probably going to get married sooner or later and I think this will be good for both of them. Just put all my personal belongings in one bedroom and I'll stay with you when I can."

"Claude...," Sophie voice was choked with emotion. She was both stunned and grateful, searching for the right words.

Claude did not give her time to respond. "You'll be doing me a big favor, Sophie. I don't know what the future holds for me, but I need time to go off and think about it. Maria was the only woman I ever loved and I'm too angry to be good for anyone, let alone a young child."

∓∓∓

When Claude returned to the mill, he was relieved to see that all was well. T.C. had picked up the mail in Clarksville and there was a letter for Claude from Mr. Ladoux in New Orleans. He wrote:

We are very satisfied with the lumber you shipped. However, we are in the process of expanding and are interested in purchasing both your mill and your timber if you would be willing to sell. We looked at the mill before Mr. Clarkson sold it to you and were pleased with what we saw. We are willing to offer you twice the price quoted to us by Mr. Clarkson. If you are interested, please come to New Orleans and we can close the deal. We have an experienced sawmill operator to run the mill, if you agree.

Claude found Jake and told him about Ladoux's offer. "I'm leaving for New Orleans. Although I'm probably going to take the offer, I'd like for you to continue running the mill until I get back," he said to his brother.

Claude returned to Indian Springs to get his traveling clothes and see his mother, Sophie, and Clovis. Clovis seemed to be happy with Sophie, but when Claude went to see his mother, he was surprised to find that she had lost weight and was looking very pale. "Mama, I'm leaving for New Orleans on business, but I'm worried about you. I don't suppose—"Claude hesitated for a moment. "Mama, do you think you could have caught consumption from Dr. Fuqua?"

"Oh, no, I don't think so. I'm just tired, Claude. Maria's passing really laid me low, but I think I'll be all right," replied Effie.

Claude's heart sank at the thought of Maria. He couldn't bear to think of losing his mother, too. "Mama, I really don't feel right about leaving you here like this."

"Well now, I'll be mad if you don't go because I want you to bring me back something pretty from New Orleans. Now get going, son!" she said with a tired grin.

Claude had a feeling that perhaps he was being overly concerned, especially after having so recently lost Maria. But at the same time, it didn't make sense to put his life on hold either. So the next morning, Claude left for Jefferson. He left Rusty and boarded a steamer heading to New Orleans.

The journey, however, was quite different this time. As he stood on the deck of the steamer, Claude observed the same passing scenery, but it had now lost all of its color. On the previous trip, he had been looking toward a new future with his wife and son. Now he stood in the shadow of Maria's death, knowing his son, Clovis, would be raised by the boy's Aunt Sophie. He did know, however, that his mother was correct and that he had to get on with his life. Someone had once told him that death was part of life; he now realized that this was true.

The trip to New Orleans was otherwise uneventful. Claude had time to calm down and think. He thought about little Clovis' future, and concluded he was right to put him in his sister's care. Then his thoughts returned to business and he began to wonder why Mr. Ladoux was willing to pay him so much for the mill. *Maybe I should keep the mill, expand it, and get into the lumber business on a much larger scale?* When he got to New Orleans he checked into a hotel and walked for hours along the riverfront; he remembered that his brother Clovis had once told him most problems could be changed, or at least helped, by hard work

When he went to see Mr. Ladoux the next morning he had decided not to sell. Mr. Ladoux was disappointed but seemed pleased when Claude asked him if he could use two or three times as much lumber as he had been sending. "Claude, we wanted to buy the mill because our business is growing and all we want is a reliable source of hard wood to sustain our growth. If you can provide what we need, we will continue to buy all you can produce.

He went back to the river to get passage north and found a boat docked, ready to leave.

When he returned to Jefferson, he saw men unloading lumber from a barge to wagons. After introducing himself to the man in charge, he learned the fellow had a large mill south of Nacogdoches and was sending the lumber to San Antonio. He mentioned there was a mill for sale in his area because the owner had died.

About that time, T. C. arrived with wagons loaded with lumber for New Orleans. T. C. seemed genuinely glad to see him. "Sho glad yuh're back. Mah mama told meh Miss Effie's real sick an' she wished you were home," said T.C. with concern.

With a sickening feeling of dread, Claude left for his mother's home immediately. As far back as Claude could remember, Effie had never been ill and he knew that if Nell was concerned, it must be very serious.

Claude pushed Rusty hard and was in Indian Springs within three and a half days. Dr. Fuqua met him at the door with tears streaming down his cheeks. "Claude, your mama is gravely ill with double pneumonia and she's been asking for you. I tell you, I've done everything I know to do and if she doesn't get better soon, I'm afraid we're going to lose her," he said.

Without a word, Claude moved past Dr. Fuqua and quickly made his way to his mother's bedroom. He could not tell if Effie was asleep or just resting. Claude was stunned at how pale and gaunt she looked, far worse than when he had last seen her. His mother's appearance was almost wraithlike; her cheeks were hollow and sunken, her skin nearly translucent in the candlelight.

At that same moment, Effie opened her eyes and Claude went to her side and lifted her hand. Her hand felt fragile in his and her skin was thin as parchment. She smiled weakly at Claude and it was such an unexpectedly warm smile, that he couldn't help but smile back.

Dr. Fuqua pushed a chair close to the bed and motioned for Claude to sit. Claude did, as Dr. Fuqua stood quietly beside him. It was several minutes before Effie broke the silence with a whisper Claude could barely hear. He couldn't make out the words, so he leaned in closer as she repeated it in a hoarse whisper that seemed to draw her last reserves of strength: "Look in the bottom dresser drawer. Don't forget what I told you about going on with your life."

Effie closed her eyes, never to open them again. Not even an hour had passed before she was gone from this world forever. Claude got up from the chair and left Dr. Fuqua alone with Effie. Once again, he found himself in the barn, weeping. He knew men shouldn't cry, but he couldn't help it. He prayed, "Why, God? Why take the only two women in this world I truly loved? Please God, why couldn't you take me instead? What have I done to deserve this?"

Dr. Fuqua took it upon himself to have all of the family notified of Effie's passing. The funeral was well attended because during her years in Indian Springs Miss Effie had helped everyone in the community at one time or another and was truly loved by all. She was buried next to her husband, Tom.

It was only after the funeral, when Claude remembered what his mother had said about looking in the bottom dresser drawer. From the cemetery, he went to Effie's bedroom and yanked open the bottom drawer. He found all of the gold coins he had given her, along with a letter:

The coins are yours. I was just keeping them for you. I've made you administrator of my estate; it's in my will and Mr. Canterbury has the records in his office. If you're reading this, I've gone home to be with the Lord. Please tell all of the family that I truly loved them.

The next day, Claude rode to Clarksville. At the law office, Mr. Canterbury offered his condolences and read to him Effie's will. Dr. Fuqua was bequeathed the house, barn, and other buildings on the property. Claude was directed to purchase 150 acres of land and deed it over to Wash and Nell; he was further instructed to divide up evenly the remaining property between Effie's surviving children.

Claude requested that Mr. Canterbury set the will for probate in case it might be contested, to which Canterbury agreed. After settling his business with the lawyer, he returned to Indian Springs and spent a day with Sophie and John. Together, the three of them discussed which property they wanted. All the while, Clovis clung to Claude, demanding attention. Claude bounced Clovis on his lap to keep him quiet, although he couldn't help wondering if the strange look on Sophie's face was one of pity or envy.

Clovis cried for him not to go when it was time to leave and it tore Claude apart inside. However, he knew he needed to visit with his other sisters to discuss the division of the property. Claude decided to save a portion of black prairie land for Jake and then rode out to Cuthand to see him.

By the time he got to Cuthand, Claude was overwhelmed with exhaustion and a deepening depression. The deaths of Maria and his mother had impacted him in ways that made every waking moment difficult. When he was not overcome with anger or sorrow, Claude felt numb and indecisive. Consequently, it left him unaware that Jake was struggling with his own guilt at not having been an attentive son to Effie. But neither one spoke of the matter. Men didn't discuss such things with one another, nor did they cry; subscribing to this same view, Jake and Claude did their mourning in private.

After watching Claude mope around the ranch for days on end, Jake finally spoke up. "You know, I think you should go by the mill and reassure the hands that all is well," he said to Claude.

Claude nodded, although it took him three more days to find the motivation to act. On the third day, he awoke refreshed, his mind made up. Claude found Jake outside and gave him a hand with carrying firewood into the house. "Jake," he said, "I've decided not to sell the mill. If you are willing to sell the black land you inherited, I'll sell you a half interest in the ranch and cattle. I would like for us to expand the ranch and upgrade the stock."

"You bet I would," replied Jake. "I'd much prefer this ranch to the black land. So if you're sure that's what you want to do, just settle the transfer with the lawyer in Clarksville."

Claude gave him a nod. "Alright then. When I finish in Clarksville, I'll come back here."

Before meeting with the lawyer, Claude stopped by the mill to visit with his employees. The men seemed to be happy to hear that Claude planned to double the size of the mill and were pleased that they would get all of the work they wanted.

When Claude arrived in Clarksville, he went to see Mr. Canterbury. In the privacy of his office, he told the lawyer he had decided to sell everything he owned except the mill and the ranch.

Mr. Canterbury blinked at him. "What are your plans? May I ask---?

Claude laughed and said, "I'm not sure what I'm going to do with the rest of my life, Mr. Canterbury, but I do know I'm not going to be a farmer."

Claude entrusted the disposal of his property and holdings to Mr. Canterbury. He also arranged for the sale of Jake's black land as well as the transfer of half ownership of the Cuthand ranch and cattle to Jake. He deeded his land and house in Indian Springs over to Sophie. After finding 150 acres adjoining the land that Wash and Nell owned, Claude bought the acreage for them according to Effie's will; he then purchased and deeded an additional hundred acres to T.C. Afterwards, he returned to the ranch and loafed around until he received word from Clarksville that all the papers were ready to be signed.

For the first time since before Maria's death, Claude actually seemed to be in good spirits. Jake even caught him whistling.

Claude rode in to see Mr. Canterbury and gave him power of attorney to handle whatever business hadn't been finished and to purchase as much timberland up the river as he could find. As he handed his pen to Claude to make his signature, Mr. Canterbury withdrew it a moment and said, "You're absolutely sure you want to do this, Claude?"

Claude sighed and said, "As sure as I'll ever be. In addition to more timberland, watch for ranch land adjoining the Cuthand property. We'll decide what to do next when I return from Southeast Texas. I've heard a big mill is for sale down there."

Mr. Canterbury replied, "Since you plan to go south, I suggest you go east down Sulphur River when you leave. I've heard there is a vast area of good hardwood all along the river. Timberland might be a lot cheaper in an area where there is no mill. Also, I have a lawyer friend in Atlanta who told me there is a big area of hardwood trees in Cass County, which lays not far to the east of Trammel's Trace. His name is John Ramsey."

When he returned to the ranch, Claude told Jake that he heard news that a railroad would be finished in a couple of years, which, hopefully, would enable them to ship lumber by train to New Orleans.

"Jake, I need you to do me a favor and check on Sophie occasionally because she's keeping Clovis and I'd like him to know his uncle better. I deeded my house in Indian Springs over to Sophie, and I left money with my lawyer to pay for Maude's help. I'll write to you when I get somewhere. I'll leave in the morning. I'm going to Southeast Texas to look at a big mill that may be for sale down there"

And with that, Claude walked away, leaving his younger brother to stand behind and watch his tall frame grow smaller in the distance.

CHAPTER 23

Claude and Sawmills
1871-1872

Claude packed a mule with supplies and headed east down the river. Mr. Canterbury was correct. He rode for miles through hardwood forest with no signs of activity. When he left the river area, he headed a little southeast where he passed through more virgin hardwood. The whole area he passed through was deserted and he was glad he was armed as he slept in seclude areas. He had all of the gold he his mother had left him in his saddlebags.

He found he was traveling a vague trail, going a little east of south. When he came to a settler's cabin, he stopped and asked if he was going in the right direction to get to Atlanta. He was told he needed to go more to the east and the trail he was on would come to another one about five miles down, which would take him to Atlanta.

When he got to Atlanta, he took his stock to the livery stable and asked that both his horse and the pack mule be fed and watered and rubbed down. He asked for a hotel, but was directed to a rooming house. After leaving his gear, he went to the barbershop for a shave and a bath. The restaurant next door to the barbershop fed him a fine steak and then he went back to the rooming house. The lady who owned the rooming house made a good breakfast and he asked directions to attorney John Ramsey's office.

Mr. Ramsey arrived at his office the same time as Claude. He seemed friendly and said, "Canterbury is a good friend of mine. He was correct. There is a lot of hardwood in the southwest part of the county."

"What I'm really looking for is a sawmill for sale. I have more business than I can supply, and I'm thinking of enlarging my mill, or adding a larger one if I can find a bargain."

"You might have come to the right place. I represent the First National Bank here in Atlanta. They had a customer who bought a new sawmill and set in on Big Cypress Creek in the southwest part of the county. He didn't have enough capital and couldn't buy enough timber to operate it. He went broke and the bank now owns the sawmill. The president of the bank is named Jim Roberts. Why don't you go to the bank and talk to him. The bank is just down the street."

Claude went to the bank and Mr. Roberts seemed glad to see him also. "Mr. Ramsey sent me to see you. I might be interested in buying a sawmill and he indicated you recently had to repossess one. Are you interested in selling?"

"Yes, I would like to convert it to cash. Do you have cash and are you familiar with this area?'

"No. I've never been here before. Can you give me directions, or better yet, do you have someone available to show me where it is. I have cash if we can make a deal."

"I have someone to show you where it is. When do you want to go?"

"As soon as your man can show me because I have no other business here."

"I assume you are staying at the boarding house. Get your gear and I'll have someone here to show you where it is as soon as you get back."

Claude went to the rooming house, paid, and then went to the livery stable and got Rusty and the pack mule. When he got to the bank, Mr. Roberts introduced him to Joe Puckett who had worked on the mill for a little while. They headed southwest.

"How far do we have to go, Joe? If I'm interested at all, I may want to stay overnight. You can go back if you want to or you can camp with me."

"Either way is okay with me. I told my wife I might be gone over night."

Claude had to slow his pace because Mr. Puckett's horse couldn't keep up with Rusty and the mule. Clause asked, "How long was the mill in operation? I didn't get any particulars and if you worked there you should know what kind of shape it's in."

"It may be a little rusty because it's been idle for almost a year. It was new and was only in operation for a few months. The first boiler was too small and is still there, but he had to stop operation and go buy a bigger boiler."

They arrived about four in the afternoon. Claude hobbled the stock so they could graze and went to the mill. He hid the big sack of gold under his pack but unpacked the coffee and coffee pot as well as bacon and beans. He suggested that Jim build a fire and put the coffee on.

The mill was more than twice the size of the one he had at home, and the boiler not in use was bigger than the one at Claude's mill. He knew he wanted it, but made no comment to Jim. Also, he didn't stay at the mill long because he felt uncomfortable leaving the gold while Jim was around.

Jim got water for the coffee from Cypress creek. Claude walked down to the creek and immediately knew even if the owner hadn't gone broke he didn't have enough water for full operation.

The next morning Claude told Jim he might stay two nights

and that he knew the way back to Atlanta. Jim decided to go back and left about eight in the morning. Claude spent the rest of the day going over every part of the mill and found it to be in good condition. He left early the next morning. When he entered the city, he left his stock at the livery stable and then checked back into the boarding house.

It was almost closing time when he arrived at the bank. He carried the gold with him.

Mr. Roberts said, "What do you think?"

"If I were to buy the mill, the big problem would be getting it to Red River County. The big boiler will be difficult to load and difficult to haul. It would take a lot of both man power and horse power and a lot of money."

Mr. Roberts said, "Why don't you buy it and operate it right where it is. There is plenty of timber available in the area."

"The mill was doomed from the start. Big Cypress creek doesn't have enough water to run a busy mill of that size. I think you are stuck with a useless big mill."

"Someone will buy it. If you want to make an offer I'll consider it."

"The mill is really bigger than I am looking for and it will be heck to move. Here is what I'll offer, and not a cent more. You have to make a decision by noon tomorrow because I plan to leave then owing the mill, or to go elsewhere to find one." Claude set the big sack of gold on his desk and Mr. Roberts opened the sack.

"When you said cash, you meant cash. I've never seen this much gold at one time before. How much is there?"

"Count it and see. I'm going to the barbershop and then to eat a decent meal. I'll see you tomorrow just before noon. If you decide to take the offer, ask your lawyer to draw up the papers. I'm not going to hang around, because if you don't take my offer I'm going to go buy a sawmill somewhere else."

⁂›ℂ‸

Claude took a bath and got a shave at the barbershop. He had just ordered supper when Mr. Ramsey, the attorney for the bank, joined him. "Mr. Roberts from the bank came to see me and asked me to talk to you and see if you would give him a little more time. If he accepts your offer, the bank will suffer a considerable loss."

"Mr. Ramsey, you and Mr. Roberts have been very nice, but the mill just isn't worth more to me than I offered. I recently sold my freight company and know the problems moving the mill will cause. If he decides to take the offer, be sure to include all equipment on the mill site and have it ready by noon tomorrow. If he doesn't take the offer I want my gold back when I get to the bank."

The next morning, Claude checked out of his room, saddled Rusty, packed the mule, and went to the bank just before noon. Both Mr. Ramsey and Mr. Roberts were waiting for him.

The papers were drawn and Claude carefully read every word. "This is alright, but I would like an agreement permitting me to leave the mill on site until I can make arrangements to move it. If you think Mr. Puckett is trustworthy, I would like to hire him to guard my property until I get back. My plan is to try to get the freight company I sold to come from San Antonio to move it. A wagon is going to have to be modified and enlarged to handle the big boiler, and it is going to need at least twelve to fourteen mules to pull it. I think you made a wise decision to sell to me and I hope I've made the correct decision to buy. Mr. Ramsey could you draw the agreement for me to leave the mill where it is until I can get it moved? I've assumed the bank owns the property where the mill is. I would like to leave as soon as you can get the agreement ready."

"If Mr. Roberts agrees, I'll go to my office and prepare the agreement right now."

In less than an hour, all papers were signed and Claude headed back to Red River County.

Thanks to Rusty and a good mule he covered about twenty-five miles a day and went directly to the Cuthand ranch. Jake came in from the mill soon after he arrived.

"Is everything okay? Any problems you need me to handle?" Claude asked.

"T. C. is gone to Jefferson with three wagons loaded with lumber and we have enough cut for him to make another trip when he returns," Jake said.

"I found and bought a mill twice as big as the one we are operating here. I also got a boiler somewhat larger than the one we have. I hope it will increase the output of our present operation. However, we have a big problem in getting it here from Cass County. The big mill was only operated for about a year and is like new. The boiler is so big we will have to modify a wagon to transport it and it will take more manpower and more mules than we have available.

"If you don't need me right now at the mill, I'm going to Clarksville in the morning to see if Mr. Canterbury has found more timber. A good meal and a night's sleep will be very welcome."

Claude fed and brushed Rusty. He was certainly glad he had bought the horse.

CHAPTER 24

CLAUDE and JAKE and BIG LUMBER
1871-1873

Mr. Canterbury was surprised to see Claude. He was under the impression that Claude had gone to Southeast Texas. He was even more surprised when Claude told him about the enormous mill he had bought. "I gather you are planning to get into the lumber business in a big way"

"What I do now depends somewhat on you. First, have you sold my property? Second, have you looked into more timber? I took your advice and went up the river and found no lumber operation, but miles of fine hardwood"

The lawyer replied, "I've sold most of your property and have the money ready for you. I went to the courthouse both here and in Bowie County to check on owners of timberland along Sulphur River. As far as I can tell, no land is for sale and none has sold recently. I have written several owners with large acreage, telling them I have an investor, a client who might be interested in purchasing their property if it was reasonably priced. Frankly, I don't know what a reasonable price is. I haven't heard from anyone, but I only mailed the letters last week. I'll push some of the people who have inquired about the land you have left and try to get cash so you will have it available when you need it."

"I plan to go to Indian Springs and visit my son and then go to San Antonio and try to hire the man I sold my freight business to and see if he'll come to Cass County and move the mill I've bought. Jake has been operating our present mill and has kept wagons on the road taking lumber to Jefferson to be shipped by water to New Orleans. Do you know when the railroad will be finished so I can ship lumber by rail to New Orleans?

"I've heard it is supposed to be finished in 1872. They seem to be moving slowly and I'm not sure they can ship lumber by rail to New Orleans. I'll try to find out by the time you get back."

Claude went to see Sophie and Clovis. He spent several days with Clovis, taking him with him on Rusty for short rides. Leaving was gut wrenching as always, but he had no choice. He had to go to San Antonio.

He went to the ranch first, visited the mill, and found his employees happy and working hard. Jake told him they were really making money and that he had a sizeable balance in the Clarksville bank. "I thank you Jake, for the good job you're doing. If we can get the big mill up here and get the logs to cut, maybe we can make some real money. I have dreams of more ranchland, and upgrading the stock, but we have to make the money first."

Claude went through Waco and Austin and tried to find places to eat and stay. He was tired of sleeping on the ground and eating what he could cook. When he got to San Antonio he went directly to his old headquarters. Pete wasn't there but was expected shortly. He was welcomed by the families of his old employees and loafed and rested for two days. Pete was very glad to see him.

"Pete, I've bought a big sawmill in Cass County about thirty or forty miles north of Jefferson and have to move it to Red River

County. The huge boiler is the biggest problem. A big freight wagon will have to be modified with an extension of an extra rear end to make it longer and to support the weight. It will also take a lot of mules to pull it. I don't have enough mules or the employees capable of moving it, but you do. If you will come move it, I'll pay for a new wagon and the cost of modifying it and add ten percent to what you would have probably made staying here."

"El Jeff, I'll try to do anything you want me to do. You were married to my sister and when you sold me the freight company you gave me an opportunity I would never have had if I hadn't met you. When do you want me to move this sawmill? I've promised to make two more trips to Galveston and will be available after that. I won't take any other freight deals until I do what you want me to do."

"When you get back from your final trip, bring four or five wagons and all of the mules you have with their harnesses. Bring a cook wagon if you still have one. Go to Jefferson and see Joe Gooch. He's the only wheelwright in Jefferson and he'll have the wagon, which I plan for him to make, ready for you to bring. I'll try to be in Jefferson waiting for you. What I plan to ask him to make, is a wagon fifty percent larger than a regular freight wagon with six extra wide wheels in tandem with extra strong axels. It has to be plenty strong to haul that huge boiler. You might be thinking, how we are going to get it loaded on the wagon and how we are going to unload it when we get to the mill site? I leave it to you and me to figure it out."

The next morning, Claude left for Jefferson and rode hard because he was eager to get home and see what Mr. Canterbury had found. He needed to order the wagon and find a mill site to place the big Cass County once he got it to Red River County.

Joe Gooch had just finished his last job and was glad to get Claude's order. "Mr. Williams I've never built anything this big. What do you plan to haul on it?"

"I've bought a big sawmill in Cass County and plan to move

it to Red River County. I would like to know how they got it to Cass County, but the former owner is gone. That thing is big and heavy, but I've got to move it."

This time he went directly to Clarksville to see Mr. Canterbury. "What is going on? I just got back from San Antonio and stopped in Jefferson and ordered a special big wagon to move the boiler from Cass County. Is any of the timberland available? Bring me up to date."

"I have contracts ready to sign for the last of your black land and have a contract ready to sign for four thousand acres of timberland. The black land is selling high and the timberland is selling cheap. You can buy three thousand acres of timber for what you get for a thousand acres of black land. I think another tract of three thousand acres can be bought for the same price."

Claude replied, "I had hoped we could get at least ten thousand acres of timber for the black land I have. Do you know a surveyor or someone who understands what I'm buying to show me what I have thus far? A location for the mill site has to be found and a lot of water has to be available to operate the necessary big boiler. If you know or can find someone to show me the property, please send him to the Cuthand ranch. I want to go from here to Indian Springs to see my son and then I'll go to the ranch."

Little Clovis was happy, healthy, and very glad to see his daddy. Claude took him riding and they went to the location where his grandfather and grandmother had built their first cabin thirty-five years ago. They also went to the cemetery and saw where his grandfather, grandmother, and mother were buried. Clovis was too young to be real interested, but he loved being with his daddy. "When you get a little older, we will get you a horse so you can go with me on short trips.

"Right now I have to go to Jefferson, but when I come back I'll take you to the Cuthand ranch and you can see the big sawmill I've bought south of here, which we're bringing to this area."

"Can't you stay a little longer? I really miss you," Clovis

replied.

He had a long conversation with Sophie and John and they told him that Little Clovis was happy and healthy. "John, I'm moving a big mill to here from Cass County. We are going to need all the help we can get. If you want to be involved, come out to the ranch in a couple of weeks."

When Claude got to the ranch, Clint Mullins, a surveyor sent by Mr. Canterbury was waiting for him. "Mr. Williams, I can't show you the exact borders of your property, but I can get close."

"Let's go. I need to find a site on my property for a big sawmill I've purchased. I'll be bringing it in within the next month or so. I need an area that won't flood, but with plenty of water close by."

"Mr. Williams, I don't think we will find what you want. There is one small creek, but it isn't near as big as Cuthand Creek, and if you get close enough to get water from Sulphur River, you'll have flooding problems. Why don't we ride right along the river?"

Mr. Mullins knew what he was talking about. They just didn't find what Claude wanted.

When they got back to the ranch, John and Jake were both there. "We searched the property I've bought and also some I haven't bought, but I didn't find a good mill site. I think the best bet is to put the big mill where our present mill is located and maybe move the mill we have down to Cass County. I plan to leave in the morning to go to Jefferson to meet the men who will move it, and then I'm going to Atlanta to see the banker. John, I would like for you go with me so you can help us load the big boiler. Jake, do you have any problems you need me for?"

"No, everything is going fine. We are shipping two or three times as much lumber as we did before you went to New Orleans. The checks from the furniture company have been deposited in your bank at Clarksville and they are sizeable."

When Claude got to Atlanta he went directly to the bank to see Mr. Roberts and told him he was thinking of moving the mill he currently had in Red River County to the site where the big mill was located. "Did the previous mill operator have any timber?"

"No, he didn't own any timberland. The only property he owned was the mill site. Times have been kind of hard around here, so he had no problem buying all of the logs he wanted. The timber region is owned by a lot of small landowners and I think you'll get all of the logs you need at a reasonable price. If you will bank here with us, I'll lease the mill site to you. We really need your operation here in Cass County."

"Please get a lease prepared and I'll stop by when we come after the present mill. If the lease is satisfactory, I'll have the movers of the big mill bring my current mill on the way back south. So far, doing business with you has been satisfactory. I would like to stay and visit but the freight company should be in Jefferson and I have to go meet them."

In Jefferson, he found the wagon complete, and he and John were able to get a shave, bath, a good meal, and a good night of rest in a feather bed before Pete and company arrived.

Pete's first comment was, "That is the biggest and strongest wagon I've ever seen. We should be able to haul anything we can load on it."

"The problem is getting the boiler loaded. Someone moved it to its present location, and if someone else was able to do it, I'll bet we can do it, too" Claude replied.

They left immediately for Cass County.

John stayed with the wagons and Pete took one wagon and he and Claude went to Atlanta to see if they could find some big timbers or get permission to cut trees to slide the big boiler onto the wagon.

Mr. Roberts was glad to see them. "I think you will be pleased with the lease. I've spread the word, so most of the mill hands who worked there previously are available and they want the work. I'm prepared to lease you the twenty acres of the mill site and there are several big trees on the property. Cut what you need. Phil

Prescott was the sawyer on the big mill and married a local girl; they still live here. I'll send for him because he was involved in moving the boiler here. He also knows the other people who worked on the mill. I'll spread the word among the landowners and you should have all of the logs you need when you get here. Mr. Prescott seems to be a good man and I feel sure he will want a job if you are interested."

Pete headed back to the mill site and Claude signed the lease after reading it. The bank really wanted a mill to be operating.

೮೦೦೮

Phil Prescott was a big man and said he would love to have a job. "I've been living in Atlanta since the mill shut down, but if you hire me, I'll move to Linden, which is much closer; plenty of housing is available there. Several of the other people who worked on the mill still live in Linden. Moving a smaller mill here is really a godsend. I was about to leave to find work elsewhere, but much prefer to be here. We never got in full operation because we didn't have enough water for the big boiler."

They couldn't travel as fast as Claude wanted to because Phil's horse was slow. On arrival, they found that Pete and John had already cut several medium size trees and were rigging them to slide the boiler on the wagon. Phil had some suggestions, but told Claude, "Your people know what they are doing and are better equipped than the people who brought it here."

In just two days, they had the whole mill loaded and were ready to go. Claude asked Mr. Prescott if he wanted to go with them. "You can talk to my sawyer who has been running the mill we are moving and tell him anything he needs to know. Also, I would like for you to oversee the setting up of the bigger mill."

They had plenty of wagons so Claude suggested they take the logs they had cut with them. "We can possibly use them to slide the boiler off the wagon like how we used them to load it."

They were all thankful it didn't rain. The big wagon was

heavily loaded, and if it got stuck, they would have had to just wait until it dried up.

Unloading wasn't near as big a job as loading. As soon as they unloaded one wagon, they started loading the other mill. Claude asked Phil, "We left the boiler you were not using at the site in Cass County. Do you think we have enough water there to use the boiler we left? I think the mill we are moving there will run better with a little larger boiler."

"Yes I do. We had plenty of water to run the boiler we left, but it wasn't big enough to run the big steam engine. I wondered why you left it."

"Phil, the next time you wonder why I do something please ask me. I may not always be right."

₧₧₧

As soon as they got the new mill up and running, they left to take the smaller mill to Cass County. Claude gave John checks for the Clarksville account and told him to pay Pete whatever amount he said was due. He had talked to Jake and told him to figure what he was due and that John would pay him. He also talked to Phil about his pay and they agreed on a pay per day worked; they also agreed on how much to pay the other mill hands and how much to pay for logs delivered to the mill.

"If the locals won't provide enough logs to keep us busy. I'll try to by timber uncut and get a crew to cut it. The only way I can make a profit is for the mills to be busy. When we are not operating, the hands don't make money, and I don't either. I have a big investment, so let's all make what we can."

Claude sat down with Jake and said, "Jake, I'm very pleased with the way you have run this operation. Please keep going and we'll take part of the profits from the mills and increase the value of the stock and the ranch as a whole, half of which you own. I suggest you turn over some of your duties to John and we'll put him on the payroll, which should give you a little relief. We are both slaving in the lumber business and I hope we can ease up a little. We are doing well because we are both working and tending to business. We can't let up too much because a business doesn't run itself. Let everybody know that we need more logs. If the locals can't provide them, at least we have timberland to the east. But I think it's best to harvest other people's timber first."

Jake sat patiently as Claude went through his plans. When he finally got the chance to speak he said, "Claude, I've met a girl who I'm very interested in and she lives in Clarksville. If I can get John to help a little, and get our hillbilly neighbor to help with the ranch a little, then maybe I can go courting occasionally."

"Nobody knows how lonesome someone cam be more than I do. Please have at it. I'm going to head back to Cass County to make sure the mill there is set up and producing. I have to write to New Orleans to be sure we have a market for the increase in production. I think we have enough mules to get the lumber to the river, but we're goin' to need more wagons. I'll get them in Jefferson. Is there anything else you need for me to get while there?"

"Nope. Get going and I'll try to take care of this end."

⊱⊰

When Claude got to Cass County, he went directly to the mill site and was pleased with what he found. Phil had the mill set up and they had enough logs to start production. Phil said, "I can begin running the mill as soon as you authorize me to hire all of the hands I need. Several of the hands from the other mill have been to see me and I can get plenty of help."

"As soon as I leave here I'm going to Atlanta and leave money with my attorney there. Send him your payroll details, and the details of log purchases. He'll send back checks to cover your costs. From there I'm going to Jefferson and buy a couple of wagons so you can send your cut lumber to Jefferson for shipment to New Orleans or elsewhere. I hope the New Orleans buyer can take all of our production, but if not, I'll find a buyer elsewhere. I'll come back here before I go to Jefferson."

৯৩

When he got to Atlanta he went directly to John Ramsey's office. Mr. Ramsey said he would be glad to handle the money for his Cass County operation. "Do you have money in the bank here?"

"No, but I plan to go to the bank now and make a sizeable deposit. The lumber we cut is going to be hauled to Jefferson and shipped to New Orleans to a furniture manufacturer who is currently buying all we can produce. I'll be around until all is goin' well and to see that you don't run out of money. I'm sure Mr. Roberts has your signature on file. I'm going to suggest that Phil Prescott send you all of the bills each week and to have the messenger wait for the checks."

Mr. Ramsey replied, "I'm glad you hired Mr. Prescott. He has a good reputation and I think he knows what he is doing."

৯৩

Mr. Roberts seemed very glad to see him and welcomed his deposit. "I think you were smart to hire Mr. Prescott and Mr. Ramsey. How about going home with me for supper tonight? I'll bet it's been some time since you have had a home cooked meal. I'd like for you to meet my widowed daughter. Her husband died two years ago and she has been taking care of me since and doesn't get to socialize much."

"I will certainly enjoy a home cooked meal. Let me go to the barbershop and get a shave and a bath and change clothes. Also, I need to check into the rooming house and take my livestock to the livery stable. You'll probably be home before I finish but, if you tell me where you live, I'll come directly there as soon as I get checked in and cleaned up."

Claude was tired. He had been on the road too long, loading and unloading sawmills without much rest. He was looking forward to an evening of no business and a good meal.

⁕⁖

Mr. Roberts' home was almost as big as the one Claude had built in Indian Springs, but on much less land. Roberts met Claude at the door and introduced him to his daughter, Diana. Claude was surprised. She was truly a beauty. She appeared to be in her late twenties or maybe thirty. Claude saw a tall, shapely, and handsome lady. She excused herself to see to the meal. Claude had been so upset with Maria's death he had hardly thought of another woman, but was mesmerized by Diana. He felt guilty to be thinking of another woman, but remembered what his mother had told him about continuing his life.

⁕⁖

Claude slept late the next morning, but went by the bank before leaving. He told Mr. Roberts he had to go to Jefferson and make arrangements to ship the lumber they had cut down the river as well as buy two wagons and some mules to take to Jefferson. "I was extremely glad to meet Diana. I lost my wife two years ago and have lost myself in work. I would like to get better acquainted with her when I return. Being alone is rough on a man or a woman."

"Diana said she would like to see more of you."

Claude found the mill running with plenty of logs to cut and a crew that seemed happy to be back at work.

After explaining his arrangement with Mr. Ramsey, he explained that Phil needed to hire someone he trusted to take the information to Atlanta and bring back the checks. "I'm going to Jefferson to buy two wagons and enough mules to deliver what you cut to Jefferson.

"If you know someone who has experience handling a freight wagon, send him to see the only wheelwright in Jefferson. His name is Joe Gooch."

"We need to get this lumber to Jefferson because I don't get paid until the lumber is delivered to New Orleans. I'm off to Jefferson now."

℠℞

When he arrived in Jefferson, Claude saw two wagons sitting in front of Joe Gooch's shop. He entered and asked, "Who belongs to the two wagons sitting out front?'

"I own them now. I'm Joe Gooch."

"How long have you had them?"

"The man who brought them in was killed in a bar fight. He had no money on him and no bank account. As far as anyone knows, he was single and had no family. The livery stable has his mules and they're for sale too. These wagons are in good shape now because I rebuilt them, including the wheels. But if his mules were treated like his wagons, I reckon you won't want them. I would sure like to sell these wagons to get my money out of them."

"Don't sell them to anyone else. I may need them. I'm gonna go see those mules; if enough of them are sound I'll buy 'em and be right back."

Claude found only four of the mules to be young and strong, but they still needed food and care. The other mules were obviously old and in poor condition He bought the four and harnesses and other equipment.

He took the four mules to a blacksmith and had their hoofs trimmed with new shoes. He then went back to the livery barn and paid to have them curried and fed extra rations.

℠℞

After a good meal and a night's rest, Claude went back to see Joe Gooch. There was a man waiting for him who said Mr. Prescott had sent him and that he was an experienced freighter. His eyes were bloodshot and he smelled strongly of alcohol. Claude said, "You are not going to work for me. You are a drinker and are obviously hung over." The man left, mumbling curses under his breath.

Claude turned his attention back to Joe. "Mr. Gooch can you tie the wagons together so I can pull them with one team? The only thing I'll be hauling will be a large quantity of stock feed and some groceries. I'll drive it to the mill myself and find someone who will stay sober to drive my lumber from there to here."

Gooch, obviously happy with the sale, prepared the wagons as requested.

Claude hooked up one pair of mules and took one wagon to the feed and grocery stores. When he returned they tied the other wagon on behind as Claude was going to pull it with all four mules. After tying Rusty and the pack mule on behind, he headed for Cass County and the mill site.

ℝ℞

Mr. Prescott asked, "What happened to the freighter I sent to Jefferson?"

"I wouldn't hire him. He'd been drinking and I don't tolerate drinkers. I'll send you some drivers. They may be black, but they will do as told and they do not get liquored up. A load of lumber represents a considerable investment and I won't risk it with some drunk. How are things going here? Looks like you've cut a lot of lumber. Any problems you need me for?"

"No. Everything seems to be working well. More hands are available than I need. And as you can see, we have quite a lot of logs ready for the mill."

"Do you think you could get two or three men to fence about an acre on the back side of the mill site? Also, please check to see that the mules are well fed and watered. They also need to build a shelter so the stock can get out of the weather, as well as a storage area for feed. The fence builders should be able to hobble the mules and take care of them until the fence is finished. I'll send more mules and two drivers from Red River County. We have to get this lumber shipped as soon as possible. I'm going to go to the other mill and send the drivers and the stock as soon as I get the material for the fence bought and delivered."

"There is a store in Linden that has fence supplies. It's closer and probably quicker. I'll take care of the operation here. Come back when you can."

The store in Linden had what they needed and said they would deliver it the next day. Claude decided that he best go through Atlanta anyway and see if they had enough money in the bank to keep operating the way they were.

"Mr. Roberts said, "We still have almost half of the money you deposited. They must be really sawing logs out there. Don't worry. After all, I'm a banker and I'll loan you money on a temporary basis as long as things are going well. I checked with your banker in Clarksville and he said cash was coming in from the big mill you moved up there. By the way, my daughter asked that I invite you back for dinner when you came back."

"I was very impressed by your daughter and appreciate the invitation. However, I must get back to Red River County and get mules and drivers to move the lumber we have cut here to Jefferson so we can ship it on to New Orleans. I don't get paid until it is delivered to New Orleans and I've been spending money like a drunken Indian. I'll be back as soon as possible. I think you will be pleased with the deposits when the money from New Orleans starts arriving."

Claude went to see Mr. Ramsey "How are things going with the mill. Is our arrangement working to your satisfaction? I just spoke with Mr. Roberts and we have enough in the bank to operate until I get back. I bought two wagons and four mules in Jefferson, but I need more mules and drivers to get the cut lumber to its final destination."

"All seems to be going well here. Is Phil Prescott satisfied with the arrangement?

"He didn't mention any problems."

"Mr. Williams, a man was here earlier today looking for you. He said his name was Shorty Spence and he mentioned he was staying at the boarding house."

"Thanks, I know him. He's a mule and horse trader. I'll try to find him right now."

Claude found Shorty at the livery. "Shorty, I don't know if I need mules or not. I think I have enough, but I have to go to Red River County before I'll know for certain. I'm leaving now but would like to have two good saddle horses and one small horse, very tame, for my six-year-old son. If you show up with what I want, go to my sawmill in the southeast part of Cass County, located just south of Linden, and they will know where I am and when I'll be back."

Claude stopped at the big mill. Jake was there and T.C. was loading two wagons for Jefferson. "Mr. Claude, we are going to have to start using three wagons to stay up with all of the lumber they're cutting. They are really putting it out."

"T. C., I need to talk to you about drivers and mules. Do you have enough mules for me to take four to Cass County? They have two wagons and four mules, but we have a big backlog of lumber we need to get to Jefferson. I'm going to give you a raise in pay and want you to supervise both freight operations going to Jefferson. We are probably going to need to talk to your daddy again and get more drivers. These drivers have made a lot of trips to Jefferson. Do you think they can make it without you? I would like for you to stay here so we can talk tonight."

"Sure, they can make it fine. I had planned for two drivers to take the wagons to Jefferson. I was gonna to try to get to Indian Springs. I ain't took no time off since Miss Effie passed on. Also, there is a young lady I wanna see."

"Fine, we'll talk tonight and you can go home tomorrow. Bet you haven't even seen the land I bought for you or what Miss Effie bought for your poppa."

⊱❦⊰

Claude had never seen a bunch of happier mill hands. They were working six days a week and had plenty of logs to cut. Jake was obviously doing a fine job. "Claude, things are going well and we are putting about three times as much money in the bank as we did with the small mill."

"That is great. I would like to look over the books tonight. Have you been using John and Ezra some as I suggested?"

"Yes, I've used them some. I hope with your permission to use them more. I'm engaged to Faye Latimer, Jim Latimer's little sister. I think she is wonderful but if I continue to run the mill and ranch we need to build better living facilities on the ranch. I doubt if she would be happy moving into the crude cabin we have now."

"The good job you are doing here along with the other operation means we'll soon have the money to build what you need. If you truly love Faye I think you should get married as soon as we get you a home constructed. Check to see if Ezra wants to work full time. I think you best turn the ranch over to him. Seems the mill needs you full time."

That night he had a good visit with T. C. After explaining the task, T. C. replied,

"We have plenty of mules left over from the half of the freight company you didn't sell. Two of the Negro drivers you hired, they can work at either o' the mills: one here, one over dere in Cass County. Daddy 'ill get us two or three otha single men to fill out the crews. Course, they'll be needin' some sort of cabin in Cass County for the drivers to live in when not outta the road. The mill hands, they be white and drivers 'ill need to have their own place.

"How soon can you start making these changes?"

"If un you'll send me one experienced man and a new one, I'll take 'em to Cass County to start haulin' lumber. Are extra mules outta the ranch?"

"Yes, and the mules are in good shape."

"The grassland at the ranch does 'em good."

"I'll round up four good ones in the morning before I go. The harness is in the shed."

"I have to go to Clarksville in the morning. I'll be back here before the hands get here."

"I'll take 'em to Cass County. It be closer to Jefferson than from here. That should handle the output there."

"If you need to, hire hands to run whatever wagons you need. The big mill is creating a lot more lumber than the old one. Tell your parents that I'll be to see them the next time I'm there. Also, tell Maude I'll be to see Little Clovis as soon as I can. By the way, if your daddy isn't working somewhere, please ask him if he would be willing to build a place for the boys you are sending to stay when they aren't in Jefferson. We'll also need to build two houses on the ranch.

"Yes, sir. I'll tell him."

"I'll be back as soon as I get things set up in Cass County."

ↄↃ

Mr. Canterbury had completely finished selling all of the black land and had bought over ten thousand acres of timber east of the new big mill. Some of the owners of smaller tracts had discovered the big mill was buying all of the logs they could deliver and all of what they were cutting now came from them.

CHAPTER 25

CLAUDE and DIANA and MORE LUMBER
1873-1874

While he was in Mr. Canterbury's office he wrote Mr. Ladoux in New Orleans:

As you can see from the amount of lumber we have been sending, we are sawing logs. Also, the amount we are sending is going to increase because we now have two mills in operation. If you can't handle all we will be sending, please let me know. I'm pleased with the present agreement, but I know we are probably going to be sending possibly five times as much as before. Please let me know by mail (in care of my attorney), Mr. Canterbury, PO Box 5, Clarksville, Texas.

Sincerely,
Claude Williams

ⅎ℧

Mr. Canterbury commented, "Claude, I'm not usually surprised by my clients, but you have surprised me. How did you do it? You have gone from a freight company owner to probably the biggest supplier of hardwood lumber anywhere in a very short time."

Claude replied, "I haven't thought of it in that way. I've learned if you have problems the best way to solve them is to just outwork everyone else. If you do the problems will either go away or a solution will present itself. When my wife and then my mother died in a short time, I was really upset. I have a seven year old son, I wanted to be able to provide for him but did not know if I could raise him and raise money at the same time. My sister in Indian Springs is raising him and I can focus on my business ventures. My hard work provides for my family and employees."

"That's very impressive."

"Well, I do have help. For example, thanks for your help and advice. Your friend, Mr. Ramsey, is currently handling the payroll and log purchases in Cass County. The mill there is really producing."

₧₨

When Claude got back to the ranch he found John filling in for Jake. Ezra was at the ranch too. "Ezra, thank you for helping us. How is your family?"

"We are all fine, Mr. Williams. I appreciate the opportunity to make a little cash. I'm trying to save enough money to fence my place, but I'll never be able to do it if I don't make some more money. Please let me know anytime I can help'"

When John came in he said everything was going well at the big mill and they were still getting enough logs to run full time.

The two Negro drivers sent from Indian Springs arrived the next morning. Ezra went with them and they got the harnesses needed from the storage shed and without much talking they headed for Cass County. When they got to the mill, the drivers camped in the pasture with the mules and Claude asked them to hitch up the teams and be ready to go to Jefferson the next morning.

Phil Prescott said all was fine. He was getting plenty of logs and said he had experienced and happy mill hands. "I'm sure glad to see you have brought wagon drivers so we can get some of this lumber on its way."

"Phil, I'm glad all is going well. Is the payroll system working to your satisfaction? As soon as I get back from Jefferson I'm going to Atlanta and to be sure all is good there. I won't be gone long. Has a horse trader named Shorty Spence been here?"

"No horse trader has been here. The payroll situation is working out. All of us appreciate the jobs."

The next morning, the drivers hitched up the teams and started loading lumber. Claude noticed that they split the teams. They put a pair of the mules they brought from the ranch as lead mules on each wagon. The mules he bought in Jefferson didn't look as bad as they had when he purchased them. They just needed to be fed.

Claude explained that he was going with them on the first load to be sure they knew the way. He was pleased to see they also had loaded feed for the stock. He had enough food for the men with him.

They made good time and stopped for the night near a small stream. T. C. must have trained them well because the first thing they did was feed and water the mules, and then hobbled them so they could graze.

While they were tending the mules, Claude built a fire and had coffee on. When they came to the fire Claude had the first long conversation with them. "I partially raised T. C. and he has done a fine job. His parents worked for my family forever and have always been free. His dad is a good carpenter and I sent word for him to come built a house for you boys at the mill and a couple of houses at the ranch if he isn't tied up. I'll buy you a tent to use until he gets here. Also, when we get to Jefferson we will buy enough groceries to last you for a while. Can either of you cook? I brought some bacon and beans and cornbread makings."

One of the men stepped forward and said, "My name is Fred and I usually do the cooking. We didn't bring much with us and we are both real hungry. I'll cook supper and make enough for tomorrow if it's alright with you. T. C. says you are the best boss ever and we both know his daddy. We are here because they say you are great to work for."

"Fred, the food is right here. I'm hungry too and I'm not a good cook. Have at it!
In Jefferson I'll buy whatever you want to eat. We should also get you some warm clothes and rain gear. Be thinking about what you will need."

When they got to Jefferson, Jim knew where to go and the people at the river dock recognized him. Claude wrote a letter to Mr. Ladoux and told him they would mark the lumber with an X that was shipped from Cass County. He told him to please send a check to Williams Lumber Company, Care of his attorney, Mr. Ramsey, Post office Box 71, Atlanta, Texas.

Then he showed Fred how to mark the lumber with an X. "You boys come with me. We are going to buy more food for you to take with you and warm clothes and a tent for the mill pasture for you to use until we can get you a house built."

They went to the same store that T. C. and Jake had used. Claude introduced himself and told them he had sold the freight company but had two sawmills and was shipping lumber to New Orleans. He then introduced Fred and told the proprietor. "My plan is to pay for what we buy today and prepay some. I'll try to stay ahead of purchases, but if Fred or any of our drivers come in and needs supplies and don't have the money, please let him have what he needs. If that happens just send the bill to Williams Lumber Co. in care of Attorney Ramsey, PO box 71, Atlanta. Texas. These men work for me and I trust them."

They bought mule feed, and enough groceries to last some time, and then started buying coats, shoes, and other clothes for the two Negros. When they finished, he told Fred to get the wagons and load all they had bought and head back to Cass County.

"Fred you now know the way so head on back to the mill, get a good night's sleep and then reload and come again. Best put up the tent because all of this good weather is going to end any time now. I'm going to head on back because I can move a lot faster than the wagons and I have to tend to business in Atlanta."

All seemed to be going well at the mill. They were working hard and producing. He visited with Phil Prescott and gave him the names and pay scale of the two drivers. Phil said, "Shorty Spence showed up yesterday and said he would wait for you in Atlanta and he would either be at the livery stable or the rooming house."

"Thanks. I'm going to Atlanta now and I'll see him there. I'm more than pleased at the progress you've made. It will even be better after the money starts coming in from New Orleans."

Claude found Shorty at the livery barn. He had two fairly good saddle horses and a small horse he wanted for Little Clovis. He checked each one carefully and found them to be sound in every way. The little horse was gray in color and was a gelding. He petted it and rubbed him all over and he stool still and seemed to like it. He and Shorty dickered awhile and Claude gave him a check and told him to take it to the First National Bank down the street and they would cash it. "I'm going to the bank now and if you will go with me I'll introduce you to the president of the bank. He's a good man to know."

At the bank he introduced Shorty Spence to Mr. Roberts. "Mr. Roberts for years I've bought a lot of mules and other stock from Shorty; he has always been honest with me. I just bought three horses from him and he needs the check cashed."

The banker called over a vice president and asked him to help Shorty. "How are things going? I checked this morning and see that you are close to being out of money in your account. Am I going to get to loan you some so I can make some money?"

"Nope. I'll make a deposit that should cover the expenses until money from the mill comes in. I just came from Jefferson where I showed my wagon drivers where and how to ship the lumber. We shipped two wagonloads and the drivers should be back at the mill by tomorrow and will immediately take two more loads. Phil Prescott has cut a lot of logs and it will take a while for two wagons with good mules to catch up.

I'm more than pleased with Prescott and know I was fortunate to get him."

"I'm glad all is going well. How about dinner tonight"

"I'd like that, but I need to see Mr. Ramsey. Then I have to go back to the mill tonight. I brought two Negro drivers in from Red River County and have to see that they are set up properly and get them back on the road. Will the invitation still be available tomorrow night?"

"Sure. I understand you have to take care of business but Diana keeps asking so we will be glad to see you tomorrow."

Mr. Ramsey indicated all was well with his part of the operation. Claude explained, "Washington Hill, a Negro, may come and need payment for lumber, and supplies for a cabin for my Negro wagon drivers. Wash Hill has worked for my family as a free man for years and is totally trustworthy. One of his sons, T. C., is in charge of transporting lumber to Jefferson from both mills. If he needs help, I'm going to tell him to come see you. I trust him completely because he has been with me most of his life"

The two drivers had returned to the mill and were trying to put up their tent. They had watered and fed the mules but were having trouble with the tent. Claude helped them with the tent and suggested they ask Mr. Prescott for some scrap lumber to fix a rack of some kind for their clothes.

Phil Prescott came down to see if he was needed. Claude told him about their need for some scrap lumber and he said he would get it for them tomorrow. Claude left with him and asked, "Do you think you will have any problem with your white mill hands because the two drivers are Negros?"

"I don't think so. I'll take care of it if we do because there are plenty of mill hands available. I'll see they keep rolling."

"Phil I have a young Negro who I have half raised and he has been with me since he was about ten years old. He is honest to a fault and is dependable and hard working. We have three or more wagons hauling lumber to Jefferson from the big mill and T. C. Hill is responsible for them and these here. He hired all of the Negro drivers. His mother and father, Washington, both free, have worked for my family for years. T. C. was born free. He'll bring some relief men for the two drivers here and I'll tell him to report to you. Let him know if you've had any driver problems. I've asked his father to come build some sort of cabin for the boys here and to also build two houses on my ranch. He is a fine carpenter. You make sure he gets whatever he needs."

⬥⬥⬥

The next morning, Claude left early for Atlanta. He checked in at the rooming house and took his animals to the livery. They had a fine horse and buggy to rent and he reserved it for the following day. He ate a good meal, went to the barbershop for a shave, and got a good night's sleep.

He stopped at the bank to find out what time he should arrive for dinner. "Will it be alright with you if I ask Diana to go for a buggy ride?"

"Sure. I'll see you tonight."

Diana was as lovely as before and served a delightful meal.

"Diana, I've rented a horse and buggy for tomorrow. Would you like to go for a ride? If you are interested, I would like to show you the mill we are operating in the southwest part of the county. Fix something for lunch if you like or we can get something from the restaurant?"

"Claude, I would love to go and I'll fix the lunch."

Claude picked Diana up the next morning and they headed for the mill. He told her about his freight hauling business, his move to Indian Springs, Little Clovis, and the unexpected death of

Maria and his mother.

She made little comment and didn't seem very interested in the mill. On the way back she told him about her husband and that he owned a general store, which she sold after his death. She asked no questions about his son or his business.

He left early the next morning for the ranch, taking the three horses he had bought from Shorty. He was disappointed that Diana showed so little interest in his son. She didn't even ask where he was living. Any women he might bring into his life had to show an interest in Clovis.

CHAPTER 26

CLAUDE and MORE LUMBER
1874

Ezra was at the ranch when Claude arrived. He turned the three horses and the pack mule over to him and headed to the mill. The mill was busy and was putting out a lot of lumber. Wash and T. C. were there and were loading three wagons with lumber.

"Wash, are you interested in doing some carpenter work? I'll pay more than you earned working for my folks."

Sure, Mista Claude. I'll do anything you want me to now and forever. I'll never forget what you done for T. C. and for me."

"T. C. says I need some sort of cabin for the two drivers he sent to Cass County. He is, as usual, correct. If T. C. is available, I would like for both of you to go to Cass County and look at the operation there. Decide where you want to put the cabin and figure out what you'll need. Then go to Atlanta and see Mr. Ramsey, the attorney who handles the payroll, and my business expenses. Mr. Prescott, the sawyer and boss of that mill can tell you where to find him. I have briefed Mr. Prescott and Mr. Ramsey. Ask Mr. Ramsey where you can get what you need to build the cabin and ask him to arrange payment. I've asked them to help you with whatever you need. I bought two saddle horses in Atlanta and left them at the ranch. I'm going there now to get the little horse I bought for Clovis.

Claude was anxious to see Little Clovis, but needed to finish his transaction first. "If you don't have saddles for the horses, come with me to Clarksville I'll purchase what you need. You can keep the horses we buy. Remind me to give you the bill of sale when I get back.

T. C. spoke up, "We don't have no decent equipment for two horses. We got here riding double on the old mare you left here before. You get us the mounts. We can leave as soon as we get these wagons gone to Jefferson."

"Let me talk to Jake while you finish loading; then we'll go."

"Jake, do you need me? Anything I can help you with?"

"Nope, things are going just as they were when you left. We're cutting a lot of logs and shipping a lot of lumber. I would suggest that T. C. put one more wagon on until we get caught up."

"I'll tell him." Claude then shared his plans for having Wash build cabins for the men. He explained he was going to Clarksville to see Mr. Canterbury and then home to see Little Clovis. "If any problem comes up, after Clarksville, I'll be in Indian Springs, I've been gone from my son for too long."

℈

Wash rode the old mare and T. C. road behind Claude on Rusty. They couldn't go fast, but they got there. They took the three horses and left for Clarksville. Claude and T. C. rode the two new horses and they left the mare at the ranch. In Clarksville, they went to a saddle shop and T. C. picked out saddles, horse blankets, and bridles for the horses.

"With the jobs both of you are going to be doing, you'll each need a horse." Once the men had mounts, Claude gave them further instructions. "T. C. go to Cass County and see how the men there are doing. If you think some of them need a break, give them some time off from the mill."

"Yes, sir."

"Wash, when you finish in Cass County, get Jake to show you where he wants his house built , and what he wants. You have a lot of building to do and will probably need one or two men to help. See that Jake gets you the help you need. I'll tell Mr. Canterbury to make arrangements for you to get windows doors, brick, and everything else you need to build on the ranch.

"When you finish Jake's house, I'll need you to build another one or two, but I'll see you before then."

"I'll take care of the building," Wash said. "Don't you worry about nothing."

"Oh yes, I forgot to mention, we will need a well dug for each house. If you know some well diggers, get them and put them to work. I also need a well in Cass County. T. C. knows where Mr. Canterbury's office is; he'll show you on the way out.

I'm going to buy equipment for the pony and then go see Mr. Canterbury. He'll be expecting you when you need the things for the ranch construction. "

"It'll all be takin' care of," Wash assured him. "You just think about spendin' time with that boy of yours."

Claude spent more time deciding on a saddle and harness for the pony than he had expected. He went to the bank and was pleased with the balance in his account. He then went to Mr. Canterbury's office and made all the financial arrangements necessary for T. C. and Washington to complete their tasks. Mr. Canterbury assured him his requests would be honored.

With the business matters settled, Claude headed west toward Indian Springs.

⊱⊰

It was late when he arrived. Maude fixed him something to eat and he went to see Clovis, who was sleeping peacefully. Sophie and Maude assured Claude that Clovis was healthy and growing like a weed.

"Sophie, I was gone a lot longer than I wanted to be, but it couldn't be helped. Have you started Clovis' learning? Is he a good student? Tell me about him."

"He is very smart and is learning a lot faster than you did. You were always too busy getting into things to be a good student."

Claude laughed and then asked, "Where is John? Is he at the mill?

"He left this morning because Jake sent a message. He is grateful for the time he gets to work. Being without anything to do doesn't agree with him. "

"Sophie, I hope you approve. I brought Clovis a pony as a surprise. I put him and Rusty in the barn and fed them both."

"Clovis will be thrilled to have his own horse."

"How is John's horse? He has to get back and forth to the mill and if his horse isn't good I'll get him one that is."

"His horse is old and slow, but he's getting along."

"I'll get him a new horse and get you a horse and buggy. With him at the mill, you need a way to get around."

Claude was very tired. He went to bed, and suggested Sophie send Clovis to wake him up after he was up and dressed.

಄ഝ

Clovis was so happy to see his father, he cried out with joy. Claude got up and dressed. After breakfast, he took Clovis to the barn to see his surprise. The little horse came over and acted like Clovis was an old friend, even holding his head down to be petted.

"Daddy, I love him! Can I ride him now?"

"Son, I'll saddle both of our horses and we'll go riding. You best go tell Aunt Sophie we are going and that we won't be gone very long."

With both horses saddled, he started to lift Clovis into the saddle but noticed a stump next to the corral and led the pony over by it. Clovis climbed up on the stump and then on the back of the horse. Claude adjusted the stirrups and showed Clovis how to hold the reins, then mounted Rusty and started walking away.

Sophie and Maude came out and watched, beaming with pride. They walked around the pasture and then out to the trail and then out on the prairie.

After about thirty minutes, Claude started back toward the house. When they got there, Clovis didn't want to get off. Claude explained if he rode too much at first his bottom would get sore, so and he needed to take it slow at first.

Claude unsaddled the horses and showed Clovis how to curry and brush his horse and told him how much and when to feed him and how important it was to see that he had plenty of water available. Claude went back into the house and left Clovis to tend to his horse.

Both Sophie and Maude were crying. They had never seen Clovis as happy as he was with his horse. While Claude was having a cup of coffee, Sophie couldn't stand not being involved and went to the barn.

After she left, Claude said to Maude, "Wash is going to build a house at the ranch for Jake. He's planning on marrying a lady named Faye Latimer from Clarksville. Jake is running the big mill and overseeing the ranch. I didn't tell T. C., but I plan to also build a house for him and a bunkhouse for the drivers.

"T. C. is overseeing all the drivers, both at the big mill and the mill in Cass County. Thought you might want to know. I'll let you tell T. C. about the house being planned for him."

Maude cried and said, "Mista Claude, the day you brought me home with you was the best day of my life. I love T. C. and knows that he loves me, but he says we can't get married until he has a place to live. I can't wait to tell him."

ℝ

Sophie had to go get Clovis for lunch. He rushed through his eating and was anxious to go back to the barn.

Claude said, "That horse is yours and it isn't going to run off. We'll go riding again later today."

"Daddy, I've finished eating and I want to go now."

"It's all right with me if your Aunt Sophie's doesn't object."

When Sophie said "yes," Clovis ran toward the barn.

Claude said, "Since Maria and Effie died I have been going ninety miles an hour, eating my own camp fire cooking and sleeping on the ground most of the time. Both of the mills are in full operation and I'm going to slow up a little. I'm going to go take a nap and I don't remember ever doing that before. Please yell if I don't wake up by mid afternoon because I promised to take Clovis riding again."

ℝ

Clovis' horse shined because he had curried and brushed him repeatedly. They repeated the mounting operation of the morning. This time they went in the opposite direction. Claude speeded up Rusty a little and was pleased that the little gray horse had a relatively fast and smooth fox trot. Clovis was delighted. "Daddy, look what my horse is doing. What is it called?"

"It's called a fox trot. It is smoother riding than a trot and covers ground faster than a walk. What are you going to name your horse?"

"If it's alright with you I think I'll name him Foxy."

"He is your horse and you can name him whatever you want to. I'm pleased with your horse and he should last you a long time. You aren't going to be able to ride him except when I'm here or Uncle John, or T. C. They'll saddle him and help you mount him. Unfortunately, I have to be gone more than I want, but with time we will spend a lot more time together. You are growing fast and soon you will be able to saddle and mount your horse without help. I don't want you ridding so much that you neglect your studies. I didn't get as much book learning as I could have and I don't want you to make the same mistake.

"Someone told me they are opening a new college south of here called Texas A & M, and when you get old enough, and Sophie has finished teaching you, we'll try to ride down and see what they are doing. Tomorrow I plan to go to Clarksville and get your Aunt Sophie a horse and buggy, and buy a better horse for your Uncle John. If you can make it there, you can ride the buggy back if you bottom is too sore. Do you want to go with me?"

"Yes sir I sure want to go if I can ride Foxy."

₧₨

They left early the next morning. Clovis rode the whole fifteen miles. When they stopped at Mr. Canterbury's office Claude lifted him out of the saddle. "Daddy you were sure right about my bottom being sore. My legs are stiff, too."

"Mr. Canterbury this is my son Clovis. He has his first horse and rode him all the way from Indian Springs."

He got out of his chair and shook hands with Clovis. "I'm very glad to meet you. Your father is very proud of you."

"Claude, I'm glad you came by. I received a letter yesterday from Mr. Ladoux in New Orleans. It's addressed to you so I didn't open it."

Claude opened the letter and read it aloud.

Dear Mr. Williams:

I don't remember if you asked me to write here or to Atlanta, I feel sure you will get it either place. Anyway, we are extremely pleased with the lumber you are shipping. You can't send more than we want because I can export any we can't use here. Please keep the lumber coming.

245

"This is great news. We are shipping five or six times as much lumber as we did when I bought the mill. I expected I'd have to start looking for more buyers. This letter takes care of that problem."

When they left Mr. Canterbury's office they walked over to the livery stable.

Claude asked the man in charge if he knew where he could buy a good horse and buggy and a decent saddle horse.

"Mr. Franks at the hardware store has both and they are for sale. They belonged to his father who recently passed away. I have them here if you would like to see them before you go see him."

Claude replied, "Yes, let take a look."

Both horses were about four or five years old and were sound. The buggy was nearly new and was in good shape. The harness for the buggy looked fine and a good saddle was included for the other horse. They left their horses and went to the hardware store.

"Mr. Franks we just looked at the two horses and the buggy you left with the livery man. Sorry about your father. We might be interested in buying the horses, buggy, and gear you left over there if you aren't asking too much."

They dickered for a few minutes and Claude wrote him a check and got a hand written bill of sale.

"Clovis, are you hungry? There is a small café up the street. Let's eat before starting back."

Claude and Clovis left Clarksville in the buggy with three horses tied behind. Nine-year-old Clovis wanted to drive and did for a little while. Then he put his head in his daddy's lap and slept until they got back to Indian Springs.

The next morning Claude felt he had to leave. It was a tearful departure and he gave in and let Clovis ride Foxy for about an hour before leaving.

CHAPTER 26

WEDDINGS, JAKE and TC, plus LUMBER, RANCH and Family 1875

Claude stopped at the ranch before going to the mill. The ranch was deserted and he thought Ezra must be away from headquarters, so he went on to the mill. The mill was running full tilt and John was there and told him Jake had gone to Clarksville and seemed very anxious to get the house built and get married.

"T. C. has four wagons taking lumber to Jefferson. Everything seems to be going well here. The mill hands are happy and working hard. I keep thinking we might run out of logs but every time we get a little low, a bunch of wagons bring more. We still haven't had to cut any of your timber."

"Sounds great, John. I'm going to walk down to the mill and tell the old hands that all is well and that I'm more than happy with them. By the way, I just came from Indian Springs and I took a small horse to Clovis. He can't saddle it yet, but he will be able to when he gets a little bigger. I also left a new horse for you and a horse and buggy for Sophie. I didn't show her how to hitch it up because I thought maybe you should do that. With you gone a lot she needs transportation."

After visiting with the employees at the mill, he went back to the ranch, got his pack mule, and headed for Cass County. About ten miles down the road he met Wash coming to the ranch. Wash said, "I finished up at Cass County and am on my way home. If ya see Mista Jake, before I do, please ask him to draw me something so I will know what I'm to build next. I didn't think I might could use a helper, but I've changed my mind. I'll talk to T. C. about it, but I would like two men to help on the ranch."

When he got to the mill T. C. and the two drivers were loading the wagons with lumber. He told T. C. what Wash had said about help. "I think you need to go to Indian Springs when you can and see Maude. I bet she'll have a surprise for you."

After visiting with Phil Prescott, he went to see the cabin and the shelter for the mules and store room for feed.

Phil said, "We've been cutting a lot of logs but so far haven't even got low. Several local residents bring all the longs we need. The wagons have made several trips to Jefferson and the piles of lumber have shrunk a little but not much. We have been lucky and haven't had any mechanical problems. Mr. Ramsey sent a note with the last payroll checks saying the money from New Orleans was coming in. All is good here and if you don't need me for anything else, let me get back to work. I'm training a new man to handle the saw when I have to do something else and I don't trust him yet."

Claude replied, "I'm going to Atlanta, but I may be back in a few days if you need me. I think you are doing a great job and I'll try to leave you alone."

₨₧

Wash had built a nice little cabin with a fireplace for cooking and heat. The hands had moved in.

Claude went back to see T. C. They had just finished loading the wagons. The drivers were not the same as the ones he had gone with to Jefferson.

"Your dad built a nice cabin. Have you found anyone to dig wells? Creek water is okay for bathing, but I think it would be much better to have well water to drink."

"I haven't found anyone yet but my daddy said he knew someone that was good. I'll get 'em when I go home."

Claude left for Atlanta. He left his stock at the livery barn and checked into the rooming house. He ate a good steak and then went to bed. After a shave and a bath and clean clothes, he went to see Mr. Ramsey. The attorney was glad to see him and explained, "I know you will be pleased. Money is coming from New Orleans and your bank account is growing. You have a moneymaking operation. Considerably more is coming in than is going out. If you want me to do anything that I'm not doing just let me know. Mr. Roberts asked about you. Let me show you the check book."

"Thanks, I'm very pleased, of course. However, I expected this to happen, and if it didn't, I would have to make changes. See you soon. If you need me or anything needs my attention please contact your friend Canterbury in Clarksville. He will probably know where I'll be."

Mr. Roberts said, "The money is beginning to come in like you said it would. I'm pleased and I know you are. Diana has been asking about you. She wanted to know if you are ever in one place for a time or if you are always riding somewhere."

"Thanks for the invitation, but when I leave here I'm going to the mill. You can tell Diana that I have a mill here and the big one in Red River County. Businesses, or banks for that matter, don't run themselves. I started with nothing and what I have, I've made by personally running my business and I don't plan to change."

After restocking his pack mule with food and supplies, he headed directly back to the ranch.

❧❦

Wash and Jake were both back at the ranch and Jake was showing him where he wanted his house. Jake said, "Wash, what do you think of using hardwood for the foundation timbers? I just mean the timbers that go immediately on top of the bricks and the timbers that hold up the floor and everything else above the floor."

Wash replied," I'll tell you tomorrow exactly what I'll need. You sure have a lot of hardwood. I'm planning to go to Clarksville and order most of the rest of what I'll need to build it."

"I haven't told T. C. yet, and I prefer that Maude tell him, but I also intend to build a house for him and a barracks' for the drivers. The lumber business is going very well and I'll have a good job for him as long as he wants it. When you get to his house be sure it is big enough for you and your wife to visit. If he hasn't already, get T. C. to get you some help or hire them yourself. This construction is far too much for one man,"

For the next few months the mills ran with few problems. They were not under cover and had to stop operations when it poured down rain or snowed. The bank accounts grew and Claude began to think about expanding and upgrading the stock on the ranch. He bought two more tracts adjoining the original ranch and explored the cost of fencing.

He took the surveys and calculated the amount t of wire he needed and the number of posts required. He ordered the wire in Clarksville and put out the word that he would buy Bois d'arc posts from anyone who would deliver them to his ranch. While he was ordering wire he included enough wire to fence Ezra's place, too.

Jake's house was finished and he planned to get married to Faye Latimer in June. T. C. came to Claude and asked if he and Maude could get the preacher to marry them also. Wash had finished three houses: one for Jake, another for John, and one for

Claude, or anyone else spending a night at the ranch. All the houses built had three bedrooms and fireplaces and all had water wells. As always, Wash had done a good job.

Jake had bought a horse and buggy and planned to bring Faye and her mother to the ranch for the wedding. He asked John to get Sophie, Clovis and Maude to come. With construction finished they had enough room for everyone.

T. C. asked, "Mista Jake, can I borrow your buggy to bring my ma and Daddy out here before you get Miss Faye and her mama?"

"Sure you can T. C. And as soon as the preacher finishes with us, I'll see that he comes to your house and ties the knot for you and Maude."

Wash and Nell still lived in their house in Indian Springs. Now that he was finished with the ranch, he planned to begin construction of a house on the land Effie had left for them.

After the date was set for the weddings, Claude stopped by their house and gave Nell money and asked that she provide a big meal after the wedding. "T. C. is going to come for you in a buggy so you can cook most of it here. I don't know how many will be attending; you better count on forty or fifty. I think some of the mill hands will show up and I'll bet some of T. C.'s drivers will also want a meal."

"Don't worry Mista Claude. I'll take care of it. Will it be all right if I ask Maude to help? That is a lot of people to feed."

"I think Maude will want to help. She is a fine young woman. I'm going to see little Clovis now and I'll mention it to her. If you find you don't have enough money, send Wash and I'll provide whatever you need."

☙❧

Claude saddled Foxy even before he went to the house. Clovis, as always, was delighted to see him. His first question was, "When can we go riding?"

"Right now, if it's all right with your Aunt Sophie."

"Please take him. He has been asking to go but I can't saddle the horse."

When they got to the barn, Clovis said, "Daddy you knew I would want to go. Let's go!"

They rode for about two hours and Clovis was having a good time. "Daddy I can get on the horse without help. Do you think it would be okay for me to try to ride him bareback? I just can't put the saddle on him yet. I'm growing and I'll bet in another year or so I'll be able to saddle and ride alone."

"I'll talk to your Aunt Sophie and see what she thinks about it. Your Uncle Jake is going to get married soon at the ranch and your Uncle John also coming to see that your Aunt Sophie and Maude come too. He will probably saddle your horse and let you ride to the ranch."

‘’

When they got back, Clovis wanted to keep riding and Claude suggested he stay on the property. He went to the house and told Sophie what was happening. He also visited with Maude and told her that Nell had asked for help preparing food for the wedding party.

When Clovis returned, Claude unsaddled his horse and told him when he came to the ranch for the wedding they would ride a lot together.

Jake went and got Faye and her mother, Ann, and brought them to the ranch three days before the wedding. Jake turned his house over to them and moved in with Claude in the other big house. Claude was surprised at how attractive they both were. Nell and Wash were already there and Nell fixed supper at Jake's house. She had plenty of food available because Jake had bought a lot. Jake and Faye couldn't keep their hands off each other and Claude was seated next to Ann.

Ann said, "Jake told me your wife died and that you live

alone like I do. My husband died shortly after Faye was born and I've been alone since then."

Claude replied, "My wife and my mother both died five years ago. I have a ten-year-old son who is staying with my sister Sophie. I find it very lonesome living by myself and have occupied my time working. I've found most problems can be solved by working so hard you don't have time to dwell on them."

"Jake said that you now have two sawmills and you have accomplished so much in the last few years."

"My sister, my son Clovis, and my brother-in-law John will probably be here in the morning. I would like for you to meet them all, particularly my son."

₧₨

As always, the food Nell fixed was delicious.

Jake had a preacher show up before noon on the wedding day. Faye and Jake were married in the living room of his new home. Claude slipped the minister a generous stipend and escorted him to T. C.'s new home to marry Maude and T. C. The weddings and the party went without a hitch. Faye and Claude left by buggy with the request that Claude see that Ann got home. He borrowed Sophie's buggy and they had a pleasant trip to Clarksville. Claude asked, "Ann, when all of the festivities are over, I would like to come see you, if you would like?"

"I would like that very much. I think we are both lonesome. I would like to get better acquainted with your son, Clovis. As you know, I lost my son, Jim, when he and Jake were down South, chasing wild cows."

When he returned, he visited with Sophie and John. "Now that T. C. and Maude are married I'll ask Wash and Nell to find someone to help you. I hope you will stay a day or two and let me visit with Clovis. I kind of promised we would ride most of the day."

Early the next day, he asked Sophie to fix them some lunch. He saddled Foxy and

Rusty and first went to the mill. The mill was in full operation and seemed to fascinate Clovis. He asked all kind of questions. Claude showed him wagons unloading logs and showed him how the logs were sawed into lumber and introduced him to several of the old mill hands that he knew.

When they left, there they rode to the back of the ranch and he saw the longhorn cows and their calves. He explained that they were in the process of fencing the ranch and buying some highbred bulls to increase the value of the stock. Clovis seemed interested.

Because he hadn't seen Ezra in several days, they next went to his cabin. Ezra was sick but said he was better than he had been. He introduced Clovis to Ezra's wife and children. As usual, none of them said a word.

They stopped and ate lunch, and then they rode past the mill down into the trees and found a man and his sons cutting logs and loading them onto their wagon to take to the mill.

"Clovis, are you getting tired?"

"Yes sir, a little"

They headed back to the ranch. When they got there, he again explained to Clovis the responsibilities required for caring for his horse. They unsaddled, watered, curried, brushed, and fed both horses. As they started for the house, Clovis ran on ahead. When Claude arrived he could hear Clovis telling Sophie all about the mill, the ranch, and how they cut down the trees and took them to the mill. Claude held back a bit until Clovis finished his adventures of the day.

&

All was going well. Both mills were busy and money was coming in. Claude made a trip to Cass County and was very pleased with what he found. In Atlanta, he asked Mr. Ramsey to mail the bank statements, after checking them, to Mr. Canterbury in Clarksville. He didn't stop by the bank.

He had been to Clarksville several times to see Ann. They

were getting along well. When he got back from Cass County he went to Indian Springs and took Clovis with him to see Ann. They had a great time together.

☙❧

They had the wire and enough posts to start building fence. Claude got the surveyor to mark the boundaries and Wash sent him two fence builders. Ezra was overseeing the construction.

Claude was more content than he had been since Maria and his mother had died. He and Clovis were having a good time. The mills were doing well and money was accumulating. He was trying to get up enough nerve to ask Ann to marry him, and, God willing, spend the next twenty-five years with him into a new century.

THE END

About the Author:

Bill Whitten graduated from the University of Texas with a B.S, in Pharmacy shortly after World War II ended. In the late 1970s he sold his pharmacies and tried to retire. He wasn't very good at retirement and started investing in real estate and operated a Real Estate Brokerage for some years. He began writing during this period. His first work, *Like Riding a Bike in the Sand,* was published in 2004. Bill now writes full time. He is currently working on a book of short stories.